SINFULLY WED

The Five Deadly Sins
Book 1

Kathleen Ayers

Dragonblade Publishing, Inc. is an imprint of Kathryn Le Veque Novels, Inc.
P.O. Box 23
Moreno Valley, CA 92556
ceo@dragonbladepublishing.com

Produced in the United States of America

First Edition May 2023
Print Edition

ARE YOU SIGNED UP FOR DRAGONBLADE'S BLOG?

You'll get the latest news and information on exclusive giveaways, exclusive excerpts, coming releases, sales, free books, cover reveals and more.

Check out our complete list of authors, too!

No spam, no junk. That's a promise!

Sign Up Here

www.dragonbladepublishing.com

Dearest Reader;

Thank you for your support of a small press. At Dragonblade Publishing, we strive to bring you the highest quality Historical Romance from some of the best authors in the business. Without your support, there is no 'us', so we sincerely hope you adore these stories and find some new favorite authors along the way.

Happy Reading!

CEO, Dragonblade Publishing

Additional Dragonblade books by Author Kathleen Ayers

The Five Deadly Sins Series
Sinfully Wed (Book 1)

The Arrogant Earls Series
Forgetting the Earl (Book 1)
Chasing the Earl (Book 2)
Enticing the Earl (Book 3)

PROLOGUE

London, 1828

FREEZING RAIN PELTED the windows of the Earl of Emerson's London home in Grosvenor Square, hitting the glass in a never-ending icy spray. The sun hadn't even bothered to peek through the clouds today, leaving everything a murky gray. Appropriate weather given the somber mood of the occupants seated in the drawing room following the burial of a peer. An earl who was much loved and would be greatly missed, at least by the six figures crowding the midnight blue damask settee.

The mourners gathered were divided into two distinct camps. The first family of Lord Emerson consisted of his oldest son and heir, Bentley Sinclair; Bentley's maternal aunt, Lady Longwood, and her husband stood next to the couple's three obnoxious, overly-indulged children. Lord Longwood, nearly as wide as he was tall, had already availed himself of the table in one corner, which held an enormous number of finger sandwiches, cakes, biscuits, fruit, and cheese. A plate piled high with food was balanced on Longwood's protruding stomach, his disinterest in the proceedings clear.

Across the drawing room, far enough from the massive fireplace centered on one wall so that the chill of the room was much more apparent, sat the earl's second *far less prestigious* family. Lady Emerson, a pale trembling wraith wrapped all in black, was reviled in London for having been first an actress, then mistress, and finally wife of the deceased. Next to the widowed Lady Emerson sat her children, Jordan, Tamsin, Andrew, Malcolm, and little Aurora. The children's reputations, unfortunately, were little better than their mother's. The Sinclairs were said, mostly by Lady Longwood, to be ill-bred given their mother's origins. Considered uncivilized by most, the Sinclair children did nothing to dissuade society's expectations with their behavior, which lacked the most basic of manners.

Lady Emerson sobbed into a handkerchief, the grief at the death of her husband visible to everyone present, especially her eldest son.

"Had he only stayed home at River Crest," she wept. "He would be with us today. Or at least he would have perished in his own bed. I'm not sure why Adam was so determined to come to town."

The earl had died, mercifully, in his sleep. Peacefully, the physician noted. A sudden attack of the heart.

"Madam." The newly minted Lord Emerson, title merely days old, addressed his stepmother in an imperious, condescending tone. One far too smug for a young man who had spent the last two years roaming the Continent while bleeding through the generous allowance provided him. "I beg you to cease your weeping if only for the sake of your children." Lord Emerson's hostile gaze slid over his five half-siblings huddled on the settee.

"My lord," sobbed Lady Emerson, reaching for his hand. "Bentley."

Lord Emerson snatched his fingers away as if her touch would taint him. "You overstep."

Jordan Sinclair, eldest of the dead earl's *second* family, gave his older half-brother a baleful look. The affection between Jordan and the new earl was nonexistent. Their dislike of each other had stirred into near loathing over the last several years as Jordan learned how to manage their father's estates while Bentley chose to indulge himself. Barely six years apart in age, the two were miles apart in everything else.

"Don't speak to her like that." Jordan's calm tone belied the rage simmering beneath his skin. There was not as much as a hint of grief in his older brother or shred of empathy for their father's widow. "You will treat my mother with the respect she deserves as Lady Emerson."

"Do not allow him into goading you, Jordy," Tamsin, Jordan's sister, murmured softly from beside him. "Bentley wishes you to lose your temper so that he can be proven right."

Jordan could be something of a hothead. His reputation as a brawler was well-earned. But he was determined to control his temper. He stayed silent, the flexing of his fists the only sign Bentley had managed to get under his skin.

"*I* am the earl now," Bentley sneered, puffing out his chest. "Head of the family, such as it is. I have leave to speak to Lady Emerson in any way I see fit."

"Toad," Tamsin hissed under her breath, forgetting the advice she'd just given Jordan.

"You will not," Jordan challenged in a calm tone. "Regardless of your personal feelings, Bent, my mother *is* Lady Emerson. Father would want you to show her the respect she is due."

Jordan's mother, who he loved dearly, was still in a state of shock from the death of their father. Long a force of nature, Lady Emerson had been a fierce mother, teaching her children to be free and follow their hearts. She'd never cared overmuch for society's rules, having lived outside them for so long. But Mother had been dealt a terrible blow. One which Jordan was beginning to realize the former Sarah Fitzsimmons may not recover from. Mother had barely eaten or slept since a messenger arrived bearing the news of Father's sudden death. She'd collapsed at the front door of River Crest and had to be carried upstairs.

"Respect?" Lady Longwood snorted in derision. She sailed forward, skirts floating above the floor with ill-concealed malice. "As she gave my sister? Flaunting her rounded form as Pauline lay dying? Is that what you would call respect, Sinclair?"

Mother shrank back from Lady Longwood like a whipped dog. Once strong and forthright, she was now a shell of her former self. "I never meant to hurt Pauline." Her voice was small. "*Never*. She was bedridden for years after Bentley's birth, well before I made the acquaintance of Lord Emerson." Mother dabbed at her eyes. "Nor did I intentionally present myself to her. Adam and I were walking in the park. How was I to know she was well enough for a carriage ride, let alone could leave her bed—"

"I don't wish to hear your lies." Lady Longwood dismissed Jordan's mother with an insolent flick of one gloved hand. "My poor Pauline was finally strong enough to leave this house only to see her beloved husband." She took a ragged breath. "With *you*. Your hands on the mound of your protruding stomach. It wasn't enough you'd taken her husband's affections, but you chose to get yourself with child." A scathing gaze ran over Jordan as he had been the child sired. "Pauline lost her will to live, hastening an already painful demise. You weren't even discreet. Brazenly flaunting the one thing my sister could no longer give—"

Mother burst into a fresh spate of tears. "I did not. I would not."

"Aunt Clarice." Bentley interrupted Lady Longwood's tirade. "The past is unpleasant to visit. I think we are all aware of what transpired."

Everyone in London knew of the scandal caused by the Earl of Emerson and the actress he kept as his mistress. Marrying so soon after the death of his first wife, barely in time to keep Jordan from becoming a bastard, Adam Sinclair had taken his new bride and retired to the country. The gossips, he'd been sure, would relent in time. Or at least forget. Another scandal would soon eclipse their own.

Unfortunately, the memory of the *ton* was lengthy. That of Lady Longwood, infinite.

Years passed before Lord and Lady Emerson attempted to return to London with their two eldest children in tow. The results were disastrous, to say the least. While Lord Emerson was received, Lady Emerson was not. It was made clear that, regardless of her title, she would never be. Jordan engaged in a series of fistfights, beating the snot out of two sneering lordlings who dared to compare his mother to one of the unfortunate women plying their trade in the rookery. Tamsin, not to be left out, assisted her brother by leaping on one of the boys and punching him in the stomach.

The Sinclairs retired once more to the country.

Mother put her face between her hands, sobbing uncontrollably, slender shoulders trembling as she struggled for composure. "I never wished Pauline ill. *Never.*"

"What a dramatic show, now that you are no longer under the protection of your husband." Lady Longwood paced behind Bentley, thin fingers twisting in the folds of her skirts. "Save your tears. You'll need them for yourself." Her eyes skittered over Jordan and his siblings as if they were nothing more than a pile of refuse. "Tell them, my lord." Lady Longwood stopped directly in front of Jordan's mother. "I wish to see her face."

Bentley's neck reddened, a flush stealing up from the edge of his neatly twisted cravat.

"Yes." Jordan's chin snapped to his brother. "Tell us, Bent."

Bentley and Father had been estranged for years. Jordan's older brother rarely visited River Crest, where the Earl of Emerson had taken up permanent residence, instead preferring to spend his time in London. Bentley made no secret of the dislike for his half-siblings or their mother. He spent flagrantly while on a grand tour of the Continent, only ceasing his pursuit of pleasure when Father threatened to cut him off if he didn't return to England and learn some responsibility. A wasted effort. Bentley had no use for ledgers or the numbers they contained.

Jordan, on the other hand, absorbed his father's lessons, learning not only to keep the estate profitable, but how to manage the tenants and other investments. He understood the responsibility required; alas, Bentley did not. Or more likely, he didn't care.

"You may refer to me as 'my lord' or not at all," Bentley snapped at Jordan in his tedious, pompous manner.

"As you wish, *my lord*." Jordan cracked his knuckles. Could he get away with punching Bentley in his perfect aristocratic nose?

"As the Earl of Emerson, I have decided that it is in my best interests to distance myself from my father's unfortunate choices." Bentley tugged at the sleeves of his coat before brushing off a bit of lint.

Lady Longwood's mouth thinned. She resembled a feral cat.

Percival, Lady Longwood's pudgy, snot-nosed son, made a face at Tamsin before stuffing a scone in his mouth.

Bentley cleared his throat. "You will not be returning to River Crest, madam." He turned a dispassionate gaze to Jordan's mother. "River Crest is the seat of the Earl of Emerson, and thus, now belongs to me."

Mother paled and fell back against the cushions of the settee.

"I cannot, in good conscience, share such an ancient and hallowed estate with those whose existence I would rather forget. I tire of living with the shame heaped upon me. As an earl, I have a reputation to protect. A duty to all those who came before me."

"What are you saying, Bentley?" Mother sniffed.

"You will address me as my lord."

Pompous overdressed peacock. Jordan's finger itched with the urge to toss Bentley to the floor and pummel him.

A choking sound came from Jordan's mother. "You would have us leave our home? He is but hours in the ground and would not have wanted this."

"*He* is dead," Bentley sneered. "I no longer answer to my father. Thankfully. Time to sweep you all under the rug. I grow weary of enduring the humiliation I suffer from the outrageous behavior of those who share my name. Your reputation," he glared at Mother, "is still spoken about in drawing rooms all over London. I am mocked at every turn."

"I would venture that you are mocked for your own actions more than ours." Jordan came to his feet and approached his half-brother. He was nearly a head taller than Bentley, broader through the chest, and had grown up wrestling and fighting the local village boys around River Crest.

Bentley took a step back, fear shadowing his smug features for a moment. "How dare you."

Jordan knew of Bentley's escapades. He spent lavishly. Kept a mistress. Gambled. His father had often despaired over the character of his eldest son. "Father may have turned a blind eye to a great many things, but I did not. I know all about your time in Paris."

His elder brother's cheeks pinked. Lady Longwood hissed like a coiled snake.

"You've no right to question the Earl of Emerson. The estate is *his*," Lady Longwood snapped. "How amusing it is to hear you make such an accusation when all of London equates the Sinclairs to a pack of wild dogs. The countryside surrounding River Crest lives in fear you'll go about terrorizing them all, to my nephew's utter mortification. Expectations were never high for any of you given your origins." Her gaze bored into Mother.

Lady Longwood also had a patrician nose, but Jordan had never once punched a woman.

Yet.

A snore erupted from one of the chairs closest to the fire. Lord Longwood, having eaten an enormous plate of pastries, had fallen asleep.

"I want you gone from London. Gone from River Crest. Our association will still be maintained, but in a much more distant fashion." Bentley took a step closer to Lady Longwood, who was likely the architect of this conversation.

"You wish to wipe us away as if we don't exist," Tamsin stated bluntly, chin lifted far too defiantly for a girl not yet sixteen. "Father would not have wanted you to treat us in such a fashion, Bent. We are your family."

"I don't care what he wanted. Again, allow me to remind you that our father is *dead*," Bentley snapped. "Buried. In the ground. *I* am the earl."

"But what about Jordan's schooling? He's—" Mother's voice trembled; her fingers clutched at the handkerchief she held.

"Been tossed out of Harrow more times than I can count," Bentley retorted before she could finish. "Unlike the previous earl, I no longer wish to bribe the headmaster to take him back."

"The headmaster is a bit of an idiot," Jordan said. "And I was only asked to leave twice."

"You've always made a great show of knowing better how to run an estate than me." A short laugh burst from between Bentley's lips. "Well, now you'll have a chance to prove what a good, responsible steward you can be. Dunnings is in dire need of management and repair."

Mother shut her eyes as if trying to blot out Bentley's words.

A collective gasp ran through Jordan and his siblings.

"Dunnings is nearly in Scotland," Jordan reminded his brother, trying to stem the blossoming panic filling his chest. "It hasn't been inhabited for years. You can't be serious." Father had spoken years ago of selling the rundown manor house, but never got around to it. Jordan wasn't even sure if there was still a caretaker in residence.

"Entirely serious," Lady Longwood uttered in a cool tone. "Dunnings is far enough from London that Lord Emerson won't need to fear an unexpected visit from the *Sins*." She glared at Tamsin, who usually drew most of Lady Longwood's ire. "Sins. What an apt title for a group of urchins who are a stain on the Earl of Emerson." One gloved hand caressed Bentley's arm. *"Deadly Sins,"* she trilled. "You've certainly made good on the name, haven't you, Tamsin?"

"I am not a sin," Aurora lisped, clutching her doll, regarding Lady Longwood with wide eyes.

Bentley's aunt smiled down at Jordan's little sister, eyes glinting with satisfaction. "Yes, you are, *darling*."

Tamsin's lips tightened, features awash with guilt. "I was only defending myself." Her bottom lip jutted out stubbornly. "What would you have had me do? Allow myself to be compromised? Have liberties taken with my person?"

"You *punched* the son of a duke. Ware's eldest. The Marquess of Sokesby. His *heir*," Bentley roared back at her, startling the entire room. "*Broke* his nose. What were you even *doing* at Gunter's alone?"

Tamsin looked down at her hands. "I merely wanted an ice. There was no one available to escort me."

Another snicker from the other side of the room. Percival stuck his tongue out at Tamsin.

"A young lady of good breeding *does not* wander about unescorted. You aren't even out yet, though I suppose given recent events, you won't be. Dear God, who would have you anyway?"

"Bent—" Jordan growled in warning. There was no need to insult Tamsin on top of everything else, but he wasn't sure what to do. He couldn't afford to antagonize or threaten Bentley, not if Jordan was to have any hope of not being cut off by his older brother. Especially if he was serious about Dunnings.

Bentley's gaze swerved to the refreshment table. Drew and Malcolm were slinking about, stuffing their pockets and mouths with biscuits as if they hadn't eaten in days instead of mere hours ago. It was the most animation the pair had shown since hearing of Father's death.

"Look at them," Lady Longwood drawled. "No better than thieves picking pockets. Perhaps instead of Dunnings, you might send them to Cheapside. They'll fit right in, my lord."

Malcolm halted, crumbs falling from his lips. A calculated look came over his face and he took a step closer to Percival, who was too busy making faces at Tamsin to notice who hovered behind him.

Behave, Jordan mouthed to his brother. *Please.*

Mother put her head in her hands, sobbing at the knowledge Bentley would evict them from River Crest and banish them all to Northumberland. Aurora was curled into her side. Even the normally stalwart Tamsin had a look of despair about her.

The responsibility for *all* of them, what remained of the Sinclairs, would fall to Jordan. He was barely more than a lad, but there wasn't anyone else. His mother might never recover from the dual blows of Father's death and being banished to Dunnings. Jordan was all that stood between his family and the rest of the world.

I won't fail you, Father.

He straightened, squaring his shoulders to look Lady Longwood in the eye, gratified when her smug smile faltered.

"I *suffered* you all while our father was alive," Bentley sneered, not ready to stop debasing them, though Mother looked as if she might faint at any moment. "Tolerated the sneers behind my back at Eton, the insults that my father had wed—" The color of his cheeks turned crimson. "An *actress* with whom he had an amorous relationship."

Bentley had stopped short of calling Mother a whore.

"I understand your dislike of me, Bentley. But I beg you to reconsider your decision for their sakes," Jordan's mother whispered. "They," she pointed to Jordan and his siblings, "*are* your family."

"No, *madam*. They are not." Bentley brushed a wave of ginger hair back from his broad forehead. He looked nothing like the other Sinclairs, but instead favored his mother, Pauline. Slight of build with narrow shoulders, Bentley wore expensively-tailored clothing with dashing bits of color. A true dandy through and through.

"You are sending us to Dunnings," Jordan said quietly. "A place none of us have ever seen, one that is in such a poor state of repair that

Father couldn't even manage to sell it. That is what you think we deserve. What about Cargave Manor?" Cargave had once been the residence of their paternal grandmother in Surrey. The house was small but well-maintained.

"Absolutely not. You'll go to Dunnings." He straightened his coat, the movement full of his own self-importance.

Jordan didn't think he could loathe anyone more than Bentley.

"The staff at River Crest has already been informed. Your clothes and other effects have been packed and are already headed to Dunnings."

The bastard.

They had been here mourning Father, grief-stricken over their loss, while Bentley and his horrible aunt were evicting them from River Crest.

"While we were at the gravesite, I took the liberty of having your trunks from upstairs loaded on the coach outside."

Aurora started crying. "My dolls," she wept into Mother's side. "What about Daisy?"

Daisy was Aurora's cat and head mouser at River Crest.

"She'll be fine, darling." Mother hugged Aurora.

"We couldn't take the risk of you absconding with the valuables," Lady Longwood added unnecessarily. "Either here or at River Crest. You've already taken so much from Lord Emerson. You are no longer welcome here. The staff has been instructed to throw you out should you attempt to return." Her triumphant gaze landed on Mother. "London will not be kind should you deign to stay."

"I'm sure you've seen to that, haven't you, my lady?" Tamsin's fingers tightened on her lap.

"I have. With great pleasure." Satisfaction lit Lady Longwood's angular features. "Lord Emerson deserves to take his rightful place in society without the *dirt,*" she said, giving Tamsin a pointed look, "clinging to the edges of his coat."

"I thought we were a *sin*," Jordan countered, sounding far more composed than he felt, sick to the very depths of his soul. The reality of the situation was that Bentley, and his unending list of ridiculous grievances, was in complete control of their future. They would be forced to subsist on his charity.

"I am not without some sympathy." Bentley took on that imperious, self-important tone once more. "Jordan could learn a trade, perhaps. Truthfully, I doubt anyone considers him a gentleman. And I feel that they," he inclined his chin in the direction of the twins, Malcolm and Andrew, "would be better suited to say… a life in the military. I will purchase a commission for each of them when the time comes," he finished with a magnanimous smile.

"How *kind*." Jordan's fingers tightened against his thighs. "And what of my sisters?"

"What of them?" Lady Longwood answered for Bentley. "I'm sure they'll both wed, eventually. Possibly a ship's captain. Or a merchant. A country squire. The lack of a dowry will be an impediment, but—"

"Father would have made ample provisions for Tamsin and Aurora's dowries. You cannot tell me he did not, Bent." Jordan watched his brother closely.

Bentley flushed once more and cleared his throat.

"You have no leave to speak to Lord Emerson—" Lady Longwood corrected Jordan.

"I'm not speaking to you," he interrupted her. "Answer the question, Bent."

"Well." Bentley coughed. "That is an item I must discuss with my solicitor. You realize that I cannot afford dowries, commissions, *and* your upkeep at Dunnings." A nervous chuckle escaped him as he looked at Lady Longwood, who gave him an encouraging nod. "My father failed to make appropriate provisions for his second family, perhaps out of lack of affection. Or pure carelessness."

No, Father would have expected Bentley to take care of his siblings.

As much of a wastrel as Bentley had been, the late, lamented Lord Emerson would never have imagined his heir would toss them out of River Crest and send them to Dunnings. It would have been unthinkable to Father that Bentley would leave his sisters without a dowry.

Mother clutched the handkerchief to her nose, rocking slowly back and forth. Tamsin put an arm around her shaking shoulders, staring at Bentley in disgust.

"That's a complete and utter lie." Jordan moved a step closer, his fists curling tighter.

"I assure you." Bentley's gaze lowered. "I've always thought that Father would come to his senses one day and realize what an error he had made—"

"One more word, Bent," Jordan said in a conversational tone. "And I'll strangle you with your cravat."

Lady Longwood placed a hand at her throat. "How dare you threaten him? I'll have you escorted out."

"What a shriveled harpy you are, Lady Longwood." Tamsin's eyes blazed pure fire at Bentley's aunt. "As unappealing as a gnawed and discarded apple core."

Lady Longwood narrowed her eyes. "You impertinent little cretin."

Sweet Jesus. Why did she have to call Tamsin a cretin? Or impertinent?

Tamsin rose to her feet. Without another word, she lifted her hand, palm open.

A tiny cake flew across the room, tossed by Malcolm.

His sister caught the cake, frosting covering her gloved fingers. "You've no idea." Then with an evil glint in her eye, Lady Tamsin Sinclair proved how barely civilized she truly was.

The cake hit Lady Longwood right on the end of her nose, splattering frosting, crumbs, and jam across her cheeks. "You horrid girl," she sputtered.

Malcolm and Drew laughed like a pair of maniacal demons. Drew tossed cakes and biscuits at Lady Longwood's two prim little daughters, who shrieked louder than their mother. Mal, with a wild roar, tackled Percival, upending the tea tray, spilling the still steaming liquid all over Lord Longwood, who woke up screaming.

Aurora stood amid the fray, picked up a discarded piece of sponge cake, and threw it, with amazing aim for such a child, directly at Bentley. "I am *not* a sin."

Bentley made to swat Aurora's bottom, but was stopped by Jordan. "Touch her and I'll break your wrist."

Mother stiffened and dabbed at her eyes. Looking about the room, she stood, a bit unsteadily, taking in the chaos her children inflicted.

"Let us be off, Jordan. Excuse us, won't you, Bentley? I don't believe we'll stay for tea."

CHAPTER ONE

Dunnings, Northumberland
11 Years Later

"Lord Emerson."

Jordan stirred, but didn't bother to open his eyes. Lord Emerson, better known as his older brother, Boring Bentley, would never lower his priggish arse to be found at The Hen, though the tavern was the finest in all of Spittal. A dubious distinction. Bentley had never once, in the eleven years since banishing Jordan to the far reaches of Northumberland, visited to check on the welfare of his half-siblings. And why would he? There was nothing in Spittal except for a lovely beach and the history of once having been the site of a hospital for lepers several hundred years ago to recommend the small village.

The Earl of Emerson lived a lavish, extravagant lifestyle, one befitting an overindulged dandy. Only London was a place worthy of Bentley's presence.

Opening an eye, the one that *wasn't* swollen shut, Jordan surveyed his surroundings. Most of the tavern remained blurry except for an enormous pair of breasts, swaying gently mere inches from his nose. Peg, The Hen's only barmaid, had an ample bosom, which she displayed to great advantage in a low-cut bodice. Modesty wasn't Peg's strong suit.

Wincing at the twinge of pain, Jordan moved his jaw, relieved to find he still could. A sticky wetness engulfed his cheek, and he caught a whiff of meat gravy. How had he come to be lying face down in a meat pie?

Ah. Yes. *Sisco.*

Thrilled to have sold several of his pigs, Jordan had taken a few coins and decided to treat himself to a bottle of whiskey at The Hen and enjoy the view of Peg's bosom. But Sisco had arrived with murder in his eye, all of it directed at Jordan.

A pea was congealed in the gravy right in front of his nose, and Jordan shut his eye in disgust.

Sisco had caught him unawares and half-foxed, which is how the sailor managed to get the better of Jordan with his fists. Elizabeth Warring was the subject of the beating who, unbeknownst to Jordan, had decided to betroth herself to Sisco. Jordan had a reputation with the female population of Spittal, though he was far from being the sort of rake he might have been in London. It wasn't as if he'd taken Elizabeth's virtue for goodness sake. She'd been free with her favors for years.

Perhaps he shouldn't have reminded Sisco of that small fact.

"Jordan Sinclair," the starched accent announced loudly above the hum of the tavern.

Not a single soul in Spittal spoke as if they had just stepped out of a gentleman's club in London. Most everyone sounded like the Scots who were a few hours' ride north of here, including Jordan. He hadn't heard such a clipped tone in nearly a dozen years.

Jordan struggled to open his good eye once more. The whiskey he'd indulged in both before and after Sisco nearly beat him half to death helped deaden some of the pain. At some point, he'd eaten the meat pie beneath his cheek. How long had he been at The Hen? Impossible to tell the time of day because there were no windows in the small tavern. Squinting into the dim interior, Jordan could just make out a lean gentleman dressed far too fine to be from Spittal. Did he owe him money?

The great Lord Emerson was a stingy bastard, especially when it came to the needs of Jordan and his family. Pig farming didn't pay nearly as much as one might think.

Pale cheeks. Hair neatly trimmed. Gloves. Whoever the man was, he hadn't come into The Hen looking for a meat pie or a tankard of ale.

"Jordan Sinclair."

No, the idiot was busy bandying about Jordan's name as if he had a right to.

Cheek throbbing, Jordan lifted his head, disgusted to see gravy dripping off the ends of his hair, which was a mite longer than it should be. He did a poor job of cutting hair, but it was better than allowing his sister to wield the shears. Tamsin left him half-bald a few years ago.

Jerking a large thumb in Jordan's direction, Edmonds, the barkeep, said, "There. The one with meat pie on his cheek. Waste of good pie, if you ask me."

A crisp, expensive coat lined with silver buttons came into Jordan's line of sight. The scent of clean linen hovered in his nostrils for a moment before being drowned out by congealed meat pie and ale. A small portfolio was clasped in one gloved hand.

"My lord." The gentleman cleared his throat.

Jordan blinked as he tried to sit fully upright, turning just slightly to take in this visitor with his good eye.

"Do I owe you money?" The coppery taste of blood filled his mouth. That last punch to the jaw must have split his lip.

"No, my lord," the gentleman informed him.

A wash of relief filled Jordan. Funds weren't only tight, but nonexistent. "Is it Andrew?" His younger brother's penchant for card games was often a cause of alarm, though he always brought the extra coin back to Dunnings.

"No." The gentleman shook his head. "I am here for you, my

lord."

Jordan shook his head, trying to clear away the cobwebs. Why did this snooty, well-dressed man keep referring to him in such a way? He and Bentley looked nothing alike. Was he misinformed? "You have the wrong brother, sir. *Bentley* Sinclair is the earl. Not *Jordan* Sinclair." He waved his hand for Edmonds to slide him another bottle of whiskey, since the previous bottle, still half-full, had shattered when Sisco tackled Jordan at the bar. "Head south until you reach London, that's where you'll find him. Number twenty-three Bruton Street, near Grosvenor Square."

Jordan tried to grab the whiskey from Edmonds, who held the bottle in a death grip.

"Pay up, Sinclair," the barkeep informed him. "You'll get nothing on account at The Hen."

Fair enough. Everyone in Spittal knew of the financial difficulties that faced the denizens of Dunnings. Jordan dug in his pocket. Nothing but lint.

"Allow me, my lord." The gentleman tossed several coins at Edmonds, who nodded and slid the bottle into Jordan's waiting hand.

"Thank you." Damn, his face hurt. A tooth felt loose. "I must have forgotten my purse." Jordan didn't actually *have* a purse because he rarely had enough coin to fill one.

"My lord—" The man cleared his throat once more. "Might I request a word with you in private? I fear it is quite urgent." He tapped the valise meaningfully with one gloved finger.

Jordan tilted his head, which did nothing for his throbbing temples. "I fear you are here in error."

"I assure you; I am not," the gentleman said. "My name is Patchahoo. James Patchahoo. I am your solicitor, my lord."

Jordan snorted. "I don't have a solicitor." The cost of the man's coat would feed Jordan's family for a week. "Can't afford one. Now, I'm quite busy, as you can see, Patchasoot." He gestured to the disreputable denizens of The Hen. "I'm sure you can find your way back to London without my help." He tried to smile, wincing at the sting to his lip.

"Patcha*hoo*, my lord. Scottish, I'm afraid. Several generations back."

"No need to apologize. But Scotland is that way." Jordan jerked his thumb. "If you're lost."

Patchahoo wasn't nearly as old as his clipped, polite way of speaking and clothing made him appear. Solicitors, in Jordan's experience, which admittedly was limited, were elderly white-haired gentlemen. The bit of hair sticking out from under Patchahoo's hat was sandy in color, as was his mustache.

"How old are you, Patchahoo?"

Patchahoo cleared his throat once more. "Age, my lord, has no bearing on my duties as your solicitor."

"I don't have a solicitor," Jordan insisted. "One must have property and the like to require your services. I'm not sure who sent you here, but they were in error."

Patchahoo waved a hand towards an empty table tucked in the dim recesses of The Hen. "A word, if I may?" The solicitor's nose wrinkled slightly as he took in Jordan's stained clothing and bruised face.

Dizziness assailed Jordan as he slid off the bar. Two Patchahoos appeared momentarily before he blinked them away. If Bentley, that pompous prick, had sent this man all the way from London to inform Jordan that funds would not be forthcoming this month, as they hadn't for the last *two* months, Bentley *could* have sent a note.

"Is this about the sum I requested for the repairs to the roof? Because I wasn't exaggerating. There is a hole the size of a mountain in the roof at Dunnings. Part of the third floor is uninhabitable. Not only because of the hole, but in general."

Dunnings was in a constant state of repair, crumbling further into decay with each year. The house had already been in shambles when Jordan and his family arrived. Mice in the walls. The hedges so overgrown one couldn't find the front door. Broken windows. Furniture rotting where it sat.

Mother had taken one look at her new home and collapsed.

The miniscule amount of funds Bentley had sent in the first few years had been barely enough to feed them all, let alone make necessary repairs to the house. There was no staff at Dunnings. Not so much as a maid or a cook. Jordan had become a master at negotiating with tradesmen while learning how to raise pigs, the only thing that would grow at Dunnings. He'd become adept at carpentry to an extent. Masonry still eluded him. Aurora kept a garden, which helped fill the larder, though they were all sick of cabbage. Clothes patched and mended dozens of times.

Anger towards Bentley, once a constant state, had faded in the face of trying to survive.

A drawn look came over Patchahoo's face. "I must apologize, my lord. I was instructed not to send your usual sum."

Jordan snorted. "Selfish prick."

Patchahoo colored at the words.

"Not you, Patchahoo." He took a sip of the whiskey, but didn't apologize. Bentley *was* a prick. A horrid one. Content to allow his siblings to struggle in Dunnings while he lived well on their collective inheritance. The papers from London did eventually make their way to Spittal, though it took several weeks. The reports of Lord Emerson and the latest purse he'd lost on some ridiculous wager or an entire paragraph complimenting the earl's new carriage were hard to miss, especially when all you were eating was cabbage.

"I admit, I threatened to come to London if Bentley didn't cough up the amount necessary for the new roof. I imagine that's why you're here. Well, you are free to inspect the damage. You tell that selfish prig that I've kept my part of the bargain. I haven't set foot in London. But

I will. I don't care if he is wife hunting."

Bentley, after an endless existence of pleasure since their father's death, had finally decided he should wed, stating emphatically that the sight of his ill-mannered half-siblings, the scourge of his existence—

That's what Bentley called Jordan and his family. A *scourge*. As if they were a bloody plague or a band of Vikings.

—would cause embarrassment and harm the chances of his lordship in making a suitable match. Bentley proclaimed, in his perfect handwriting, that it had come to his attention it was time to provide an heir for Emerson. Because he certainly, and Bentley had underscored the word several times, couldn't *afford* to allow Jordan to inherit. He couldn't risk anyone recalling his unfortunate association with the *Deadly Sins*, else he would never make a match.

Prick.

Jordan had written back that they were living in the very backwater of England. How the bloody hell did they pose any embarrassment to his lordship?

By existing, Bentley had written back. *Your very birth taints the Sinclair name. You are the offspring of our father's paramour, one who is to blame for my mother's early demise.*

Jordan took a large swallow of the whiskey. Well, his mother was dead now too, unable to survive the loss of her husband and Dunnings. Shouldn't that make him and Bentley even? Jordan drummed his fingers on the table, remembering the whistle of the wind as his mother lay dying, wrapped in every spare blanket they could find at Dunnings. He had been unable to save her.

"My lord."

"I need funds for the roof. Bentley can't expect us to sleep in a house with the cold and wet dripping in."

"I fear this has nothing to do with the roof."

Jordan took a deep breath; if it wasn't the roof, the situation could be infinitely worse. "It's my sister, isn't it?"

Tamsin *had* bested the Earl of Richland's son in a horse race two weeks ago. She'd been riding astride and wearing leather breeches that had once belonged to Andrew. Horrifying nearly everyone. But the race had been a private one. Only a dozen or so onlookers. Surely, the news hadn't reached all the way to London. Richland's son had been a good sport.

"This has nothing to do with Lady Tamsin."

"Tell my brother, Patchahoo—"

The solicitor slapped the small portfolio he carried on the bar. "I am here to inform you that Bentley Sinclair, twelfth Earl of Emerson is dead. You are the new earl." Patchahoo took out a handkerchief and patted the sweat from his lips. It was warm inside The Hen.

The glass of whiskey hovered at Jordan's lips. "You're joking." Bentley was too insufferable to die. He'd stay alive purely to keep the title from Jordan.

"My lord—"

"Stop calling me that." Jordan ran a hand through his hair, disgusted to find a bit of potato above one ear. "Bentley can't be dead. And do I look like an earl to you?"

"I realize this is unwelcome news."

The solicitor had no idea how unwelcome. "How?" Jordan downed the remainder of his glass.

"The axle on Lord Emerson's barouche broke apart. The vehicle was new and not the sort meant to take such sharp corners, especially when driving so fast. The road was narrow and bordered by a stone wall on the right. When the axle snapped, it threw Lord Emerson against..." Patchahoo paused long enough to brush a half-eaten chicken leg off the table. "The stone wall, breaking his neck. If it is any comfort to you, my lord, I do not believe your brother suffered. It was...very quick. I've made the necessary arrangements on your behalf, but you are expected in London. The house on Bruton awaits your arrival. I took the liberty of informing the staff at River Crest as well."

"He hadn't been to River Crest in years. Not since my father's death." Bentley rarely visited the place where Jordan and his siblings had been born and raised. Bentley had evicted them purely out of spite.

"No, my lord. To my knowledge, River Crest has stood empty for some time. There is only a small staff in place."

Jordan sat back, fingers curled around his glass. Bentley was dead.

He hadn't seen his brother since the day Bentley sent the entire family to Dunnings, unceremoniously escorting them to a waiting carriage only hours after burying Jordan's father. They hadn't even been allowed to return to their rooms, enduring Lady Longwood's insistence that Malcolm and Drew be searched for any valuables they might have taken. It had been an altogether humiliating experience.

"I'm only surprised Bent was driving himself."

"I believe Lord Emerson was attempting to impress a young lady." Patchahoo gave an awkward cough.

Jordan raised his brows. "One he hoped to wed?" The gossip column in the last paper from London, months old, dedicated an entire paragraph to the dashing earl who had at last decided to secure a match.

"No, my lord." A blush stained Patchahoo's neck above his cravat. "Another woman of your brother's acquaintance, one whom he had an existing relationship with. May we continue this conversation at Dunnings, my lord?"

The Hen's other patrons were a curious lot. Edmonds was already giving Jordan and Patchahoo a curious look. Peg was hovering a bit too close, trying to overhear their conversation. No one in Spittal needed to know that the impoverished pig farmer they knew as merely Sinclair was now the Earl of Emerson.

"Agreed, Patchahoo. Let us retire to Dunnings."

CHAPTER TWO

JORDAN SAT BACK, reaching for the bottle of whiskey he'd brought back to Dunnings from The Hen. Pulling out the cork, he splashed the amber liquid into a chipped glass and swallowed a mouthful. On the ride, Patchahoo had quietly related a number of important details to Jordan concerning Bentley's finances.

Now Jordan's face hurt, his head ached, and he was mildly dizzy from the news Patchahoo had related. It seemed that Bentley had not been content with the insults he'd served to his half-brother for the last decade; no, he wished to continue making Jordan's life hell from the grave.

"You're sure?" The whiskey wasn't helping. He hoped Drew had some brandy stashed somewhere.

"Positive, my lord. I handled Lord Emerson's affairs personally as he didn't employ a secretary."

Bentley's letters, when he cared to write something, were filled with accusations and vicious diatribe towards Jordan and his mother. There was barely enough to keep him in the style befitting an earl, Bentley insisted because Lady Emerson had squandered enormous sums on furnishings for River Crest. Demanded the finest clothing and jewels for herself.

That claim had been Jordan's favorite. Outside of her wedding band, Mother rarely wore any adornment.

Poor investments, Bentley insisted, were the fault of their foolish father who emptied the coffers to provide for his greedy "second" family. *Leeches*, Bentley called Jordan and his siblings, bleeding him dry of funds so they could maintain themselves at Dunnings. The frugality Bentley forced upon them wasn't *his* fault, but theirs.

He had assumed all Bentley's posturing was little more than an excuse to punish Jordan further. Nothing more. When Bentley insisted he needed to wed, there had been no hint that the urgency was anything more than his brother's determination to have an heir so that Jordan might never inherit.

Bentley had always liked to gamble, though he rarely won. Horses were a favorite. Hazard. Making ridiculous wagers, which rarely paid off. In the last two years, Bentley had sold every piece of property not entailed with the exception of Dunnings.

Loathing and disgust for Bentley filled Jordan at Patchahoo's careful recital.

Bentley never visited River Crest because the house had been stripped bare of anything but the basest furnishings. A handful of other properties Father once owned, including a textile mill, were gone. Everything that was not entailed, excepting Dunnings, had been sold. He continued to keep his two mistresses in lavish style, providing both with their own houses, staff, and carriages. Clothing. Jewelry. Only the house in London had been left virtually untouched because Bentley was determined to maintain appearances.

Bentley had *needed* to marry.

He took another swallow of whiskey, wishing this entire conversation was the result of being hit too hard in the head by Sisco. Jordan would wake up surrounded by his pigs to find it had all been a horrible dream and Patchahoo a figment of his imagination.

"I am ill-equipped to become an earl."

Jordan knew what was required, or at least he had vague memories of him and his father reviewing the accounts together and visiting tenants. But the last ten years had been spent barely surviving, drowning his bitterness at Bentley with too much whiskey, and brawling. His manners, never spectacular to begin with, were now rusty. There was no need for niceties when one was a pig farmer. He didn't even know how to dance, at least not properly. Had only a rudimentary knowledge of his peers and few polite conversation skills. The idea of going about with a cravat strangling him every day wasn't the least appealing.

"Nonetheless, you *are* Lord Emerson."

"Then as Lord Emerson, I beg you to stop reminding me of my changed status. How long before the duns come beating on the doors?"

"The sum from the upcoming sale of the homes your brother kept his—*companions* will be enough to see to your needs for the time being. Clothing, for instance." He took in Jordan's much-mended shirt and nearly soleless boots.

"You didn't answer my question Patchahoo. What am I to expect in London?" Maybe Jordan should just pack up the entire family and flee to the Continent. Malcolm was floating around France somewhere as a mercenary. Or, at least, his last letter mentioned Paris and swordfights. Or Venice? He couldn't recall at the moment. "How enormous are my brother's debts, now mine? Do I owe half of London? Come now, it can't be any worse than what you've already told me."

"You've only one creditor, my lord. He holds all of the previous Lord Emerson's markers. And there is the matter of Miss Odessa Whitehall. She is the heiress your brother had agreed to wed." Patchahoo frowned. "Though Lord Emerson had suddenly become convinced he could no longer do so."

"Bentley is dead, which I think voids his obligation to Miss White-hall. She'll have to find someone else to wed." Jordan shrugged. "Is there a point to this? I'm more concerned with the entire amount of Bentley's debts being held by one individual."

"May I avail myself of a glass of whiskey, my lord?" Patchahoo nodded to the bottle.

"Of course." Jordan pushed an extra glass towards the solicitor, checking first to make sure it was clean.

"Mr. Whitehall, Odessa Whitehall's father, *is* your sole creditor, my lord. Not only has he collected every marker of Lord Emerson's, but your brother also owed Whitehall a substantial amount beyond that."

"Who is Whitehall that he would lend money to Bentley?"

The sides of Patchahoo's mouth turned down in distaste. "I suppose the politest way to describe Mr. Whitehall is to say he is a financier of sorts. He has a reputation for providing loans to titled gentlemen, those who cannot, for various reasons, ask for large sums on their own without drawing unwelcome attention. The interest Whitehall charges is usually three times the amount of the loan. Those who become involved with him often find themselves in a delicate, tenuous situation."

There was a shady fellow who lingered about the docks in Spittal, offering his assistance if a cargo had been lost or otherwise compromised. Many a merchant had found themselves beholding to him, often to their detriment. "He's a sharker." At Patchahoo's look, he said, "A moneylender."

"He is, or at least, he once was. Mr. Whitehall attempted to become a legitimate man of business once he wed the daughter of a viscount. The viscount, coincidentally enough, also found himself in the same straights as your brother; at least that is my understanding. Whitehall now owns a variety of businesses and is well-known, but not well-liked, in London for obvious reasons. Which brings us back to Odessa Whitehall."

"And me, I assume." A dreadful, oily feeling was seeping into Jordan's stomach.

"The previous Lord Emerson reached an agreement with Whitehall to wed his daughter."

"Please refer to him as Bentley. I think that far easier."

"As you wish, my lord. Whitehall wants a title for his daughter. I believe he assumes that it will gain him acceptance into society, something he greatly covets. The usual ways to find a suitable match for Miss Whitehall have failed."

"No one wants to wed a sharker's daughter."

"Correct, my lord. It is my belief that Bentley found himself in a difficult financial situation caused by his own excesses. An understanding was reached in which Bentley's debts would be erased. Whitehall even advanced your brother a sum as a show of good faith. Ironically, those same funds were used to purchase the barouche which led to Bentley's demise."

Bent. You fucking idiot.

"So am I to understand that Bentley indebted himself to a well-known sharker in London and was going to wed the chit?"

Patchahoo took a sip of the whiskey, wincing at the taste. The Hen didn't stock the finest spirits. "Shortly before his demise, your brother informed me that he no longer wished to wed Miss Whitehall under any circumstances and to find another way to repay the debt to Whitehall. After a few brief visits," Patchahoo cleared his throat, "Bentley declared Miss Whitehall to be…repulsive."

"Repulsive? In what way? Is that why Whitehall couldn't marry her off before Bentley?"

"I'm afraid your brother didn't elaborate." Patchahoo coughed at another sip of whiskey. "He insisted that I find a buyer for Dunnings immediately, which was nearly impossible given the estate's," Patchahoo waved a hand about, "disrepair. I believe he meant to inform Whitehall of his change of heart, but he—"

"Died. Leaving me with this mess to clean up." Bentley had meant to leave his half-siblings homeless. Why was he surprised?

"In regards to Miss Whitehall, I can find nothing which proves or disproves your brother's claim as to her appeal. But to be honest, there are few families, my lord, titled or not, who would wish to be associated with Whitehall. Fewer still who would openly admit to an association. Only the most desperate of gentlemen would consider doing so. Perhaps that is why Bentley changed his mind."

"Let me guess." Jordan raised his glass, peering at the solicitor over the rim. "One Emerson is as good as another in Whitehall's estimation."

Patchahoo reddened. "Mr. Whitehall has expressed his desires to me."

Jordan stared out the window, allowing the bitterness towards Bentley to burst and spread across his entire being. It hadn't been enough for his brother to bankrupt the estate. Now Jordan must wed a repulsive heiress to make his family whole once more. Unfortunately, he had never responded well to being forced to do anything. His record at Harrow was proof of that.

"I object to be dictated to. Like some sort of trained dog." The urge to tell Whitehall to piss off was a strong one.

A drawn-out sigh left Patchahoo. "May I speak freely, my lord?"

Jordan nodded.

"Your brother left you in dire circumstances. There is nothing left to sell but Dunnings, and the amount this estate would fetch isn't enough to even touch the amount owed Whitehall. I strongly urged your brother to wed Miss Whitehall. As I must also urge you. I see no other way out of this situation at present."

Jordan considered that. "I've no other options?" It was a ridiculous question. If there had been any other option, he guessed Patchahoo would have already found it.

The solicitor pushed aside his glass and leaned forward. "Your reputation in society, my lord, though you haven't visited London in many years, precedes you. And the current Season is half over. Given those two factors, it is highly unlikely that you would find another heiress of Miss Whitehall's magnitude before Whitehall makes good on his threats. Lady Longwood has been particularly vocal in her," he hesitated, "opinions."

"Good to know Bentley's aunt remembers me with such fondness. Does Whitehall realize I am damaged goods?" Jordan gazed at his solicitor. "My reputation is little better than his."

"There is no comparison, my lord. Whitehall is reviled. You are an earl, and regardless of the opinion of Lady Longwood—"

"Shared by most of London."

"You are still much more highly regarded than someone of Angus Whitehall's origins. You will have a seat in Parliament. A house on Bruton in Grosvenor's Square." Patchahoo held up a hand. "You may not see it, my lord, but despite your tattered standing in London, you are still leagues ahead of what Whitehall could ever hope to have despite his wealth. He covets that which was bestowed upon you at birth. For all that Whitehall detests the aristocracy, he desires more than anything to be a member of it." Patchahoo's voice rose just a tad. "I don't like Mr. Whitehall, my lord. But I *do* understand."

"So all I must do is wed his unappealing daughter and the debts are erased?"

"You will also receive Miss Whitehall's dowry, which is significant. As I've explained, repayment of the debt is not Mr. Whitehall's true objective. The marriage contract is favorable to you, my lord. You could hardly do better."

"Are there any stipulations placed on me after we are wed?" Jordan had no intention of residing with this Odessa Whitehall, let alone bedding her. "Children, for instance?" Whitehall would be sorely disappointed if he assumed the grandchildren of a sharker would inherit the title of earl.

"I don't believe so, my lord. The marriage and having a title bestowed upon his daughter seem to be his main concerns."

"Make sure of it, Patchahoo. Whitehall gets *nothing* else. I want no restrictions placed on me once I'm wed. I can leave her anywhere in the world and it won't make a whit of difference."

"Yes, my lord."

"I hope it wasn't quick, Patchahoo," Jordan said after a few moments.

"What, my lord?" The solicitor's brows drew together.

"Bentley's death. I hope he lived long enough to feel the pain and know he was dying. I hope he knew that everything he'd done to me was for naught and that I would inherit." The loathing for Bentley, for what he'd done, sparked along Jordan's skin as if it were alive. "We'll return to London, Patchahoo, but not in time to see him buried. Lady Longwood can mourn him." It was petty. Cruel. The gossips in London would hum with the news. Jordan didn't much care.

Patchahoo nodded. "Do you think that wise, my lord?"

Boots sounded on the chipped tile of the foyer moments before the double doors to the drawing room burst open. One of the doors hung onto its hinges for dear life.

Tamsin stomped into the room, dropping mud from her boots all over the threadbare rug. She paused to gaze at Patchahoo with interest before tossing her hat onto the nearest chair. A great mass of chestnut hair spilled over her shoulders. Tilting her chin, she raised a brow in question. "Who's this?"

Patchahoo's eyes widened, taking in Lady Tamsin Sinclair in riding breeches and marching about like a Valkyrie.

Jordan splashed another finger of whiskey into the solicitor's glass. "Trust me," he said under his breath. "You'll need another swallow of whiskey."

Tamsin was an acquired taste.

"Mr. Patchahoo," he said as the solicitor came to his feet. "May I present my sister, Lady Tamsin. Tamsin, this is Mr. Patchahoo," Jordan informed his sister. "My newly acquired solicitor. Bentley is dead."

Tamsin's mouth popped open. She fell back against the cushions of the ancient sofa, releasing a cloud of dust. "Bentley is dead?"

"He is."

"Lady Tamsin. A pleasure." The solicitor bowed politely, trying not to stare at her. There was intensity to Jordan's sister, one that both attracted and terrified any male in her vicinity, akin to a hurricane which decimated everything in its path. The last man who had bowed to Tamsin had likely done so because her fist had made contact with his stomach.

"Mr. Patchahoo." Tamsin greeted the solicitor politely, but did not offer her hand.

"I understand we have a guest." Andrew appeared a moment behind Tamsin, strolling casually into the drawing room, the green of his eyes landing squarely on Patchahoo, then Jordan. Malcolm and Andrew were twins, though not identical, but both had inherited Mother's eyes. An arresting green, which sometimes took on a grayish hue. Like moss fading on a rock.

Drew let out a low whistle as he took in Jordan's swollen eye and bruised cheek. "Who got the best of you?" He glanced at Patchahoo. "Certainly not your new friend here."

"No, this is Patchahoo. My solicitor." Jordan tapped his cheek. "Captain Sisco."

"I thought he was still out to sea." His brother carelessly slumped into a chair. "Your lack of skill in fending off that brute is shocking. You've got a pea clinging to the back of your head, Jordan." Drew peered at Patchahoo. "We have a solicitor?"

"*I* do." Jordan said. "He's—

"I bring wonderful news," Drew interrupted; a smug look fixed itself on his face. "I've the funds to fix the roof; no need to go to the Evil Earl and beg him."

"It's just as well." Jordan held up a hand. "Bentley is dead, so begging him for anything would prove useless. Thus, the appearance of his former solicitor, now mine, Mr. Patchahoo. If you haven't guessed, Patchahoo, this is one of my brothers, Andrew Sinclair."

"Mr. Sinclair." Patchahoo gave a small bow. The solicitor was eyeing Andrew's shiny new boots and expensively-tailored coat, probably wondering, given the state of Dunnings, how his brother had managed to afford them. Gifts, no doubt, from Drew's current lover, Mrs. Pryce.

"Forgive me, we don't often entertain at Dunnings." Andrew shook the solicitor's hand. "My manners are lacking. Patchahoo? Scottish, isn't it?"

"It is, Mr. Sinclair. A pleasure." Patchahoo smiled in return, instantly charmed to his starched core by Drew.

There wasn't a soul alive who didn't enjoy making the acquaintance of Jordan's younger brother. Charming, attractive, possessed of a quick wit, Drew was an expert at cards, often taking in enough from his wanderings to supplement the meager bit of coin Bentley had tossed in their direction. It was Drew who'd won Tamsin's horse in a game of whist, which in turn allowed his unconventional sister to challenge well-heeled young lords to a race now and again.

Jordan didn't begrudge Drew his older, wealthy lovers or his propensity for gambling. Surviving Dunnings had been difficult for all of them.

"He really is dead then?" Drew seemed less surprised than Tamsin to hear of their brother's demise. "Jordan's the earl?"

"It would seem so." Tamsin answered. She stood and made her way over to the bookshelf where an assortment of unmatched goblets, teacups, and chipped crystal were displayed. They didn't have a proper sideboard. Not at Dunnings.

Picking up an ancient-looking tin cup, she walked over to the bottle of whiskey between Jordan and Patchahoo and poured out a healthy amount before returning to her perch on the sofa.

Patchahoo turned pink, blushing like a schoolgirl.

"Mr. Patchahoo." Jordan turned towards the solicitor. "I assume you've taken rooms in Spittal, or at least I hope you have. The rooms there are far better than what you'll find here. If you will make our travel arrangements, I would be appreciative. We'll leave at the end of the week once I've tidied things up here. I'm sure Lady Longwood will be more than comfortable with our absence at the funeral."

Patchahoo opened his mouth to protest, but just as quickly pressed his lips into a thin line. "Of course, my lord. I'll see to everything." He bowed once more, and exited, carefully closing the broken door behind him.

Tamsin leapt up from her place on the sofa. "London? But Jordan—"

"There is a perfectly good house waiting for us, one that doesn't have a hole in the roof and is fully staffed. You can't expect me to brave Lady Longwood and her minions alone, can you?"

"No, but, well you *can't* be serious." Tamsin held the whiskey to her lips. "Society isn't fond of me. Nor am I overly fond of it. You can't think to send me to balls and such. Or make polite conversation," she said in a rush. "I'll remain a spinster, thank you. But I suppose Aurora deserves a come out, doesn't she?"

Tamsin was lovely. Beautiful, even. The young lords she often challenged to horse races only agreed because doing so meant being in Tamsin's presence. Even without a dowry, Jordan was sure he would have been inundated with offers for her hand except for Tamsin's difficult nature. "You need never wed if you don't wish it," Jordan reminded her. "I've said as much. And you are beyond the age for a proper come out. At least, I think you are. But I would appreciate you playing along, Tamsin. For Aurora. You want her to make a proper match one day, do you not?"

Tamsin nodded; her gaze fixed on her whiskey. "I do. She should have the future Bentley denied her. And she possesses a romantic nature."

Jordan regarded his sister with a great deal of sympathy. Tamsin blamed herself for their banishment, though he'd told her many times she wasn't at fault. Even if she hadn't broken a lord's nose, Bentley still would have sent them to Dunnings.

"She'll be the most distressed about Bentley," Drew said. "Aurora has always been convinced that someday he would turn into a proper brother and arrive at Dunnings with a trunk of books as an apology for sending us all here. What utter rubbish. But Bentley's done something worse than banishing us to Northumberland, hasn't he, Jordan?" Strolling over to the shelf, Drew grabbed a chipped teacup and splashed it full of whiskey.

Jordan wasn't sure how to answer. He was still adjusting to his own swirl of emotions since Patchahoo arrived at The Hen.

"There were quite a few guests from London at Mrs. Pryce's little gathering, none of them decent at cards. I won an obscene amount at whist alone. Sir Thomas Glascomb," Drew waved his cup about, "is much better at gossip. He's also an unmitigated arse. Glascomb made a point of informing me that Bentley's mistress, he had two I believe—"

A snarl of disgust left Tamsin. "Two. While we starved at Dunnings."

Drew raised a brow. "Both expensive creatures, according to Glascomb. However, one of these delightful young women was currently on the hunt for a new protector. Her modiste bills weren't being paid and Bentley had informed her that she would be limited to one carriage instead of two. She found the situation intolerable, as Bentley had spent so freely before."

"Wonderful." Everyone in London would know Jordan was desperate to wed an heiress because the gossip of Bentley's financial difficulties was already making the rounds.

"When you can no longer satisfy your mistress, word tends to get out. Bentley had stopped receiving credit at any of the gaming establishments he frequented. Bills went unpaid, though it's rumored

Lady Longwood took care of Bentley's household expenses. Then there is the speculation, at least by Glascomb and his cronies, that our brother became involved with Angus Whitehall."

"What do you know of Whitehall?" Jordan drained his glass once more. The pounding in his temples hadn't receded a whit.

"According to Glascomb, titled lords who find themselves with no other choice but Whitehall often end up either embarrassing themselves or taking the honorable way out." Drew made a motion of cocking a pistol near his temple.

"Bentley wasn't the least honorable. His barouche overturned," Jordan replied. "But he was gracious enough to leave me to deal with Whitehall, which I will with Patchahoo's assistance. Our brother was deeply indebted to him."

Drew sighed and drained his cup. "Of course he was. The idiot."

"We can sell Dunnings." Tamsin set down her cup and looked at Drew. "You can gamble more. We—"

"Tamsin, stop. Whitehall isn't looking for repayment of the loan." Jordan rolled the half-empty glass of whiskey about in his hand. "He wants a title for his daughter. Something dear Bentley promised to see to, but had the audacity to get himself killed instead. It's more than a fair trade," Jordan insisted before his sister could protest further. "The truth of the matter is that Bentley left us in poor circumstances. Even if there was no Whitehall, I would be forced to wed a wealthy young lady with all expediency. An agreement with him ensures that not only are all debts erased, but I will also receive Miss Whitehall's dowry, which according to Patchahoo, is obscene."

"But Jordan," Tamsin leaned forward. "You can't agree to wed a girl you've never met. Not even for our sakes."

"I can and I will. Aren't you tired of being impoverished, Tamsin? I know I am. Stretching out every farthing. Eating cabbage." A vision of his mother, trying to be brave as she stepped into Dunnings, appeared before his eyes.

"This won't be so bad, my loves. At least we're together."

"My marriage," he said firmly, "will be nothing more than a business arrangement. No different than most of those in the *ton*." Jordan ran a hand through his hair, dislodging another pea. "I'm not the only title who has had to wed due to pending impoverishment, nor will I be the last. It is the way the world works. This saves me the trouble of trying to find my own heiress."

He sounded so bloody rational. Sensible. Logical, even. Jordan didn't want to mention that Bentley had wanted to reject Miss Whitehall because she was less than appealing for some reason. No need to inform his siblings their new sister-in-law would likely be a troll of some sort. Nor did he want to express any of his other, unkinder, decisions he'd made where Odessa Whitehall was concerned.

Whitehall would get *nothing* but a title for his daughter. That would be the extent of their association. If he had visions of attending balls and the like or a crop of titled grandchildren to bounce on one knee, he would be sorely disappointed.

Jordan didn't spare a thought for Odessa.

"Bentley is dead?" A delicate voice came from the entrance of the drawing room. "And you're marrying some horrid girl none of us have met so we won't be poor?"

He, Tamsin, and Drew all looked up to see Aurora watching them, a basket filled with berries clutched in one hand. His youngest sister didn't look upset, only annoyed she was the last to hear the news.

"I would like to clarify, for the room." Aurora tossed her thick plait of dark hair over one shoulder. "That I gave up wishing for Bentley to rescue us long ago. I know you all think I'm fanciful, but not where he was concerned." She frowned. "I don't mean to say I'm not distressed at Bentley's passing. He was my brother. But I'm far less upset than anticipated."

Tamsin held out one hand, urging her to come sit. "You have a wonderful heart, Aurora. Bentley doesn't deserve you mourning him. And we don't know that Miss Whitehall is horrid."

"Yes," Jordan added without emotion. "She might be perfectly lovely."

CHAPTER THREE

"T HIS IS MOST welcome news."

Miss Odessa Whitehall perched on the edge of the sofa in her father's drawing room, nibbling on a currant scone. Amazing how much better a scone could taste when it was coated with relief. The Earl of Emerson, her unwanted, despised suitor, the third in little over a year, had perished when his barouche overturned.

"A gentleman is dead, Odessa." Her great-aunt and chaperone, Miss Charlotte Maplehurst, looked up from the book in her lap. "I do not think his untimely demise is a cause for celebration."

"It isn't as if I'm dancing about or giddy with delight. But you must agree that Lord Emerson was *beastly*. Each visit was more awful than the last."

"Yes, but you became more…*revolting*, niece. Your conversation grotesque at times. So much so that I am only relieved when your father didn't see fit to be present when Emerson visited. Any gentleman, when faced with such *adversity,* would find it hard to control his feelings. I feel I must point this out."

"I expected disgust from him, but he was overly cruel, don't you think? Condescending. Comes from being overindulged and privileged your entire life. I've more character in my pinky finger," Odessa held up her hand, "than Lord Emerson possessed in his entire body. Thankfully, the fates sought to rescue me. I didn't even have to resort to eating a strawberry to dispel him from my presence."

"A truly fortuitous turn of events."

Odessa wasn't trying to be unkind in regards to Emerson; it was only that she hadn't liked him. Overly pompous and possessing an extravagant ginger mustache, Emerson behaved at each visit as if Odessa were in the presence of royalty. He was the very *worst* suitor Papa had ever sent her way.

"Papa's obsession with having me wed some titled, limp-wristed fop in the hopes it will make society accept me, and thus him, is an absurd notion. No acceptance was forthcoming after his marriage to Mama and no doors opened for me since. And Mama was the daughter of a viscount. Do you recall how he strong-armed Lord Norris? Forcing an invitation to his lordship's ball?"

That ball was several years ago, before the parade of suitors. An event at which Odessa had been an unwelcome guest. Lord Norris's ball had been the first real indication of her standing in London society. Or lack of standing. She'd planned her gown weeks in advance, a pale pink tulle, the skirts covered in tiny brilliants. Fresh roses had been woven into her hair. She'd been so excited.

"I do," Aunt Lottie answered.

"What a travesty. Not one gentleman asked me to dance." Requests for an introduction were nonexistent. Odessa's presence was ignored completely. She had stood along the farthest wall, her hopes for dancing and perhaps a stolen kiss fading faster than the blasted roses in her hair. Possibly if she'd been a great beauty, some young lord might have risked paying Odessa some attention, but she was, at best, only passably pretty. Yes, her dowry was enormous. Papa liked to boast about the obscene amount at every turn, which did nothing to endear Odessa to society. No titled lord that Season had been desperate enough to allow their line to be tainted with the likes of the low-born Angus Whitehall or his somewhat plain daughter.

Papa, undeterred, changed tactics, hand selecting Odessa's suitors.

"Now I face a stream of impoverished lords. My preference is not some titled nitwit who finds me so beneath him socially that only my dowry would induce him into my presence."

Odessa had a stubborn streak and a great deal of determination. Papa's choices of husband for her were, at best, *repellent*. Her romantic nature was partially to blame because she could not even contemplate the idea of feeling affection for the sort of man Papa thought appropriate. Or possibly, it was knowing the misery that awaited her from a marriage made for financial gain and status but little else. Her own parents had been trapped in such a union with disastrous results.

"Honestly, I don't know why Papa assumes I want a gentleman, especially one with a title. Who cares if he can trace his line back to William the Conqueror? I certainly don't. Lolling about doing nothing but gambling, dressing well, and attending balls." She made a disgusted sound. "There isn't anything wrong with *working*. Papa is self-made."

"Angus doesn't see it that way."

"Which is why I've had to take matters into my own hands."

Dire circumstances often inspire enormous creativity. She had extracted a tear-filled promise from Papa, demanding that at the very least, she was to be courted by the man she would wed. If Papa were so determined she be a lady, shouldn't Odessa be treated as such? Polite calls. Walks in the park. Possibly a carriage ride. Didn't she deserve to have at least the semblance of affection?

A flood of tears had erupted from Odessa as she tried to convince her father.

She could not wed a complete stranger, or a man who loathed her. Odessa would do her part to foster a sense of companionship, but if the gentleman in question didn't find she suited *him*, then Papa must accept the decision. There was a shoe for every foot, Odessa reasoned. She must be allowed to find the right fit.

Reluctantly, Papa agreed.

Tears, Mama often said, were a lady's greatest weapon.

But guilting her father with tears would only last so long. The trick was to rid herself of these unwelcome suitors while finding a man that appealed to her. Or find a way not to wed at all, a much more difficult proposition.

"Angus will realize sooner or later what you've been up to, Odessa," Aunt Lottie gently reprimanded. "Your methods will not go unnoticed."

The first test of Odessa's newfound strategy had been a viscount whose name she couldn't recall. Yet another self-important twit, more concerned with the cut of his coat than anything else. The viscount visited Odessa once, but never returned. It had taken little effort on her part to deter him. Some wool padding and the morbid tale of a man in Germany who gruesomely baked his wife into a pie had done the trick.

A few months later, a baron arrived to call. Lord Malfrey. He'd lasted a full two weeks before throwing up his hands and announcing to Odessa he would rather stay impoverished than wed her. An onion was used to great effect. A story about Madame Guillotine's victims. More wool padding.

When questioned by Papa, Aunt Lottie pretended utter mystification over Malfrey's sudden change of heart. Odessa put her hands to her face, sobbing, and pretended to be despondent over Malfrey's rejection. The matter seemed to rest, especially when the baron up and wed the daughter of an earl barely a month later.

Relieved, Odessa had gone about her usual routine, secure in the knowledge that she had outsmarted her father and his ambitions once more. A great deal of Odessa's time was spent either at the museum or at one of several booksellers she favored, feeding her fascination with oddities, macabre tales, and other strange amusements to be found in London. She adored a good ghost story or haunting, particularly if the area had witnessed a notorious murder. Creatures not of this earth that walked the London streets at night. Deaths caused by bizarre misfortune. She read and memorized the details of every execution and horrible crime in London contained in the criminal broadsides she devoured as if they were sweets.

A strange hobby to be sure, for a young lady, but without the constant lure of dozens of invitations for the Season, or anyone having the slightest inclination to pay a call upon her, Odessa had to keep herself busy. And she wasn't any good at embroidery. Madame Tussauds wax exhibition was her new favorite activity. She'd visited the gruesome display of victims of the French Revolution three times alone in the last month.

"I don't expect to continue this way forever, only until I have an opportunity to present a gentleman of *my* choosing to Papa. Or better yet, convince him to allow me to remain unwed."

"A dream, Odessa. Angus will never allow you to remain unmarried, nor will he accept the sort of man you would choose yourself." She shook her head. "You are simply delaying the inevitable."

Aunt Lottie was wrong. Odessa had met a dashing cavalry officer a few months ago. Appealing to her in every way. A bit rough. Masculine. Unpadded shoulders. Lacking the scent of pomade. She'd been so *terribly* excited.

Then Lord Emerson appeared like a rotten, wormy apple in an otherwise perfect basket of fruit.

"I do not want some over-indulged fop who spends his time putting pomade on his hair and worrying over his waistcoat, title or not. Emerson quite possibly put me off well-bred gentlemen forever." Drastic methods had been required to force Emerson to beg off. And he did. Or, at least, Odessa was certain he would have if his barouche hadn't overturned.

"Odessa, there you are."

Angus Whitehall's voice filled the air as he stepped inside the drawing room, making the area seem that much smaller with his presence. Not because of his size, for he was no more than average in height and build, but from the sheer confidence he exuded. He was handsome, which drew the eye. Fit. Possessing a full head of silver hair and a well-groomed mustache and beard. Blue eyes, which twinkled and charmed a person within minutes of an introduction.

All of which Mama had often said belied his true nature and made one forget Papa was more wolf than gentleman.

Odessa had never seen evidence of Papa's ruthless side, not until his determination to have her wed a title had surfaced. Society simply didn't like him because he was low-born and self-made, which was incredibly unfair. But marrying her off to a title wouldn't fix things.

"Good morning, Papa." Odessa tilted her head as he pressed a kiss to her cheek.

"I'm here to speak to you concerning Lord Emerson." Papa came forward and settled into the chair beside her, eyes shining like cut sapphires and just as hard. No twinkle today.

"Lord Emerson?" Her brows drew together in confusion. The barest hint of dread, like a swirl of smoke, caught around her. What more could there be to discuss? Emerson could hardly wed her from the grave. "But he has…*died*, Papa."

"Unfortunate, to be sure."

"I—am sorry that our association came to naught. You had such high hopes that I become a countess. In truth," she added, "I was looking forward to being one as well." The lie slid easily off her tongue. "I haven't yet sent a note to Madame Theriot." Her voice held just a touch of sadness at informing the modiste she would no longer need an expensive trousseau. "But I will do so today. I promise."

"There is no need." The brackets around her father's mouth deepened as his lips drew taut into a grim, determined line.

"But Emerson is…dead, Papa." Another sprinkle of dread made its way over Odessa's shoulders. Had Emerson somehow managed to survive? Odessa had heard macabre tales of corpses about to be put in the ground suddenly coming back to life. Beating on the lid of the coffin, begging to be released before a shovelful of earth fell. Odessa had once even broached the subject with an undertaker, much to Aunt Lottie's dismay.

"Bentley Sinclair *is* dead." Papa gave a flip of his wrist. "You don't recover from a broken neck. Fortunately, he has a younger brother who inherited the title. *Also* unwed."

Odessa's fingers froze on the folds of her skirts, unable to as much as twitch. "A brother?"

Aunt Lottie slammed her book shut. "Angus, you can't be serious. What you are suggesting is—"

"Entirely acceptable. Odessa and the first Emerson weren't wed. Or even officially betrothed. I doubt he even touched her hand."

"But you cannot merely switch one brother for another." Aunt Lottie looked askance at Odessa. "The very idea is distasteful."

"You will refrain, Charlotte, from sharing your unwelcome opinions with me. Indeed, the matter is already settled. Emerson is open to wedding Odessa."

"But Papa." Odessa's fingers twisted together, trying to swallow back her panic. "His brother has only been gone for a few weeks. And—what if Lord Emerson and I don't suit? You promised—" She hesitated, afraid to show her hand lest Papa become suspicious. "The new Lord Emerson can't possibly wish to court me so soon after his brother's demise." This was *terrible* news, but not insurmountable.

Papa shrugged. "As I said, Emerson doesn't share your concerns, and matters necessitate he wed sooner rather than later. Just like his brother." A dark sound came from Papa.

Amusement, Odessa realized. The blue of his eyes, usually so affectionate when they landed on her, now gleamed with cold satisfaction. "But—"

"You'll get to know each other as I promised." He tucked his finger beneath her chin. "Have the opportunity to find common ground. I know how important it is to you, Odessa. But I am *assured* you and

Emerson will get on. I think him a perfect match for you." Another guttural sound of amusement, as if Papa were laughing at a joke only he was privy to. "You'll be Lady Emerson before you know it."

Odessa looked away, afraid the anger coursing through her veins would show on her face. She had already decided to seek out the dashing cavalry officer, Captain Phillips, as soon as possible with the intent of inducing him to call upon her. Composed a speech to convince her father of his suitability because, though Phillips wasn't titled himself, he was related to a marquess on his mother's side.

"You'll see, Odessa, that this is a good fit."

"Yes, Papa." She studied the toe of her slipper, already contemplating the steps that would need to be taken to rid herself of this new Emerson as quickly as possible.

"Lottie, you'll welcome Lord Emerson and act as chaperone as you have the others. Unless you wish me to, so your tender sensibilities aren't offended."

"No," her aunt said quickly. "I'm pleased to extend an invitation to Lord Emerson for tea."

"Wonderful." Papa stood, obviously finished now that he'd delivered his unwelcome news. "I have an appointment and won't return until dinner. Have Cook make a cherry tart for dessert, Odessa. I know it's your favorite."

"Yes, Papa." She didn't dare look up from her slippers.

"Until then, Angus." Aunt Lottie inclined her head. "I'll send a note to Lord Emerson within the hour."

CHAPTER FOUR

L ONDON WAS EXACTLY the way Jordan remembered, right down to the sneering look on Lady Longwood's painfully sharp features. The hatred for Jordan and his siblings which had simmered for years now threatened to boil over with the death of Bentley.

She had the audacity to be seated in Jordan's drawing room, sipping *his* tea, when the Sinclairs trudged into the house on Bruton Street, exhausted after the long journey from Dunnings.

Percival, Lady Longwood's sniveling son and now Viscount Longwood, sat by her side, stomach protruding from his waistcoat. He barely looked up as Jordan entered, too engrossed in stuffing the pastries from Jordan's kitchen into his mouth.

Lord Longwood didn't feel the need to stand when Jordan's sisters entered the room; apparently, the tart he held in one pudgy hand was more important than his manners.

Drew cast him a murderous look.

Bentley's butler, a snobbish sort who introduced himself with great reluctance as Hart, took Jordan's hat with a disdainful flip of his wrist, informing them all, in a snippy tone, that the household had been caught unawares with the news of Lord Emerson's arrival. Rooms were still being prepared.

A blatant lie since Patchahoo had informed the staff on Bruton Street before he'd ever come to Dunnings.

Hart, as well as the remainder of Bentley's staff, would soon be seeking other employment very soon. Jordan wasn't about to tolerate such blatant insubordination, nor have a household full of servants whose loyalty was to Lady Longwood. If Bentley's aunt thought banishment to Northumberland had cowed Jordan or the rest of the Sinclairs in any way, she was mistaken.

"Lady Longwood," Jordan drawled with just the right amount of insolence. "What an unexpected pleasure to find you *and* Lord Longwood in my drawing room."

"I wanted to be the first to welcome you to London." She bared her teeth at his tone.

"You shouldn't have gone to such trouble. But possibly, Percival needed to be fed." Jordan circled her chair.

"No trouble at all." Her fingers, long and thin, rippled over the damask-covered arm of the chair, lips pursed in distaste. "You don't look very different after so many years."

Percival chomped away on a sandwich, crumbs dangling from his mustache, a sneer on his lips as he shot his mother a look. "Just like a pig farmer."

"I've a pen that should fit you," Jordan advised Percival, delighted when the fattened lord reddened.

"My lord, how lovely to see you." Tamsin, clearly forgetting the half-dozen promises she'd made during the trip to London to behave in a manner befitting a lady, nudged Percival's rounded form in passing. The plate he held, filled with tiny sandwiches, tilted and bits of cucumber spilled over his shoes.

Percival sniffed, glared at them all, and kicked a slice of cucumber across the rug.

Jordan, Tamsin, Drew, and Aurora all stared pointedly at the cucumber, then at Hart who stood silent, gaze fixed forward.

A bit of watercress dropped. Percival ground it into the plush thickness of the rug with the heel of his boot, watching Jordan the entire time. A smirk crossed his bulbous lips before he deliberately chewed the remainder of his sandwich.

"My lord," Hart the soon-to-be-sacked butler intoned. "Lombard has advised me that due to your unexpected arrival, dinner will be sparse tonight and begs your apology. He had no time to create a proper menu. A stew of some sort. Fresh bread, of course."

"Lombard?"

"The chef, my lord." The butler refrained from looking Jordan in the eye and kept his gaze away from the mess Percival had created.

The size of the tea tray arranged for Percival could have fed a small army.

"Odd that the larder wasn't lacking in refreshments for Lord Longwood. Since we are so unexpected," Jordan's sarcasm filled the room, "I don't wish to trouble Lombard further. Drew, would you send a note to Patchahoo for reinforcements? After, if you wouldn't mind ridding my kitchens—"

Hart stiffened. "My lord—"

"I don't care for French cooking, Hart. Drew, you might also inform Lombard and his minions below that no references will be forthcoming. At least from me. Lady Longwood might be induced to provide one since he was in her employ."

Bentley's aunt set down her cup of tea, rattling the saucer.

Drew gave a small bow "As you wish, my lord."

The drawing room remained silent for some moments while Jordan and Lady Longwood glared at each other. What sounded like vile curses, all uttered in French, broke the quiet.

At least Jordan assumed them to be vile. He didn't speak a word of French.

Lady Longwood's thin lips twisted into a sneer. The chef was but the first volley fired in her little war against the Sinclairs. Lombard was merely cannon fodder for her next assault. Jordan was sure had Lombard been permitted to remain, dinner would have been a greasy stew and moldy bread.

"I expected your arrival sooner, my lord. But possibly you stopped to dance upon my poor Bentley's grave before coming here." Lady Longwood's clipped, icy tone filled Jordan's ears. "Couldn't even see him properly buried, could you? Disgraceful." She drew out the word. "No, your only concern was to invade Bentley's home as soon as possible with the rest of your herd."

Lady Longwood. So superior. Strident. More bitter than any un-ripened fruit. How Jordan despised her.

"Bentley's home? Emerson House belongs to *me* now. Not even you can take that away, my lady. And as for dancing on Bentley's grave, I don't dance. At least not well." He cast a glance at Percival, who looked very much like one of Jordan's pigs at the moment. "Do you dance, Percival? Or merely roll around?"

"At least I don't muck about with farm animals," Percival sneered.

"You tampered with Bentley's barouche, didn't you?" A manic look entered Lady Longwood's eyes. "Or did you enlist one of your brothers?"

So that was her purpose in being here. In addition to all the other slurs leveled against Jordan, Lady Longwood wished to add the accusation of murder.

"I was in Northumberland, as you well know. A place my family and I were banished to immediately after the death of my father, by dear Bentley. You remember the day well, don't you? The feeling of triumph as you insulted my mother?"

Her fingers curled over the arms of the chair, thin, brittle fingers tapping on the wood.

"I haven't been to London in at least a decade until today," Jordan reminded her. So your accusation, as amusing as it is, has no merit, my lady."

"You paid someone to harm Bentley. I'm sure of it." Lady Long-wood leaned forward with a small sob. "You've *always* coveted his title."

"You mean *my* father's title? You behave as if the queen created it especially for Bentley and it belonged to no one else. His only claim was that he was born first, my lady. And paying someone to harm Bentley? When our very existence was dependent on his dubious charity? You must be joking. We barely had the funds for coal let alone paying an assassin. Pig farming doesn't pay as well as one might think." A laugh came from him.

Lady Longwood reddened. "You will never be the earl that he was. Never be able to fill his shoes."

"Good God, I should hope not." Jordan strolled over to the sideboard, pleased to see that there was a nice selection of expensive spirits and cut crystal with which to drink it from. "I've no desire to bankrupt a previously wealthy estate and gamble away my fortune on horses and hazard while keeping two mistresses. Bentley will always be far better at those things than I."

Lady Longwood inhaled sharply. Percival finally stopped stuffing himself.

Apparently, this conversation wasn't going how they imagined. Jordan was supposed to be brow beaten after his years away. Pathetic and defeated. Terrified of the great Lady Longwood and her influence.

"And I would *never*, no matter my own feelings, banish my siblings to a far-flung estate and force them into poverty while I continue to pursue my extravagant lifestyle. I owe Bentley no shred of kindness for doing so. Or respect. Dancing on his grave is the least of what he deserves."

"I wish you had all perished at Dunnings, but I suppose that was too much to hope for." Her voice shook. "The Sinclairs are nothing more than a pack of beetles that find their way into your flour." Lady Longwood's face turned puce, an unattractive hue in clothing as well as skin. "Well, you won't find a warm welcome in London." A smug smile pulled at her lips. "And you'll need to make a decent match to save you. Which is now an impossibility. Not one young lady who possesses a decent fortune will look your way, nor will her family accept you. I've made sure of it. You'll stay impoverished. Unwelcome. The Sinclairs will fade into obscurity, as they should have years ago."

Strange that Lady Longwood didn't know about Angus Whitehall. Or Bentley's involvement with the man.

"My beloved nephew was in dire straits because of *your* mother's flagrant spending." She continued her tirade. "Bentley inherited an already teetering estate. He was forced to borrow large sums from me just to maintain appearances. Leeches, that's what you are. You sucked the lifeblood from Bentley with your constant demands." Lady Longwood glanced at Percival, who nodded in agreement. "I've paid the staff at Emerson House for years and I will no longer do so."

"Do you hear, Hart?" Jordan said in a mournful tone. "You've lost your position. Just as well, you were going to be sacked today at any rate. I hope you receive a recommendation from Lady Longwood."

Hart puffed out his chest and finally looked to Bentley's aunt, who pointedly ignored him.

"How odd," Tamsin interjected. "My mother has been dead for *ten* years. I wonder how she managed to fritter away Bentley's fortune on dresses, furniture, or other fripperies from the grave. I hadn't known she possessed such skill."

"And the estate was solid when my father died," Jordan added. "I saw the books, my lady. Bentley was a pathetic wastrel. A gambler. A man who had little charity in his heart and will not receive an ounce of it from me now that he is gone. A terrible earl and a worse brother. Good day, Lady Longwood."

The sound of an enraged animal came from her at the dismissal. Had there been a knife or other weapon handy, Jordan would have found himself murdered in his own drawing room.

Tamsin glared at Percival, kicking him in the ankle. "Get up. You've overstayed your welcome, my lord."

Percival came to his feet like a great toad, crumbs rolling off his stomach to litter the floor. He lumbered to stand behind his mother, thick fingers patting her shoulder protectively.

"Do not invade my home again. Either of you. Do I make myself clear, Lady Longwood?" Jordan considered, briefly, breaking each one of Percival's sausage-like appendages. This was what society deemed an example of a well-bred gentleman? Percival? Bentley?

I'll have none of it.

"I never pressured Bentley to repay me." His adversary stood and smoothed her skirts. "He was my family. But you, Lord Emerson, are not. I'll expect all debts, along with the gifts I've given him over the years—"

"Good day, Lord Longwood," Jordan said again, chilly and polite. "Lady Longwood." He would toss her out the door if need be. Her sour presence spoiled the air in his reclaimed home. "I beg you to not trouble yourself by calling upon me again, or I won't be responsible for Lady Tamsin's behavior."

Lady Longwood sniffed and took Percival's arm. "Out of the goodness of my heart, I came today to check on your welfare and offer my assistance as you re-enter society because that is what my beloved Bentley would have wanted. I was dismissed and told to leave. Escorted out of your home." That ugly, feral smile once more broke across her sharp features. "I'll make sure everyone knows of your unkind behavior towards me. You'll rue the day you came to London, Jordan Sinclair."

Jordan raised his glass to her. "I already do."

CHAPTER FIVE

"MY LORD, MR. Whitehall awaits you in his study."

Jordan rubbed a finger against his temple, willing the ache to subside. He hadn't slept well his first night in London, owing to the fact that nothing at Emerson House had been readied. Patchahoo's instructions had been deliberately discarded by a staff instructed by Lady Longwood. He couldn't fault Hart or the number of servants under his guidance; after all, Bentley's aunt had been paying their salaries. She'd probably instructed Hart and the others on how to deal with the Sinclairs. Ready themselves if Jordan ever made good on his promise and unexpectedly appeared on the steps of Emerson House.

Hart was unceremoniously and immediately sacked after Lady Longwood's dramatic exit. The butler sputtered, protesting his departure until finally gathering his things and exiting the premises. The upstairs maids, Bentley's snobbish valet, three footmen, and two grooms were all shown the door. Jordan kept the driver Patchahoo had hired for the trip to London and the stable boy who was promoted to groom. A scullery maid also survived the purge because she'd been hired only last week. Not enough time to be infected by Lady Longwood.

Patchahoo, bless him, perhaps anticipating the day's events, was prepared. He sent a note that Lord Emerson was not to worry. Assistance was forthcoming in the form of a plump, amiable older woman named Mrs. Cherry who had recently lost her position due to the death of her elderly employer.

Mrs. Cherry arrived like a small whirlwind, taking charge of the kitchens and the lone scullery maid, declaring that no matter what else might transpire, Lord Emerson and his family would eat well. The larder had not been depleted.

Additional staff would be forthcoming. Patchahoo had already started inquiries.

Jordan tugged at the cravat around his neck. Damned thing felt far too tight. Or perhaps it was the thought of Whitehall leading him about on a leash.

He studied the fine wood paneling and mellowed cream walls of the Whitehall residence, thinking that if he didn't know it was the home of a sharker, Jordan would think it that of a lord or a wealthy merchant. Certainly not a gentleman of Whitehall's reputation. The house itself stood at the edge of a still fashionable area of London, one inhabited with well-bred families whose standing in society had faltered along with their fortunes. Snobbery hung in the air, along with the scent of the roses from the park across the street. He doubted Whitehall was overly friendly with his neighbors.

Jordan followed the butler, who introduced himself as Burns, to a polished oak door at the end of the hall.

What had Burns done to land in such an undesirable post as butler to Whitehall? Murder? Theft?

After a short knock, Burns opened the door and bowed. "Lord Emerson, sir."

Angus Whitehall stood, standing behind a massive desk of oak. He made no move to come forward and greet Jordan, and there was little welcome in the blue of Whitehall's eyes. Only calculation. The snaggle-toothed sharker who'd lurked about the Spittal docks often greeted his own victims with the same expression. Whitehall's appearance as a gentleman probably allowed him to slip into the waters of society unnoticed.

Whitehall smiled, showing a line of crooked teeth. "My condolences on the loss of your brother, my lord." He managed to sound sympathetic.

False platitudes. Jordan wasn't fooled.

"Thank you. It was a shock to all of us." He doubted Whitehall had spared Bentley a moment's thought after discovering Jordan's existence.

Burns shut the study door with a soft click.

"I confess, my lord. I was growing concerned at your continued absence in London. I expected you to arrive to bury your brother. I worried you had decided to reject my offer."

Offer? More threat. Jordan had little choice but to comply.

"Apologies I kept you waiting." Jordan shrugged. In his opinion, Whitehall was little better than some thief operating in the rookery, only he hadn't thrust a pistol into Jordan's back to get what he wanted. "Business matters."

Whitehall's smile faltered at the blatant insincerity. "You should have informed me, my lord."

"My solicitor assured me he relayed the information." Jordan's fingers curled into his palms, struggling with the urge to take out his frustration at Whitehall with his fists. A foolish desire to be sure. Whitehall held all the cards at present, and it would do Jordan no good to let this petty criminal see his hand.

"Business? In Spittal?" The glittering blue of Whitehall's eyes mocked Jordan. "Did you find a good home for all your pigs, my lord?"

Why did everyone feel it necessary to remind Jordan he'd been a pig farmer while waiting to become an earl?

"Mostly," Jordan answered.

Turning, Whitehall lifted a decanter of brandy, splashing the amber liquid into two glasses, one of which he pushed across the desk. "You may sit." Whitehall took his own seat.

Bentley might have been obedient, but this prick would find Jordan far different. He was not some pampered lord who had the bad sense to become involved with Whitehall.

Dunnings and Spittal had molded Jordan into someone far different.

Jordan didn't sit. Nor did he touch the proffered brandy he hadn't asked for. Presumptuous of Whitehall, a man who was obviously enthralled with his own power and assured Jordan was trapped by it. Resentment filled him, for Whitehall and his unseen, unappealing daughter.

Whitehall frowned. Drummed his fingers along the edge of the desk. Waited impatiently for Jordan to speak first. An intimidation tactic of sorts.

Jordan clasped his hands and regarded Whitehall blandly, to the other man's growing annoyance. The ever-efficient Patchahoo had prepared an entire file on Angus Whitehall, criminal and blackmailer. The list of wealthy, affluent gentlemen, nearly all titled, who found themselves ruined by Whitehall was lengthy. He'd used the desperation of others to great effect. Wealth seemed to be his primary objective in the beginning, possibly some petty revenge on his betters. After a time, Whitehall wanted to be part of society instead of merely bleeding it.

Whitehall wanted acceptance. Laughable, really, considering he'd caused the "honorable" deaths of a handful of lords. Put others in his debt forever. Even though his business dealings were by now of a more legitimate nature, Whitehall still demanded favors from his acquaintances, some of whom despaired they'd ever rid themselves of him. His marriage, to the youngest daughter of Lord Maplehurst, an impoverished viscount, hadn't brought Whitehall any closer to the acceptance he so desperately craved. He'd pushed his daughter into the marriage mart, hoping to use his dead wife's connections, but to little success.

No one wanted Whitehall at their parties. Or his daughter.

Holding the brandy against his chest, Whitehall took a sip and leaned back in his chair, taking Jordan's measure. Drummed his fingers some more. Finally, he grunted, "Your solicitor informed me he is reviewing the contract once more. I won't tolerate another delay, my lord."

"Mr. Patchahoo is incredibly thorough, which I cannot fault him for, given the circumstances."

A tiny sneer lifted Whitehall's lips. "You seek a way out. I assure you, there is not one."

Jordan had decided at Dunnings there wasn't a way around wedding Miss Whitehall, but he didn't care to be reminded of it by the charlatan before him. A great deal of money would be required to dig the Sinclairs out of the hole Bentley had made, and an heiress of Odessa Whitehall's magnitude would be required. Once the debt was erased and Odessa's dowry in his hands, Jordan had every intention of discarding his unwanted wife and ensuring Whitehall didn't invade his existence again.

Patchahoo would scrub every inch of the marriage contract before Jordan signed it.

"How did you come to be acquainted with my brother?" he asked, knowing it couldn't have been accidental. Whitehall was the type who liked to play with his food, taking stock of his victims and knowing exactly what he wanted from them before pouncing. Bentley's markers had been all over London, and his financial situation worsening.

"We both enjoyed wagering on horses and happened to be doing so at Newmarket."

Horse racing. One of Bentley's favorite pursuits, though he wasn't a good judge of horseflesh. His brother would have been deep in his cups, bemoaning the fact his horse had lost once more, demanding he be extended every courtesy because he was Lord Emerson. So full of his own self-importance he wouldn't have seen the trap Whitehall set for him.

At some point in the last year, Whitehall must have realized the usual methods of dangling Odessa's enormous dowry to nearly impoverished titles hadn't worked. So he'd resorted to blackmail; after all, according to Patchahoo, it was how Whitehall acquired his wife.

"The previous Lord Emerson wasn't any better at picking horses than he was at anything else," Whitehall said in a bland tone. "Begged for my assistance after a time."

There was no point in debating the absolute *stupidity* of Bentley Sinclair. Nor would he defend his brother. "And you were happy to offer it."

Whitehall's gaze bored into him. "I could hardly do less."

"You realize I'm not much of an earl, Whitehall. My reputation isn't exactly that of my brother's, despite his obvious deficits. It is doubtful that becoming my countess will elevate your daughter," Jordan stated bluntly. "Or allow her to be received."

"You're trying to weasel out," Whitehall snapped in a guttural tone, showing a flash of the refuse-strewn alley he had no doubt been born in. "I assure you, my lord. That would be a terrible mistake."

"You misunderstand, Whitehall. I merely wish to manage expectations. The *ton* has a long memory."

"You mean they haven't yet forgiven your father for wedding his mistress?" A bark of laughter, curt and brittle, escaped from Whitehall. "A woman known more for being a bit of a lightskirt than her acting abilities. You're no better than I am, in many respects."

Jordan didn't consider himself much better than most, but he was leagues ahead of Whitehall. His jaw hardened, the only indication the insult to his mother bothered him. But far worse had been said about the late Lady Emerson.

"I only wished to be made aware of the inevitable challenges that will be faced by you and your daughter. And my inability to stop them."

"What is *inevitable*," Whitehall slammed down his fist, "is that you will wed Odessa. You will make her a countess. Guide her into society. Show her every ounce of courtesy and respect. Make her feel as if you suit. Her happiness is important to me, Emerson. You will take the time to court her." He waved his hand. "Or I'll ruin you and your bloody family. Bring you to your knees. Do we understand each other?"

Jordan picked up the brandy and took a sip. Expensive. French. "You hold my bollocks in your fist," he said crudely. "There isn't any need to continue with your threats."

Whitehall sat back. "Good."

"Were my mother here," Jordan said, glaring at him, "she would tell you that you can be poor as a church mouse so long as you are *well-bred* and from the right family."

"You take me for a fool. But I am not. You see, my lord, one day, *my* grandson will inherit an earldom. *My* granddaughters will be ladies. Accepted. Sought after. The memory of society is indeed lengthy, but eventually, they'll forget."

Whitehall favored a long game. Just how did he expect to have these grandchildren conceived? Hold a pistol to Jordan's head to ensure he performed his marital duties?

"I'll bestow an additional sum on you for each child born. Put it in the contract."

Ah. That was how.

Thank goodness. Jordan didn't perform well under pressure. "How generous."

Did Whitehall realize he resembled a crocodile when he smiled in such a toothy manner? He had no intention of siring this man's grandchildren or even living with Odessa once they were wed. Under no circumstances would Jordan give Whitehall that which he most desired. At first glance of the marriage contract, there didn't seem to be any provisions for Odessa *after* the marriage. No references to

Jordan and Odessa even residing in the same city, let alone the same house. Whitehall assumed bribing Jordan with money for each child would be enough. It would have been for Bentley.

"You'll be wed at the end of next month." Whitehall continued, now that he was assured Jordan had been put properly in his place and he would get what he wanted. Instead, he'd just doomed his daughter to a life of loneliness. A countess without an earl. No one bearing Whitehall blood was going to inherit Jordan's title. He had two brothers.

"You aren't nearly as stupid as your brother, Emerson. I didn't care for him."

And yet you were willing to give him your daughter. Just as you are me. For your own ambitions.

"I am *nothing* like Bentley." Jordan swallowed the brandy and set down his glass on the desk. "You would do well to remember that, Whitehall. I'll see myself out."

CHAPTER SIX

"E MERSON WILL ARRIVE any moment, Odessa." Aunt Lottie turned her about. "Are you sure you wish to go through with this farce once more? Your luck in deceiving each of your suitors will only last for so long. Angus will be furious if he finds out."

"Then I will have to be extra careful that he does not find out. Papa met with Lord Emerson and has assured me that his lordship agreed to a courtship of sorts, in order that we may know each other better, just as the others did. He seems to be certain Emerson will find me suitable." A short laugh came from her. "But if Emerson is *anything* like his brother, or Lord Malfrey, he'll be so disgusted by my appearance and so self-absorbed, deception will be the last thing he guesses. The onion will keep him from getting too close, at any rate."

Odessa stared at the peeled onion sitting on the table beside the mirror. The smell emanating from the small, white ball was so strong her eyes watered. She took up the onion, hesitating only for a moment before taking a bite. The acrid taste burned her tongue as she chewed.

"Dear lord, that is pungent." Aunt Lottie waved a hand in the air.

Odessa made a face as the pulpy mass slid down her throat. "My mistake, aunt, was not indulging in an onion the first time the previous Lord Emerson visited. It might have put him off that much quicker. He never listened to anything I said, and thus I wasted several of my more lurid observations on him."

"Yes," Aunt Lottie drawled. "You're a great observer of human nature, particularly the more horrid bits."

"The point is, I had to tolerate Emerson for several visits before he was properly dissuaded. I see no point in prolonging the process with his brother."

Odessa regarded herself in the mirror, checking to make sure her usual slender form was hidden beneath rolls of wool. "Do you think I need a larger bump along my hip? I want to appear as stout as possible." She pulled up her skirts, toying with the fabric tied along one thigh. "Fleshy, even. That's sure to repulse him."

"You are quite lumpy." Aunt Lottie shook her head. "And...savory. I worry that one of the servants will mention your appearance to Angus. Or he'll catch sight of you himself."

"Not today he won't. Papa is in Manchester, if you'll recall, which was why today is the perfect time to have Emerson visit." She patted her hip with a frown, the onion taste rolling around her mouth. "All it took was my lumpy figure to deter the viscount and the story of Herr Keigal. The viscount—I can never recall his name—"

"Lindhaven."

"Lindhaven possessed a weak constitution, and he fairly sprinted out of the drawing room after catching sight of my enormous, fleshy hips. I only recall that he was balding with yellowed teeth. Malfrey was far worse. That lisp, aunt." Odessa made a disgusted sound. "I giggled every time he spoke. The way his gloved hands, barely larger than my own, fluttered about as he pontificated on every dull topic that came to mind. He tested the very limits of my patience. He insulted my interests."

Aunt Lottie raised a brow. "Most young ladies prefer to pursue hobbies a little less macabre, Odessa. You can hardly blame Malfrey for asking why you couldn't simply garden."

"He learned quite a bit about the uses of belladonna."

"While you belched onion at him, dear."

"The onion causes stomach distress. I can't help what escapes.

Unexpected expulsions of gases are an added benefit." Odessa turned once more in the mirror. Her figure was broad. Sturdy. Like the trunk of a tree. The flaps of her hips jutted out like a ridge just above her buttocks. The sheer *girth* had made the last Lord Emerson avert his gaze, unable to look directly at her. "It is a sound strategy."

"Unless your father becomes suspicious."

"I only need banish this last unwelcome suitor." Odessa puffed out a breath, making her aunt step away. "Emerson won't come within two feet of me, not with the smell. If he peers too closely at my unappealing form or attempts overly polite conversation, I will put a stop to his efforts by burping at him. Getting an heir on me will be so repellant he won't possibly consider wedding me."

"What if you find *this* Emerson appealing?"

"Based on Papa's choices thus far, his only consideration in choosing me a husband seems to be a title, a pompous self-important personality, and the need of my dowry. I'm sure Emerson's carefully trimmed hair will smell of some odorous pomade. I expect his shoulders to be padded to give him a manly form, as was the previous earl's, his brother. His skin is bound to be softer than mine. At least I imagine his hands will be."

"A gentleman's hands should be the least of your concerns."

"I have a weakness for such things." Odessa's fascination with the shape and size of a man's hands stemmed from her adoration of a junior groom in her father's employ when she was fifteen. Jacob had been his name. Upon seeing him shirtless, accidentally, Odessa had nearly fainted. She flirted relentlessly with Jacob, encouraging a forbidden kiss. Large, rough hands, nicely callused, had gripped her chin as he turned her lips to his. The smell of leather and hay had filled her nostrils. Odessa had even boldly run her hands down his chest, very nearly ruining herself in the process.

"Odessa." Aunt Lottie snapped her fingers. "Your thoughts wander."

Gentlemen didn't possess such hands. Her taste in the male species had been very firmly formed after Jacob's kiss. Men who got dirty. Earned the hardened muscles often glimpsed bulging beneath shirtsleeves and coats. The very thought of such…territory to explore made Odessa lightheaded. She could never settle on some titled dandy who barely had the strength to lift a glass to his lips.

"I find such gentlemen as Malfrey, Lindhurst, and the previous Emerson unappealing. Nor are such titled lords interested in me. Only my money. I would love to be a spinster, traveling about, visiting the world. Did you know there are catacombs in Paris? There are scores of bones stacked high beneath the city."

"How lovely." Aunt Lottie gave her a sympathetic look. "Another macabre oddity which fascinates you, which I've no desire to see. Nor does anyone else."

"I do not wish a marriage of quiet loathing. Mama drifted about this very house, never laughing. Miserable."

Aunt Lottie pressed a kiss to her cheek. "It wasn't entirely loveless. Emily had you."

"I would rather not wed at all, but if I *must*, my husband should be of my choosing. I wish to *like* the man I wed. Have him bear me some affection. Not belittle my fascination with dreadful things or mysteries at large. Captain Phillips told me his family estate possesses a ghost." She blinked at Aunt Lottie. "Can you imagine?"

Odessa also expected that Captain Phillips possessed lovely, rough, callused hands. His palms had been broad, fingers strong as he took her hand and led her to the dance floor. The scent of shaving soap and leather had emanated from him, with just a bit of horse.

Perfect.

"Captain Phillips? The soldier you danced with at Lady Curchon's? Once? You barely know him."

"He is a cavalry officer. Captain Phillips and I have much in common." Or, at least, Odessa thought they might if he were permitted to court her. She may have also allowed the good captain to steal a kiss on the terrace at Lady Curchon's. Bold of her, to be sure. But Odessa had been quite taken with him.

"The very same. Even you said he filled out his uniform well."

"Well, yes, he does." Aunt Lottie's cheeks pinked. "But Angus would *never* allow you to wed a soldier, even one who is as well-connected as Captain Phillips appears to be. He wants a title for you."

"He will if there is no other choice."

"One dance and a stolen kiss," Aunt Lottie said, "does not constitute a courtship. If anything, Captain Phillips probably regards you as far too bold for allowing him to do so. You court ruination with such behavior."

"Exactly." Better than being wed to what seemed to be an endless assortment of desperate titles who only considered the daughter of Angus Whitehall because of their impending poverty.

"Odessa—enticing a man to ruin you in order to avoid another is not wise."

"I prefer to have Captain Phillips court me in the proper way, of course. But he'll hardly call on me if an earl is doing so. Thus, I must rid myself of the new Emerson. It is only my poor luck the previous Emerson possessed an unwed brother." She took another defiant bite of the onion. "I have no other recourse."

"Odessa, this entire scheme is madness."

Odessa made a face as she chewed, finally setting aside the gnawed vegetable on her vanity. If she had to, Odessa would ensure she and Phillips were caught in a compromising situation. It was incredibly dishonest of her, but he had shown great interest in her at Lady Curchon's. Papa would be most distressed, but he would have no other choice but to accept Phillips. The last time Odessa had seen the dashing Phillips, it had been from a distance while attending the theater. He'd caught sight of her, smiled, and bowed in her direction.

"Phillips and I would suit far better than this Emerson I must greet.

Do I look and smell appropriately disgusting?"

"You stink for certain," Aunt Lottie answered. "And your appearance is that of a lumpy pear. Even I find you undesirable." Her aunt took the remainder of the onion and tossed it out the open window.

"Perfect. He should find me repulsive within moments. I may try to appear demure at first, barely speaking, only belching in his direction."

"Let us get on with this." Aunt Lottie went to the door, cracked it open, and cast a gaze down the hall to make sure no servants lurked about. "Hurry and get down to the drawing room before Burns sees you."

CHAPTER SEVEN

J ORDAN STOOD IN the foyer of the Whitehall home, once more greeted by Burns, before being shown to the drawing room to make the acquaintance of Miss Whitehall and her chaperone, Miss Maplehurst.

The bitter taste of Whitehall and his schemes filled Jordan's mouth. He reminded himself to be polite at all times. Cordial. Engage the little twit in conversation and pretend great interest. Whitehall must assume Jordan to be completely trapped beneath his thumb. Obedient. Which he meant to be, up to a point. Patience had been forced upon Jordan at Dunnings. A hard lesson, but one he'd taken to heart. Besides, he'd raised pigs for God's sake. Wallowed in the muck. Earned a purse or two by fighting in tavern brawls. Marrying some spoiled, unappealing chit to restore his fortunes was rather dull in comparison.

He'd done far worse for a bit of coin.

The reputation of the Sinclair family was another matter. Yesterday, Jordan had taken Aurora and Tamsin for an ice at Gunter's. Aurora, against his protests, insisted on leaving the safety of their carriage to venture inside, thrilled to be at the fabled confectioners. Gunter's quieted the moment Jordan set foot inside with his sisters. As they made their way to the wide counter, a low hiss came from one group of matrons having tea to their left. The air hummed with dozens of whispers all directed at the Sinclairs. The incident of Tamsin punching the Duke of Ware's son in the nose years ago was repeated loudly enough for all the patrons to hear.

Tamsin's back had stiffened upon hearing her name mentioned, but her steps never faltered. She ordered her ice in a calm, clear voice, and kept her chin lifted, not bothering to give the gossiping harpies so much as a glance.

Aurora lit up with so much pleasure as she was handed her treat, was oblivious to the scathing remarks directed at her. She'd giggled and held out her spoon for Jordan to taste.

The Deadly Sins. A bark of laughter. *What gall they possess.*

The words were murmured in a low, scathing tone by a finely-dressed lady. She pointedly tugged her skirts away from Jordan and his sisters as she passed.

A pig farmer, now an earl. Can you imagine? His brother, bless his soul, must be rolling in the grave.

The elder sister is a brazen hoyden. Punched the Duke of Ware's eldest years ago. Too bad the act can no longer be avenged.

Maybe there's hope for the youngest. But she is a product of—

Jordan had firmly pushed his sisters back outside. Aurora did not deserve to have her day spoiled. Thankfully, she appeared far too absorbed with her ice to give any notice to what was being said.

Not so Tamsin. The toe of his sister's half-boots connected with the lady's shin on the way out to the carriage.

Burns waved him forward, silently guiding Jordan to a pair of double doors. Swinging them open, he bowed. "Lord Emerson."

Jordan blinked as he entered. The room was unusually dim, and the air held an unpleasant aroma beneath the usual smells of beeswax and fresh cut flowers.

The curtains of each window had been drawn tightly against the sun attempting to brighten the drawing room. A bare slit of light sliced across the toe of one boot as his feet sunk into the plush Oriental rug beneath his feet. A rug far finer than any at Emerson House. He peered through the poorly-lit surroundings, finally landing on a large watercolor of lilies above the fireplace. No family portrait, of course. Whitehall couldn't possibly have any prestigious ancestors, or at least none that merited a portrait.

Jordan sniffed the air once more. What was that acrid scent? Familiar yet out of place in the drawing room. He turned to the two figures awaiting him. A young lady, hands clasped perfectly in her lap, sat on the settee. Or rather, her *girth* was spread across the blue tufted cushions. Miss Whitehall appeared to be quite fleshy. Her hips alone covered most of the settee.

An older woman, who must be Miss Maplehurst, was forced into the furthest corner of the settee to avoid her niece's expansive form.

Miss Maplehurst's lips lifted in a smile at seeing Jordan. Steam rose in the air from the teapot before her, obscuring, blessedly, her niece for a moment. Scones, along with an assortment of other pastries, all set out on tiny plates completed the picture.

"Lord Emerson. Thank you for accepting my invitation to call. I am Miss Maplehurst."

"My pleasure, Miss Maplehurst," he returned politely, moving to take her hand.

Miss Whitehall's aunt was a lovely elderly woman. The sort that reminded Jordan of finely spun Flemish lace with her silver hair and nearly translucent skin.

What is that smell?

"My niece, Miss Odessa Whitehall."

Onions. *Raw* onions. *That* was the odor emanating from the settee.

He glanced at the tray assuming it to be the scones…possibly? He couldn't imagine the smell would be coming from anywhere else. Jordan's gaze slid over the robust, bulbous figure of Miss Whitehall.

Or anyone else.

Miss Maplehurst hadn't yet let go of Jordan's fingers. Her shrewd, assessing gaze traveled the length of his body from the tips of his boots up to the shock of hair falling over his forehead. Taking his measure as if he were a bloody horse at Tattersalls. He half expected her to ask to examine his teeth.

A tiny, knowing smile lifted one side of Miss Maplehurst's mouth.

Jordan had garnered that look from any number of women, but never from one who could well be his grandmother. Flustered at her unexpected perusal, he turned to Miss Whitehall. Hair a nondescript golden brown, the same color as the honey he'd drizzled on his toast this morning. Delicate ears. Oval face. No pockmarks or warts. Not that he could see. That at least was a good sign.

"A pleasure," he said taking her fingers. Surprisingly slender and graceful for a young lady who was so—

Thick. Not so much as a curve to indicate a waist.

Her thighs, he assumed, would be chunky. Ankles only slightly smaller than the legs of one of his pigs. The breasts pushing up against her bodice appeared ridiculously small when taken in comparison to the rest of her overly generous form.

The onion smell hit Jordan square in the nose.

"My lord," Miss Whitehall said in a shy voice, lips barely moving. "I am pleased to make your acquaintance." She jerked back her fingers as a small, unladylike belch left her mouth, spewing out a cloud of onion in Jordan's direction. "Pardon," she whispered.

Words failed Jordan. No wonder Bentley had wanted to beg off. The last ten years of Jordan's life had been spent in Spittal, a village filled with fishmongers, day laborers, farmers, and sailors. Not *once* had he been burped on. At least not by a young lady.

Struggling not to pinch his nose, Jordan forced a polite smile to his lips and settled himself across from Miss Whitehall, wishing he could pull the chair halfway across the room. Possibly seat himself outside in the garden and merely converse through the window. Eyeing the spread of Miss Whitehall's skirts, he wondered what other horrors hid beneath the fabric. Hooves? An overabundance of hair, perhaps?

Another soft belch filled the air, followed by a puff of onion.
Dear God.

"Tea, my lord?" Miss Maplehurst asked, seemingly oblivious to the smell emanating from her niece.

"Yes, thank you," he answered. A shot of whiskey would be more welcome.

Miss Whitehall rolled awkwardly on the settee, wiggling the enormous wings of her buttocks, trying to force her strange body to maintain a seated position. She twitched, bottom tilting to one side before straightening once more. Miss Whitehall didn't seem to be completely in control of her faculties.

A pair of grayish-blue eyes, like a piece of wet slate, snapped to his. The sky over the ocean before a hurricane comes ashore. So lovely and fierce. Impossible they belonged to such a creature.

An unwelcome ripple of sensation shot through Jordon as those orbs met his.

Dislike for Jordan splintered across the blue-gray, like dark clouds gathering before a storm. Miss Whitehall's lips parted slightly once more and she breathed out the smell of onions at him.

Purposefully.

"Please accept our deepest condolences on the death of Lord Emerson." Miss Maplehurst frowned. "The *previous* Lord Emerson. I beg your apology." A hand flew up to her lips. "Goodness, how strange that sounds."

It would be better if Miss Maplehurst covered her niece's mouth rather than her own. Wasn't there a sprig of parsley or mint handy?

"Don't distress yourself, Miss Maplehurst," Jordan returned smoothly, determined to remain courteous when every instinct begged him to flee. "The situation is awkward at best. Did you know my brother well?"

"He only called upon me a handful of times," Miss Whitehall answered, oddly slender fingers grasping her teacup; she took a sip.

Jordon prayed the tea would lessen the onion on her breath, but he wasn't hopeful.

"Three times, I think," Miss Maplehurst interjected.

"Lord Emerson and I had little in common. I expect you and I have less," Miss Whitehall spoke, the air filling with the caustic stench of onion once more. The slate of her eyes hardened as if daring Jordan to challenge the assumption.

Hostile and a troll. Delightful.

Whitehall expected Jordan to be respectful and behave as an ardent suitor. The words had been part of the contract Jordan signed only this morning at Patchahoo's office. But nothing of how he must behave after he and Odessa were wed.

Ambition often makes a man blind to all else.

Today's meeting only strengthened Jordan's resolve that his marriage would be one of distance.

"I'm recently arrived in London." Jordan struggled for a topic of conversation. Polite discourse had never been his strong suit. "Haven't visited in years. But you've lived here your whole life, haven't you, Miss Whitehall?"

Miss Whitehall's pert little nose wrinkled like one of his pigs scenting the scraps he'd set out. Annoyance flashed across her face before she looked down at her lap.

"I was born in Reading, my lord, but we always kept a house in London," she replied, lips barely moving. Miss Whitehall, for all that she was a troll and smelled horrible, had a lovely speaking voice.

"Then you must know the city quite well. Better than me, at least. I've taken my sisters on a variety of carriage rides through the city, but the usual amusements are rather dull."

Miss Whitehall wiggled about as if a bee were caught under her bum.

No bee. Just a great deal of fleshiness.

"Are there other recommendations you might make? Something unusual, perhaps? Off the beaten path, so to speak."

"I suppose I might make a suggestion, though I do not leave my home often." Miss Whitehall's nose wrinkled once more, annoyed at having to converse with him. Or perhaps she'd only caught a whiff of herself. "Everyone visits Gunter's. Or takes a ride through the park to see and be seen. Or the museum if you are inclined towards more academic pursuits."

"Is there nothing more exciting to be had in London than an ice or spying into a carriage rolling through the park? And I would only take my sisters to the museum if there are mummies on display."

A spark of something very much like interest lit in Miss Whitehall's eyes. Mummies were of more interest to this strange creature than Gunter's.

Another puff of onion was launched in his direction, but the slate blue of her eyes gleamed with interest. "A fine collection of mummies resides at the museum, along with a host of instruments used in the embalming process."

Jordan nodded, thinking of Tamsin, who liked history. And mummies.

"Have your sisters visited the London Colosseum in Regents Park?" Miss Maplehurst spoke up. "There is a panoramic of the city which is quite divine."

He gave a roll of his shoulders. "A possibility. I think they'd prefer the mummies."

"I sense you are looking for entertainment that is out of the ordinary, my lord." Miss Whitehall leaned towards Jordan.

Gazing back at her, he was struck again by the color of her eyes. So beautiful and wholly out of place considering the appearance of her. There was intelligence hovering in the slate blue, along with a great deal of passion for the current topic. Her features had softened, making her *almost* pretty, though Jordan thought it more a case of dim lighting.

"Tamsin and Aurora are inquisitive by nature, Miss Whitehall. As am I. We've taken in the usual sights and found them tolerable, but not worthy of acclaim." Dunnings should have made them greedy for things like a modiste shop. A confectioner. A walk through the park. Tamsin declared them all mundane pursuits which lost their luster quickly. "Is there nothing else you can recommend besides the mummies?"

"You *must* take them to the wax exhibition. On Baker Street," Miss Whitehall said, enthusiasm spilling out of her.

"Wax?" The first thought Jordan had been that she was suggesting a trip to a candle maker. Fitting because her body seemed to simply *melt* around her on the settee. Many women had generous forms, something Jordan appreciated. But not like…this.

"Madame Tussaud." Those slate eyes shot him a look of disbelief. "Well surely, you've heard of her?"

"I've only been in London a fortnight, Miss Whitehall. I'm not familiar with everyone in society, having been gone from it for so long."

"Madame Tussaud is a legend," she said in an awed whisper. "A creative genius. Her medium is wax. She toured the Continent and all of England with her exhibit before deciding to settle in London."

Jordan shrugged. "I've never heard of her."

Miss Whitehall's eyes popped wider in disbelief. "She makes…effigies. Lifelike reproductions from wax. As a young woman in France, she began by making death masks of Madame Guillotine's victims. Some are quite…gruesome."

A bloodthirsty troll who smelled of onions. No wonder Whitehall had to blackmail someone to wed her. Next, Miss Whitehall would tell Jordan she enjoyed gravedigging.

"There is a section," she said, bouncing in excitement, "of the exhibit, which is rather horrifying." She placed one hand on her throat, probably to stop herself from dancing about in glee. "A *complete* reproduction of those that perished so tragically. Blood and all."

Miss Maplehurst cleared her throat.

"Sounds intriguing." Thank goodness he had absolutely no intention of bedding Miss Whitehall. If the mysterious horrors beneath her skirts didn't terrify him to death, he was just as likely to awaken with a knife at his throat.

"Not everyone relishes such grim details, Odessa." She placed a hand on Miss Whitehall's arm. "I apologize, my lord. The waxworks are a particular favorite of my niece. There are other figures on display which are not so… shocking to one's system."

"Have you ever heard the tale of the German baker? He baked his wife into a pie."

"I have not." Jordan would definitely not be residing in the same home with Miss Whitehall. Never mind being murdered in his sleep. She was just as likely to make a death mask of him or put him in the pudding.

She took a deep breath, prepared to recite the entire terrible story to him, when Miss Maplehurst's fingers tightened on her niece's arm. "Odessa, not everyone shares your fascination for such things."

Miss Whitehall lowered her gaze, though Jordan didn't think her chastised. She burped. And wiggled her giant bum about some more.

"I'll take your suggestion of Madame Tussauds under consideration." Jordan took in her fingers, now twisting about gracefully in her lap. Shouldn't a woman of Miss Whitehall's large proportions have plump digits?

She looked up, catching him watching her from beneath her lashes. Scratching rather forcefully at her midsection, as if infested with fleas, Miss Whitehall expelled another burp in his direction.

Deliberate.

"Oh," she murmured, covering her lips. "I must apologize, my lord."

Though Jordan thought he would likely regret asking, he said, "You are…fond of onions? I confess, Miss Whitehall, the aroma is difficult to miss."

"I am not *intentionally* fond of onions, my lord." Her lashes fluttered down once more to brush her cheeks. "If we are to wed, I suppose I should confess. I do not wish our relationship to start with dishonesty."

Their entire acquaintance was nothing but dishonest, from start to finish.

"My niece has an affliction," Miss Maplehurst offered quickly. "Of the skin. Most unfortunate."

"Involving onions?" Jordan had never heard of such a thing.

"The onions are only a temporary cure for my affliction." Miss Whitehall pursed her lips, drawing Jordan's attention to her mouth. Her bottom lip was unusually plump. Made for nibbling and pulling between the teeth.

Jordan exhaled slowly and reclined further in the chair. The smell of onions had made him mad.

"There is no permanent cure, I fear. An onion must be consumed every day to avoid the condition, according to the physician." Miss Whitehall shook her head sadly. "I understand if you find the idea repellant." The slate blue eyes stayed lowered. "Unfortunately, onion also causes a host of unpleasantness, stomach distress, for instance."

"The gases," Miss Maplehurst added in a helpful tone, "must be released."

"Most would wish to avoid such unpleasantness." Miss Whitehall once more lowered her gaze, sounding more mournful with each passing moment. "I would understand."

The smell of Miss Whitehall's breath permeated across the tea tray, completely blotting out the aroma of the currant scones, once Jordan's favorite. Could he wed a woman who reeked so horribly? Or worse, released the odor from various points of her anatomy?

Jordan had little choice. Whitehall hadn't mentioned a word about the strangeness of his daughter or her affliction, but the marriage contract had already been signed. He'd have Miss Whitehall's dowry and Bentley's debt erased. Miss Whitehall could have her onions and her grisly wax exhibits.

Separate houses. He'd already decided to depart for River Crest after the wedding.

"There isn't any other remedy for this affliction?" Jordan inquired politely. "Besides a daily onion?" Admittedly, he knew nothing about diseases of any sort unless they involved animals, mainly pigs. It was just Jordan's luck that in addition to—he held his breath as she belched again—her appearance and unwelcome interests that she be diseased as well.

"The best physicians in London have examined my poor niece and they all agree," Miss Maplehurst informed him. "It *is* rather unfortunate. Terribly distressing."

Whitehall had been more desperate than Bentley. It wasn't just her father's reputation that kept Miss Whitehall unwed. He glanced once more at the spread of her skirts, trying to restrain the urge to shudder.

"I must ask for your discretion, my lord. We don't speak of Odessa's affliction. Mr. Whitehall becomes incredibly upset at the mere mention of her defect."

And no bloody wonder.

Miss Whitehall's shoulders trembled. "I so hate to disappoint my father. I am an embarrassment to him."

"I completely understand," he murmured. Jordan may not be considered a gentleman by most, but he would never be deliberately unkind. He'd promised to see this through, be polite. Courteous. Besides, Jordan felt sorry for Miss Whitehall. She was also at the mercy of her father's endless ambition. Constant rejection had to be difficult. He may not like the situation, detested Whitehall with every fiber of his being, but until the wedding, Jordan could be pleasant. At least now he understood Whitehall's demands to treat his daughter with respect. "I am the soul of discretion."

Those slate blue eyes gleamed at Jordan, brows drawn together in consternation, before lowering once more, almost as if she were angry at his courteous behavior. Perhaps she hadn't much experience given…obvious circumstances. Bentley would have been cruel to her.

"Thank you." But she didn't sound grateful.

"In time, I'm sure to grow accustomed to the scent of onions." He had the smell of manure and pig excrement. After a while, he wouldn't smell her at all. Maybe. "I promise to be considerate of you and the challenges you face."

Until the wedding. Then his consideration would come from leagues away.

Miss Whitehall's gaze returned to her lap, fingers twisting once more. Her lips drew into a taut line, as she continued to burp incessantly while Jordan turned his attention to Miss Maplehurst.

"I confess, my lord." Miss Maplehurst fluttered her hands over a biscuit with pink frosting, ignoring the sounds and smells coming from her niece. "I wasn't aware of your existence prior to Mr. Whitehall's announcement. The previous Lord Emerson never made mention of a brother or any siblings. How kind of you to honor your brother's commitment to my niece and consider a match."

Miss Whitehall stayed quiet.

"Sadly, we were not close." Jordan saw no duplicity in Miss Maplehurst's lined face, but maybe she had no idea what Whitehall had done to secure a marriage for her niece. Surely, she must suspect.

"I do not see a resemblance between you and the previous Lord Emerson, if you don't mind me saying, my lord," Miss Maplehurst said, tapping her chin with one finger. "You look nothing alike." Her smile told Jordan she thought that a point in his favor.

"I do not mind, madam. Bentley was my half-brother. I am the product of my father's second marriage."

"Oh, yes, of course." Miss Maplehurst made a small sound of recognition. "How could I have forgotten? I remember Lord and Lady Emerson quite well. Lovely couple." She regarded him quite intently for a moment, likely remembering the horrible scandal his parents' marriage had caused. He waited impatiently for a thinly-veiled insult to be lobbed at him, but none came.

Miss Whitehall looked at her aunt in surprise, then back at Jordan briefly before lowering her gaze to her lap. "You made no mention of such, aunt."

Miss Maplehurst patted her niece's clasped hands. "Slipped my mind. I never made the connection. You look like your sire," she finally said, eyes running over his shoulders once more. "Lord Emerson was quite handsome, as I recall."

Jordan shifted at her flirtatious tone. Miss Maplehurst must have been quite brazen in her youth.

"And Lady Emerson a great beauty. Stunning, as I recall."

"How kind of you to say." It was the nicest thing *anyone* in London had said about his parents since Jordan's arrival. He liked Miss Maplehurst all the more for it, despite the lascivious glances she shot in his direction. "I would like to suggest a carriage ride, the day after next, if your schedule permits."

Miss Whitehall's chin jerked up, staring at him in disbelief. "A carriage ride, whatever for?"

"So that we may know each other better before wedding, don't you agree? You can point out various points of interest to me," Jordan replied.

Miss Whitehall wasn't at all pleased. She twitched rather dramatically. Her far too slender shoulders—

Shouldn't her arms be plump and fleshy like the rest of her?

—tensed in annoyance. "I don't know that there is anything of significance to show you. I've already told you about the wax exhibit."

"A carriage ride only then," Jordan replied smoothly. "As it turns out, I've only driven through the park once with my sisters in tow and would like to visit without their chattering." A blatant lie, but if he had to sit inside this drawing room again with onion being thrust upon him, Jordan might go mad. At least in an open-air carriage, there would be clean air to breathe.

And Miss Whitehall, bloodthirsty little troll that she was, intrigued him against his better judgment.

"With your permission, of course, Miss Maplehurst."

"We would be honored to join you, my lord." Miss Maplehurst stood, a signal Jordan's call had come to an end.

"Wonderful." Jordan smiled. Miss Whitehall's digestive issues had increased in frequency. There may have been some…flatulence erupting from her a moment ago. His dismissal had come at an opportune moment. Patchahoo must be consulted about Miss Whitehall's condition. Perhaps recommend another physician or an entire army of them to examine her.

What will it matter? She can eat as many onions as she wishes once we're wed and I'm no longer in London.

Miss Whitehall lumbered off the settee to wobble politely as Jordan took his leave. She extended her fingers briefly but did not look up at him. Annoyance showed in every line of her stout little form.

Jordan bowed. "Until our carriage ride. Miss Whitehall. Miss Maplehurst. I bid you both good day."

CHAPTER EIGHT

"You have been outmaneuvered." Aunt Lottie pulled a sprig of mint from the cushions of the settee and handed it to Odessa as the sound of Lord Emerson's carriage pulled away. "Chew. Thoroughly. Please."

Emerson was an entirely unwelcome surprise. The gentleman she'd burped onion at for the last hour was nothing like his superior nitwit of a brother. Far more attractive, for one thing. The tangle of dark hair wasn't styled artfully but worn far too long. The strands appeared uneven, as if cut haphazardly by a blind valet. If Emerson possessed a valet, which in observing the twist of his cravat, gave Odessa doubts. Coat moderately expensive, but not tailored with much care for his broad-shouldered form. The fabric pulled taut with each movement of his arms, suggesting an abundance of muscle with no hint of padding.

A nose which might have once been considered patrician, excepting for the bump at the bridge. Broken. At least once. The nose combined with the wild tangle of dark hair, and the ill-fitted coat gave Emerson a more roughened, wilder appearance than Odessa had expected. Manners decidedly rusty. No hint of anything soft about him.

Emerson was horribly, *terribly* masculine. Odessa's midsection had curled pleasurably every time he spoke or looked in her direction.

"Not what you expected, niece?" Aunt Lottie motioned for her to keep chewing the mint. "Emerson is not the self-indulged fop either one of us thought would arrive. He doesn't look the sort to spend his time drinking and playing cards. His cravat wasn't even tied properly. *Big* hands. And did you see the size of his feet?"

"Aunt Lottie," Odessa admonished, though she was used to her aunt's blunt way of speaking. "What a wholly inappropriate comment for a woman of your age and station."

"Pah. I'm not dead, Odessa. I can appreciate a handsome gentle-man caller."

"Yes, but you must not appreciate *this* one. The intent is to drive him away. Remember?"

"Determined. That is my initial impression of Emerson. He has the look of a man who has never shied away from a fight. You don't break your nose wandering about discussing the weather."

"Hmm." Odessa pulled out the sprig of mint. "Better?" She breathed in her aunt's direction.

"Mildly." Aunt Lottie waved a hand before her nose. "I suggest you use a tooth powder when you return to your room."

"You know quite a bit about his family, which you neglected to share with me. Papa told me a great deal about the previous Lord Emerson. His connections and such, but nothing about *this* Emerson."

"*This* Emerson's father committed the great sin of marrying his mistress, an actress of little note but great beauty, a short time after his first wife died. Had he wed her any later, *this* Emerson would have been born a bastard."

And saved Odessa a great deal of trouble.

"The first wife was a sickly thing who rarely left her bed. Well-bred, modest, ladylike, but tedious with a poor constitution. Emerson would have wandered even had she not been ill. Quite the scandal. Not the part about taking an actress as your mistress, of course, but marrying her and making her a countess. Lady Emerson was rarely received after their marriage. The family departed from London to reside in the country, visiting only when necessary. Once Emerson died, his second family disappeared. Having met Bentley, I can say he struck me as petty. Seems like something he might do, banishing his half-siblings out of spite. Likely somewhere far north of here. Emerson's high-browed accent slips now and again. Did you notice?"

"I did. You feel sorry for him."

"Somewhat, though I doubt Emerson would care to have my pity. He is not *quite* an earl, is he? Wild-looking. A bit savage." Aunt Lottie shivered with delight. "Much more so than your cavalry officer."

"Phillips is a man of my *choosing*, which makes him far more attractive in my opinion." Odessa stared at the drawing room door, frustrated that this new adversary would prove harder to dispel than she originally anticipated. "Why did you accept his invitation for a carriage ride?"

"He would have thought it odd had you refused," Aunt Lottie said with a sigh. "I don't wish to give him any reason to speak to your father about your *affliction*, though I have the impression he doesn't care for Angus. Or has any inclination to curry favor with him. Unlike those other suitors you found so unappealing. Despite your burping at the poor man, he was unfailingly polite to you. Cordial, even. Curious. He didn't blink at your description of Madame Tussauds exhibit, though his brother turned green at the mention."

"I suppose his constitution is stronger. Doesn't mean a thing."

"You've stubbornly set your cap for Captain Phillips after only one dance some months ago. Foolish, Odessa. Perhaps Emerson deserves a chance."

"I will not be bartered off to some titled nitwit—"

"Emerson is the farthest thing from a nitwit," Aunt Lottie interrupted.

"If not Phillips, then someone else." She would need to hurry. Papa would only find another destitute title for her. "When he calls for our carriage ride, I want you to pad me excessively. Make it appear as if my stomach is about to burst the seams of my gown."

"Odessa—"

"He *must* beg off. Find me unsuitable as the others did. He is already disgusted with my appearance and my smell. Emerson only requires a more forceful push."

"What if Emerson cannot beg off," Aunt Lottie said quietly. "Have you considered it? The previous Emerson was in far more dire financial straits than your previous suitors, if the rumors are to be believed. I cannot imagine the situation has improved."

"There are other heiresses in London, Aunt Lottie. The Season is not over. He would find one in an instant. Besides, Papa can hardly *force* an earl to wed me. What would he do? Hold a pistol to Emerson's back?"

Aunt Lottie looked away, pretending great interest in the view of the garden. She said something under her breath and shook her head before once more facing Odessa. "Angus will not welcome a cavalry officer. Nor a barrister. Or a wealthy merchant, should those be your next options."

"Tar, I think," Odessa said, choosing to ignore the unwelcome feeling Aunt Lottie's hesitation stirred in her about Papa. "That should do the trick. I don't know why it took me so long to think of it."

"Tar?"

"I was careful not to part my lips overmuch today." Mainly to build up the reek of onion before breathing it on him. "He has not seen my teeth. But he will. And the tar will make them appear black with rot."

Aunt Lottie pinched the bridge of her nose. "Odessa."

"Few gentlemen want to see a wife with a mouth of rot across the breakfast table. Spoils the appetite. And I must eat a minimum of two onions. What do you think of garlic?"

"Aromatic."

"I'll be burping the entire carriage ride."

"The other suitors *were* terrible, dear. I concur. But—" Aunt Lottie waved her hand over Odessa's thickened form. "Emerson seemed to want to know you better, even if it was out of politeness. You could do worse than a man willing to treat you kindly in spite of—your perceived deficits."

"He wants to know my dowry better, not me. He's as desperate as his brother only more masterful at hiding it. And *you* promised to help," Odessa reminded her aunt.

"I did. A decision I regret each time you eat an onion. But very well. The tar will need to be applied right before you come down to greet him. You'll have to refrain from looking or smiling at any of the staff, even from a distance. I'll get Burns out of the way before he catches a whiff of you, lest he report back to your father. He's already curious. You'll have to take great care, as the tar will slide off your teeth each time you speak."

"The onion and garlic should keep him a good distance. I'll be careful."

"Even so, you must choose your smiles wisely."

Odessa nudged her aunt with an elbow. "I knew you would agree. Papa would have wed me to Malfrey. Or the first Emerson. You avoided marrying your father's choice for you. How can you expect me to do less?"

"The gentleman my father decided I should wed was a putrid turnip, Odessa. Legs like twigs and a bulbous body." Aunt Lottie shivered. "Had he presented someone as splendid as Emerson, I might have agreed. Or as dashing as Captain Phillips." Odessa nodded sagely. "Surely if a handsome cavalry officer called upon you—one who had engaged your affections—"

"I find it interesting that you continue to fixate on a man you barely know merely because he lacks a title and Angus Whitehall would never approve him."

"That isn't why—"

"I disagree. You have ascribed a host of character traits to Captain Phillips, all of which he may not possess. He becomes larger in your mind with each conversation. Your affections have *barely* been roused." Aunt Lottie took her hand. "I do understand what it is to be a young woman with no say in her own life. To feel forced into a situation not to your liking. Your father's ambitions do not need to be yours. But I like Emerson, Angus's choice or not."

Odessa turned away. She refused to consider Emerson.

"I find him arrogant. And I will run away and join a traveling troupe of circus performers before wedding him."

"Stubborn. You may need to do more than run away if your father catches wind of this scheme to replace an earl with a soldier. Be very careful, Odessa."

CHAPTER NINE

"HOW WAS MISS Whitehall? As horrid as you imagined?" Tamsin sat perched on the edge of the settee, back ramrod straight as if facing an execution. A tea tray sat before her with two cups. "I'm practicing decorum. Aurora and I have been properly sipping tea with a book balanced on our heads to ensure our posture is correct."

"How did you do?" Jordan asked as he strolled further into the drawing room.

"Poorly. Aurora did much better, though she became bored. She decided to read the book perched on her head rather than use it to maintain a straight spine. I believe she escaped to the garden."

Mrs. Cherry was firmly in charge of the kitchens and had taken on a kitchen maid in addition to the scullery maid left over from Bentley. An upstairs maid, Mrs. Cherry's niece, had started just yesterday. But otherwise, Jordan's staff was still woefully lacking. They didn't even have a butler.

"Mrs. Cherry is a treasure," Tamsin declared, biting into a biscuit. "These are divine, by the way. Drew declared himself in love after breakfast. Mrs. Cherry blushed like a schoolgirl. I doubt she'll ever leave us."

Thank goodness. Though Aurora had taken on kitchen duties in Dunnings, she wasn't but a passing cook. Nor should an earl's sister be found in the kitchens preparing cabbage soup.

"Oh, I found a butler." Tamsin relaxed against the cushions. "Holly is his name. Hired him on the spot."

"Holly? Like the shrub?"

"Indeed. He's quite a big fellow. Reminds me of some of the dockworkers in Spittal with his size. A mite terrifying, which should be helpful if Lady Longwood or her terrible son attempt to call once more."

"Are we in fear of that?"

"She sent a note demanding some of Bentley's things." Tamsin waved about the overly-decorated drawing room. "Claiming they were family heirlooms and should be given into her keeping. Conveniently enough, there is no longer anyone here who can say differently."

"Don't allow her to set foot in this house. Did you check references for this Holly?"

Tamsin raised a brow. "He was the only one who applied for the position of butler. And I did ask for a reference and was provided one."

"*One* reference? Hardly acceptable, Tamsin."

Jordan made his way to the sideboard, hoping a healthy glass of whiskey would dispel the scent of onion clinging to his clothes and tongue. Unlike Dunnings, there *was* an actual sideboard in this drawing room. And clean glasses of matched crystal.

"I was surprised that no one else applied for the position of butler, but I assume that hag, Lady Longwood," her lip curled slightly, "has put out that it would be undesirable to be in the employ of the Earl of Emerson because no one else dared come to the door. Holly has had a checkered past, and thus isn't overly concerned with gossip. He asked for a chance, and I decided to give him one. The lone reference in his possession was very favorable."

Jordan paused. "Whiskey? You look as if you are exhausted with tea."

His sister nodded. "And decorum. I'd forgotten how dull I find this."

Splashing whiskey into two glasses, Jordan sat across from his sister and the remnants of the tea tray. Snatching up a tiny sandwich of watercress, he popped it in his mouth and waited for her to continue.

Tamsin took a sip of the whiskey, smiling to herself. "Oh, that's lovely."

"Holly," Jordan reminded her.

"Yes, well, Holly had an altercation with his previous employer, Lord Belmont. He may have spent some time imprisoned for a time due to a false claim made against him."

"Might have?"

"Very well, he was definitely imprisoned, but the accusations against him were false. Before Belmont, he was in the employ of Lady Carver, who wrote favorably of Holly."

"I see. Did he steal from Belmont?"

"He did not. Belmont insisted Holly had taken a pair of cufflinks studded with rubies, but those were later found in the possession of Belmont's valet. Stuck in a shoe. Holly was released, but his reputation was ruined, largely because Lord Belmont decided that Holly must have taken something, though he was incorrect about the cufflinks." Tamsin rolled her shoulders, stretching her neck. "His lordship was overly familiar with Holly," she said in a low tone, though there was no one about to hear her. "He told me in confidence. But Holly refused his advances. I'm not sure why Belmont would ever think for a moment—well, you'll understand when you meet Holly. This." She held the whiskey aloft. "Is much more appealing than ratafia."

Tamsin had been attempting ratafia as of late, because that is what a lady *should* drink, but thus far found the overly sweet wine to be a terrible substitute for whiskey.

"You don't have to change yourself completely, Tamsin. Or at all."

"But I do, Jordy. Here I am, Lady Tamsin. And there is Aurora to consider. I'm trying not to add more fuel to the fire of Lady Long-wood's hostilities towards us."

His sister was a stubborn sort. Now that she decided to conform to society, Tamsin was full of determination to master the skills required of her. She hadn't yet been sixteen when the family was banished to Dunnings, and possessed the basics. As much as Lady Longwood liked to preach that the Sinclairs hadn't been raised with an ounce of respectability, Mother had insisted her children possess manners and know the correct way to hold a fork, but she hadn't been overly concerned on which fork should be used. Like a muscle that isn't used often enough, the trappings of society had faded away when confronted by the reality of their situation in the remote wilds of Northumberland. After all, there had been no reason to be Lady Tamsin in Spittal.

"I want to show I am capable. Be a lady. I refuse to prove Lady Longwood correct."

Ah. So that is where his sister's resolve came from. Lady Longwood detested all of them, but Tamsin in particular. Probably because his sister so strongly resembled their mother. "What happened?"

Tamsin flopped back against the cushions of the settee. "Aurora and I visited a modiste as you instructed. A lengthy undertaking, Jordan. Far more than I remember. Apparently, neither Aurora nor I have anything proper to wear as sisters of the Earl of Emerson. The modiste nearly fainted at the sight of our underthings." A breath left her. "At any rate, once our measurements were taken, I purchased some ready-made dresses until our wardrobes are finished. A large order. Madame says we are woefully lacking everything. Gowns. Dresses for paying calls. Gloves. Riding habits."

Jordan snorted.

"I didn't have the heart to explain to Madame Theriot that I ride astride and prefer breeches. She was dreadfully excited about the emerald velvet she was holding up to my cheek." She bit her lip. "I *might* have also exchanged pleasantries with Lady Longwood."

So, today's decorum lesson was a sort of penance. "Should I make the assumption that pleasantries can be interpreted a myriad of ways?"

"Correct."

Jordan took another deep breath, gently pinching the bridge of his nose. He adored Tamsin. She was stalwart. Loyal. Brave. Overly protective. He would never have survived Dunnings and the responsibilities heaped on his shoulders if not for his bold sister. Aurora, especially, would be drifting about without a tether. But those same qualities could also make Tamsin combative, although he was not one to point fingers given his penchant for enjoying a good brawl. It had taken Jordan years to get his temper under control.

He stood and returned to the sideboard, and this time, brought over the entire decanter of whiskey, setting it before his sister on the small table between them.

Tamsin swallowed down the remainder of her glass, eyeing Jordan.

"Go ahead. I doubt seriously anyone in this household would care if you indulge in the middle of the day. Certainly not Holly, who apparently has his own challenges."

"Holly isn't the slightest judgmental." Tamsin sniffed, accepting another splash. "I was trying so *very* hard, Jordy."

Jordan didn't doubt it. Lady Longwood had all but openly declared war on the Earl of Emerson and his siblings. Even before the incident at Gunter's, Drew and Aurora had been cut during a walk in the park, though only Drew took note. Jordan was not greeted warmly at the same club his father and Bentley had once frequented. The lack of applicants for employment as footmen and maids was the least of their concerns.

"Aurora and I were admiring a fine bolt of silk. Keeping to ourselves. Not difficult under the circumstances, I assure you. Aurora was so happy. Spinning about Madame Theriot's shop, eyes wide. She'd never witnessed such finery. Whispers sounded behind us." Tamsin met his eye. "Very like the day we were at Gunter's, though no one accused me of punching anyone."

"Go on." Jordan nodded.

"Lady Longwood and her eldest daughter were standing next to Madame Theriot. I can't recall the daughter's name. The more horrid one."

Lady Longwood had two daughters. Both were equally distasteful and not shy about offering their opinion of the Sinclair family, but one was worse than the other. "Helene."

"Yes, Helene. She should be fortunate Madame's shop was full of customers. I nearly hit her with a bolt of fabric. I don't care if she eyes me as if I am a pile of refuse, but I won't allow her to be so awful to Aurora. Lady Longwood, sour thing, declared in a loud voice, that she could not in good conscience allow Madame Theriot to extend us credit without at least trying to spare the modiste from the misery of becoming yet another one of our creditors."

Slate blue eyes flashed before Jordan, along with the odor of onions.

Not for long.

He didn't care if Miss Whitehall resembled a toad and smelled like horse droppings; he was still going to wed her. Because Aurora and Tamsin deserved to be treated with *bloody* respect when being measured for gowns and underthings.

Tamsin took a deep swallow of the whiskey, wiping her mouth in a most unladylike manner. "I had to defend our honor, Jordy."

"I expect nothing less."

"I may have referred to Lady Longwood as a bitter old witch. Loudly."

"I hope she heard you."

"She did. As well as everyone else at Madame Theriot's establishment."

The familiar rush of anger filled Jordan as he looked up at the self-important portrait of Bentley hanging over the fireplace. Bentley, in all his glory. The artist had taken some liberties, strengthening his brother's chin, for example. That smug smile Jordan so detested graced Bentley's mouth, as if even from the grave he was still passing judgment on his siblings.

Sins. That's what you are. Tainting an otherwise respected line.

Years ago, there had been a portrait of Jordan's parents hanging in the drawing room, painted just before the birth of Tamsin. His mother had been standing amid a field of wildflowers, the artist's obvious attempt at hiding her rounded form. Father tickled a daisy beneath her chin. The love they'd shared, no matter how distasteful the snobs in London found it, shone through in that portrait.

Lady Longwood refused to let go of her bitterness, and Jordan was done with being made to feel less because of it. He and his siblings had struggled at Dunnings. Mother died in squalor, coughing out her life into a scrap of linen. All while that prig—he glared at the portrait of his brother—bled the coffers dry. Bentley barely gave them enough to live on while he frittered away a fortune on expensive knickknacks and the objects d'art scattered around this very room. Pretentious French wines. *Two* mistresses. A portrait of himself, which wasn't close to revealing what a bloody prick he'd been.

Jordan abruptly jerked to his feet. Setting down the whiskey, he dragged the chair he'd just vacated over to the fireplace. That painting of Bentley was coming down. *Today.*

"My lord. May I offer assistance?"

A mountain dressed as a butler stood with hands clasped at the entry to the drawing room. His massive form, head nearly brushing the top of the doorway, inched into the room.

"Holly, I presume."

"Yes, my lord." The mountain nodded, coming forward. Jordan had inherited his father's height, but Holly was still half a head taller. He could easily reach the portrait of Bentley without the assistance of a chair.

Splendid.

"I would like this portrait removed." Jordan jerked his chin at the supremely smug Bentley. "Immediately. I don't care what you do with it."

Holly bowed. "As you wish, my lord."

"Also, how is it possible a uniform was found to fit you on such short notice?" Holly would be the perfect butler for the household of Lord Emerson. His size alone would put off a great many people. Lady Longwood and her insipid son, Percival, for instance.

"Lady Tamsin assisted me." The mountain gazed at Tamsin with utter adoration before lowering his eyes. It was clear the butler would do anything for Jordan's sister.

Good.

Tamsin shrugged. "I sent Holly to a tailor Mrs. Cherry recommended. It was not difficult." She bestowed a smile on the butler.

Jordan had never seen a man of Holly's imposing stature blush in such a way. He liked Holly already. Wandering over to a side table, Jordan ran his fingers over an ornate sculpture of a horse and rider made entirely of blue john. Blue john was rare. Exceptionally expensive. The sheer cost of this sculpture alone would have kept Jordan and his siblings well-fed at Dunnings for a year, possibly longer.

How you must have hated us, Bent.

Holly took down the portrait with little effort, stuck it under one muscled arm, and bowed to Jordan. "Will there be anything else, my lord?"

"Yes. I want you to accompany Lady Tamsin when she sells this." He tapped the hunk of blue john. The sculpture wasn't even especially good, which somehow made things worse. If Bentley were still alive, Jordan would be tempted to beat him with it. "Can you do that for me, Holly?"

"Of course, my lord." Holly looked at Tamsin.

"I passed a shop earlier today on my way to Madame Theriot's that deals in such things," Tamsin interjected. "An antiquities dealer.

Should I take anything else?"

"Anything that is not to your taste or just too Bentley. Leave only what you believe our parents purchased, or if the piece has sentimental value. Not things like this." Jordan nodded at the sculpture. "Father never would have wasted such a sum on this terrible piece. This house is filled to the brim with our brother's excess. I find it insulting."

"Given Dunnings," Tamsin said softly.

"After you are finished, have Holly escort you back to Madame Theriot's," Jordan instructed. "Whatever sum you are given by the antiquities dealer, offer it to the modiste for your wardrobe. A show of good faith. If the modiste does not wish to deal with you, find another. Do whatever is necessary to ensure you and Aurora are well turned out. Leave a bit for Drew and me." He looked down at his own clothing. A nice coat, not specifically tailored for Jordan, but one that had been ready-made and not overly expensive. Patchahoo had insisted Jordan and his siblings stop on the way to London and outfit themselves properly, advancing them a sum to do so, but the frugality Jordan had learned over the years kept him from spending all of it.

Now, it didn't matter. He was going to wed the smelly, odd troll known as Miss Whitehall.

Tamsin finished her whiskey. "Why don't you rid yourself of that, Holly?" She nodded at the painting of Bentley. "Before we go out on our adventure."

"Yes, my lady." A ghost of a smile crossed the butler's mouth before he departed, Bentley secured beneath his arm.

Jordan wondered what Holly would do with the portrait, and couldn't find it in himself to care. The proper thing would have been to send it to Lady Longwood, but he wasn't feeling gracious towards the old harpy. Not after what Tamsin and Aurora endured earlier.

"You never answered my question, Jordan. About Miss White-hall." Tamsin stood and examined the sculpture of the horse, running a finger over the tail. "He must have paid a fortune for this. How could he?" Moisture gathered in Tamsin's eyes. "Mama was so ill. You begged him."

Jordan shook his head, not willing to allow that particular wound to reopen. "Bentley was a terrible person, Tamsin."

"And Miss Whitehall?" She wiped at one eye. "Is she as awful as we anticipated?"

"Suitable. She's suitable." He considered how much he should say to Tamsin and decided not to burden his sister. Tamsin might take it in her head to confront Whitehall or his daughter, which would never do. Jordan had made his decision. Signed the contract.

"The agreement is favorable to me," he assured her. "We will wed at the end of next month after a short courtship."

CHAPTER TEN

ODESSA LOOKED OUT over the park, turning her head so that she could discreetly push a bit of tar further against her bottom teeth. The tar, terrible tasting and sticky, had been applied after eating an onion along with a clove of garlic. Standing before the mirror in her room, Odessa had arranged the tar so that it appeared she possessed two rotting upper teeth and two below.

Aunt Lottie, after her initial disgust, advised remembering which teeth she'd put the tar on, in case she needed to do so again for Emerson's benefit.

Impossible. He'd be horrified.

Her smile, once bestowed upon the troublesome, far too handsome earl, would be hideous. The smell of the onion and garlic so pungent, Emerson wouldn't dare get too close. Even Aunt Lottie had kept her distance. The added precaution of rubbing an onion beneath each of her arms had been taken.

After the carriage ride, which Odessa prayed would be brief once Emerson caught sight of her teeth, she hoped he would deposit Aunt Lottie and her at home and *never* return.

A bonnet, oversized, unfashionable, and ugly, had been donned and pulled tight around Odessa's face in case Emerson's carriage crossed paths with someone she knew. Captain Phillips was known to ride in the park, and it wouldn't do for him to recognize her.

Odessa wiggled her bum on the padded leather seat. Beads of

moisture dripped between her breasts and rolled down the sides of her ribs. The day had grown warm. Perhaps she should have insisted on something other than wool to pad herself, but only the bulk of wool provided the proper girth. And as itchy as the thick padding was rapidly becoming, Odessa didn't need to fake the constant jerking of her body.

Emerson might think had some sort of nervous tic.

Perfect.

"Something amuses you, Miss Whitehall?"

Emerson, far too attractive for her liking, asked from across the carriage. Hazel eyes, more green than brown, took her in before putting a finger to his nose, not bothering to hide the fact that he found her odorous though Emerson had wisely suggested putting the carriage's top down.

Odessa, too, was having difficulty ignoring her own scent. The garlic may have been a bad choice. At the least, she should have refrained from rubbing the onion beneath her arms. She would need to soak in a hot bath the moment she returned home.

"Not at all." Odessa itched along the side of her ear where a tiny curl of honey brown hair dangled. "Only a squirrel."

A gentle breeze blew through the carriage, entirely welcome on such a warm day, though it did little to cool Odessa's body swaddled in wool. It did, however, succeed in forcing the aroma of onions and garlic into Lord Emerson's nostrils.

Aunt Lottie discreetly raised a handkerchief to her nose.

"Squirrels are curious creatures," Emerson said. "Not when they are nesting in your eaves or attic, grant you. But in the park, I find them rather delightful."

What a curious comment. "Nesting in your eaves?"

"I've lived in the country for most of my life, Miss Whitehall. Squirrels often take up residence in one's home. I imagine they try to do so in London, but there are all sorts of footmen and the like to dissuade them."

Odessa considered his words. Papa had hired a ratcatcher once because they could hear tiny feet running in the walls, but nothing about squirrels. Possibly Burns would know. Aunt Lottie had said Emerson and his family had been living far from London. She pictured a glorious country estate with a full staff, not a place where squirrels and the like invaded one's home. But his comments led her to believe otherwise. She couldn't fathom Malfrey, for instance, even knowing what an eave was.

"I haven't been down this path since my last visit to London." Emerson's rough, chiseled features clouded for an instant, nose wrinkling as the smell of her hit him once more. "But that was many years ago." A thick, errant wave of dark hair fell over his forehead, but he didn't brush it away. Only allowed the wind to toy with it.

Emerson was nothing short of splendid, which Odessa considered completely unfair. He was still a titled twit, of course, her father's choice and interested only in her dowry. An unwelcome suitor. But admittedly, under better circumstances, Odessa might have found herself drawn to Emerson.

He turned his gaze to the pond littered with ducks. Wistfulness drifted across his face, along with a hint of sadness. He resembled a distraught angel, albeit one with massive shoulders strewn with muscle.

"Does the area around the pond have some special meaning for you, my lord?" She silently cursed herself for speaking once more. The trick to keeping the tar in place was not to open one's mouth over-much. She didn't want to know him better or why he grew melancholy over a pond.

"As I said, I was raised primarily in the country. London has never held much appeal for me. But my father liked to bring me and my brothers here when we did visit. I've two younger brothers in addition to two sisters. Twins, as it happens, though my brothers look nothing alike."

Odessa had always been intrigued by twins. She'd read they could communicate without speaking. Some developed their own language.

She wished Emerson would shut up and cease to be interesting.

"We came here to sail the tiny boats out of newspaper we'd created the night before. Our day was ruined, however, when Malcolm decided to wade in after his boat because it had been attacked by a duck and sank to the bottom. He didn't swim well at the time. I'm not certain he does now." Emerson's fingers, large and roughened, trailed along his chin.

His hands were...*beautiful*. Deliciously graceful and strong. The nails neatly trimmed. How had she only now noticed he had taken off his gloves? A soft flutter pressed down the length of her chest, even beneath all the horrid wool.

"Father dove in after Malcolm. Drew followed merely because he was told not to. And he couldn't bear to be separated from Mal." Emerson's strong features grew dark with emotion. It was clear he had a great deal of affection for his brothers and greatly missed his father. "They refused to leave each other's company. But now, of course, Mal is on the Continent while Drew is with me."

"And you, my lord?" A bit of tar slipped, and Odessa discreetly covered her mouth, pretending to cough. A gentle push of her finger forced the tar back onto her tooth.

"I sat right there." He pointed to a spot in the grass. "And laughed. The pond isn't very deep, you see, and Drew knew how to swim. After a bit of flailing about, I helped pull them out."

Odessa was struck by the broad shape of his hand. There was a rough spot on his palm, along with a thin scar. She recalled the ill fit of his gloves when he'd called upon her previously.

He doesn't care to wear gloves. At least not the proper kind.

The sort of gloves a gentleman wore in polite society. No, Odessa sensed that the gloves that *did* fit Emerson were worn, dirty leather.

Not polite in the least.

Another flutter occurred in the region of her midsection, definitely not onion related.

Placing a hand on her stomach, or at least where she supposed her stomach lay beneath all the wool, Odessa strengthened her resolve. She was not supposed to moon over Emerson but rid herself of his presence. A wide smile pulled at her lips, one she had practiced the last few days before the mirror to get the angle correct. Across the carriage from him, it would appear half her teeth were rotted. She burped, blowing a bit of onion at his glorious face.

Emerson didn't flinch. The big hands settled on his thighs, fingers stretching across the fabric of his trousers as he stared back at her.

Drat.

Odessa, filled with determination, scratched at herself in great dramatic fashion. Rather impolitely. She wasn't entirely pretending. The wool had balled up around her hips and grown increasingly itchy with the heat of the day.

Emerson regarded her blandly, before the hazel eyes fell on her waist. There was no revulsion in his gaze, only curiosity.

Odessa's fingers rubbed against a troublesome spot on her thighs. He should be cringing in horror after seeing her smile. That was the entire point of rotten teeth, to be disgusted. Emerson should be holding a handkerchief to his nose and ordering the driver to turn the carriage around.

"You don't seem well, dear," Aunt Lottie announced.

"The rocking of the carriage distresses my stomach," she replied in a contrite voice, hoping Emerson would take the hint. Maybe the threat of Odessa casting up her accounts on his boots would persuade him to take her home.

Emerson rapped on the driver's seat behind him, halting the carriage. "Then perhaps we should walk a bit to help settle you before returning."

Oh, good grief. He cannot be serious.

Odessa glanced at her aunt for help.

"A short stroll will set you to rights," he said politely, already hopping down. His coat flapped just a bit, enough so that Odessa caught sight of what was a spectacular pair of carved—

"Oh, my," Aunt Lottie said under her breath.

There would be no help from that quarter.

Emerson held out his hand to Odessa, meaning to help her down. "Come, Miss Whitehall. We'll take a quick turn about the pond and return to your aunt. Will that suffice, Miss Maplehurst?"

Her traitorous aunt, undoubtedly still struck by the curve of Emerson's buttocks, agreed. "I shall enjoy the view from the carriage."

Having no choice, Odessa allowed him to assist her out of the carriage, which was difficult at best given the excessive padding and the difficulty in moving properly. At least the park wasn't overly crowded. Wobbling slightly as her feet made contact with the path, she tried not to look directly at Emerson. He was breathtaking up close.

When Emerson tucked her hand into the warmth of his elbow, a jolt of sensation shot up Odessa's arm at the polite touch of his masculine, *very naked* fingers.

The wool tied to her hips had started to list beneath her petticoats, sliding about with every step. She tried not to panic. Things were secured, of course, but Odessa hadn't planned on strolling about the pond.

Drat.

"Isn't this better, Miss Whitehall?" Emerson glanced over at her.

He could not be unaware of his effect on her, or any woman he came in contact with. "Is what better?" she snapped, appalled when a bit of tar flew out and she barely had the presence to cover her mouth. Odessa quickly pulled her lips together.

"Why, to be out of the rocking carriage. Are you feeling better?"

"Yes, quite. I appreciate your concern," she mumbled, glancing back at Aunt Lottie. "Thank you, my lord."

Her traitorous aunt waved at her from the carriage.

Emerson lifted his head. "Miss Maplehurst recalls my parents, so too, the resulting scandal." He leaned over just enough for his shoulder to brush hers. "Has your aunt shared the story with you?"

"In passing." Aunt Lottie hadn't been terribly forthcoming.

"My mother trod the boards at Covent Garden before meeting my father. All of London is aware. A great sin, apparently, in the eyes of society, to be an actress." He gave a careless wave with one glorious hand. "At any rate, Mother was very fond of the theater, but growing up in the country, such entertainment was in short supply." A smile lit his features along with the appearance of a dimple in one cheek.

Her heart, as traitorous as her aunt, flapped about Odessa's chest in response.

"Unless a traveling troupe of actors came through," Emerson laughed softly. "Which happened every summer. I'm sure my father paid them to stop at River Crest. My country estate," he added.

"How interesting." She itched at her stomach with her free hand, wishing Emerson would make his point. The tar was fighting the onion to see which could leave a more horrible taste in her mouth. Thus far, the onion was winning.

I hadn't expected we would ever be so close.

"Mother was fond of Shakespeare. *A Midsummer's Night Dream* was one of her favorites. Do you know it? We, my siblings and I, all took turns playing a part. I'm familiar with costumes and disguises." His voice dipped. "The art of pretending to be someone else."

Odessa was fond of Shakespeare as well, though admittedly, putting off what seemed to be an unending stream of Lord Emersons had kept her from reading much as of late. "Your brother," she gave him a careful glimpse of her rotted teeth, "never mentioned playing dress-up and the like."

"Bentley, as you'll recall, was my *half*-brother, Miss Whitehall. We didn't grow up together. He rarely visited River Crest."

A distinction that was becoming more apparent as time went on. The first Lord Emerson had been everything Odessa despised with his pretentious mannerisms and snide politeness. Papa only saw that Emerson had been an earl, and little else. But *this* Emerson, in addition to his annoying attractiveness, was incredibly kind. Rough around the edges. And his hands—

"I must apologize, my lord," Odessa spit out, demanding her skin stop tingling so deliciously. "You did mention Bentley was your half-brother during our first meeting, but I'd forgotten. I'm terribly forgetful at times. My aunt insists I write everything down," she ended with a tiny trill.

Now she'd declared herself a simpleton in addition to smelling terribly, burping, and resembling a rotting pear. Surely, *that* would deter him.

"You've so many challenges, Miss Whitehall. I must confess—"

"Yes?" *Please beg off. Please.*

The brown of his eyes warmed her, the bits of green sparkling at her in the dappled light filtering through the trees. "I've nothing but admiration for you. What a courageous young woman you are to be yourself when faced with such challenges."

Wait.

Odessa stumbled and Emerson's grip on her arm tightened. He couldn't possibly be serious.

"How understanding you are, my lord." Odessa turned her face to his with a smile, gratified to see the quivering of his nose and the gleam of disgust as he took in her rotting teeth.

"What happens if you do not avail yourself of onions on a daily basis?" Emerson turned his attention back to the pond, pulling her gently in the direction of the waiting carriage.

Aunt Lottie leaned over the side watching. At least she had the decency to look guilty.

"It is too frightening to contemplate. The onions are the only thing which staves off my affliction." Odessa took a whiff of herself, which forced the moisture to gather in her eyes. Dear God. She was truly quite pungent.

"So, you've said." There was a curious tilt to his head as he glanced at her from beneath his lashes, which were longer and far more lush than such a slightly wild-looking earl should have.

A burp came from her lips. "Pardon."

"No need for apology, Miss Whitehall. I only wanted to inquire what I could expect if you don't indulge in your onion. I'm quite sympathetic to your plight and will do everything in my power to ease it." Emerson sounded sincere, but there was an undercurrent of steeliness in his pretty speech. "Would you forego an onion? Just once, mind you, so that I can gain more understanding of what you face. And only if it will not put you at great risk."

Damn him.

"I can try for your sake, my lord." Odessa looked straight ahead, her steps full of grim determination.

A strawberry it is.

Tiny pustules would appear in clusters across her skin. The rash, red and raw-looking, would spread across her entire body, but especially her cheeks, chin, and forehead. Aunt Lottie had an ointment which would help the worst of it, but Odessa would itch and scratch for days.

Worth it, though, if Emerson truly realized his alternative to a foul-smelling wife was one who looked like she had the pox. It might be the inducement he needed to end their association.

"Did you enjoy your stroll?" Aunt Lottie asked once Odessa was settled beside her again. "Do you feel better, dear?"

She was put out with her aunt for allowing the walk with Emerson. A burp erupted and Odessa blew the resulting odor directly into Aunt Lottie's face.

"I feel much better. Lord Emerson is most accommodating."

Odessa gave Emerson a flirtatious smile to reveal more of the rot. The effect was ruined by a small coughing fit when a piece of tar became stuck in her throat.

"Miss Whitehall, would you care for an ice before returning home? I know that you've mentioned you aren't particularly fond, but the day is warm." Emerson wasn't smiling, more…*smirking* at her. The small grin, unabashedly sensual, had Odessa's heart nearly leaping from her chest. An image of Emerson in only shirtsleeves pushing a plow across a field flashed before her. Those powerful, callused palms grabbing at—

"Odessa?"

Aunt Lottie's elbow nudged her in the ribs, barely felt through all the padding Odessa was wrapped in.

Good lord, I've been staring at Emerson's hands.

"Very kind, my lord. But I think it time we returned home," Aunt Lottie announced. "My niece still looks a bit pale. The walk helped, but—"

Another burp erupted from Odessa, giving credence to her aunt's words.

The lift of his lips twisted up further. "I agree, Miss Maplehurst. But I enjoyed our time together nonetheless."

The carriage rolled forward, and Odessa fell back against the seat, not daring to look at Emerson again. Fighting the urge to study his glorious hands.

Emerson pointed to another squirrel running alongside the carriage, and her eye followed the movement, as if he knew of her strange fascination with those elegant but roughed fingers.

Drat.

"My youngest sister, Aurora, once kept a squirrel as a pet," he said, watching the creature scamper about the grass, an acorn held in one tiny paw. "I can't recall what she named him. He preferred walnuts to acorns as I recall." He turned to her. "I myself like pigs."

"Pigs, my lord?" Odessa blinked in surprise.

"Pigs," he stated again, a perfect row of white teeth gleaming in the sun as he bestowed a breathtaking smile on her.

Emerson was the most infuriating man she'd ever met. First squirrels and now pigs. Despite Odessa's best efforts, he refused to treat her with anything but polite respect, nor did he give any indication of disgust. Odessa was quite annoyed.

"Your brother preferred horses, as I recall," Aunt Lottie mused. "It seemed his favorite topic."

"Yes, but I'm not my brother, Miss Maplehurst." His gaze drifted once more over to Odessa. "It would be best for all concerned if we keep that pertinent fact at hand." The edge to his words, impossible to miss, seemed out of place with his polite manner, offering a glimpse at a man who was nothing like the nitwit dandy Odessa had originally imagined him to be. For the first time since Papa had mentioned *this* Emerson, doubt trickled down her spine. Her efforts might well fail.

Emerson was *not* his brother.

"Why pigs, my lord?" Odessa murmured, refusing to raise her eyes to his or look at him directly. Doing so had an unwelcome effect on her.

"Why not pigs?" Emerson countered. "They are surprisingly intelligent creatures."

"I've never known a gentleman such as yourself to express the slightest affinity for a pig." Her interest in him was piqued once more. She wished Emerson would stop that. Being so different that she was forced to pay attention to him. Another piece of tar moved from her tooth, and she had to twist her lips to keep it in place.

"I think we can both agree you've not met a gentleman such as me before, Miss Whitehall." He shrugged. "At any rate, while intelligent, pigs can have a vicious temper. Sows, in particular, can be territorial. I nearly lost a finger once. Didn't move quick enough." He held up his palm where the scar she glimpsed earlier lay in a stark, whitened line against his skin.

"You've been in their immediate vicinity?" she found herself asking.

"I raise them." The green in Emerson's eyes sparkled and deepened, like the murky depths of the pond they'd so recently strolled about. "Or at least I did until recently. But I might again. I miss doing so, you see. Never thought I would."

How incredibly shocking. And mildly, at least for Odessa, stimulating. That blasted flutter took up once more between her breasts.

She could clearly picture Emerson stomping about a pen of grunting, vile-tempered pigs. He'd be muddied. Trousers stretched deliciously tight across those muscled buttocks glimpsed earlier. Shirtsleeves rolled up, showing off what Odessa imagined were broad, muscular forearms. The wild tangle of his hair would be damp with his exertions, clinging to his forehead and cheeks. Curling a bit around the edges, as it was doing now during the warmth of the day.

She jerked her eyes over the side of the carriage, praying rather desperately for another squirrel to come into view and dispel such improper thoughts of Emerson. Anything to keep Odessa from staring at his hands. His thighs. Or any other part of his magnificent person.

"Where did you raise these animals?" Aunt Lottie inquired. "May I guess, my lord?"

A tiny grin fell over his lips. "You may, Miss Maplehurst."

Odessa's aunt made a soft giggle, delighted to have Emerson's attention.

Ugh.

"I knew a gentleman who lived just to the south of the Scottish border once. Somewhere in Northumberland, I believe." Aunt Lottie leaned towards Emerson just a tad. "You sound at times remarkably like him."

"You are correct, madam. Northumberland. Specifically, an estate of my father's called Dunnings, which sits just outside of Spittal." At their twin looks of confusion, he said, "A small village on the coast. My family…" He hesitated, the carved lines of his face sharpening. "Took up residence there after the death of my father. There aren't many activities for a *gentleman* such as me in that part of England. Pig farming seemed as good a hobby as any to keep myself busy and make a bit of coin." The clipped, patrician accent dropped completely.

The previous Lord Emerson *had* banished his father's second family from London; that much was apparent even if Emerson hadn't said so. And admitting to not only liking pigs but raising them? For money? A proper earl would never—

Odessa's opinion of titled lords and fine pedigrees had become firmly fixed after that first terrible ball hosted by Lord Norris. Stricken and alone, save for Aunt Lottie, horrified that no matter how expensively Odessa was dressed, every gentleman in attendance knew her to be Angus Whitehall's daughter and beneath notice. No matter the obscene amount of her dowry. Even with such inducement, those gentlemen steadfastly turned their noses up at her. The rejection, the knowledge she would never be considered good enough for a bunch of fops, pained her. Odessa didn't *want* that sort of man, or any marriage offered out of desperation. One of coldness and financial gain. Chosen by her father.

It was a matter of principle.

"And your family, my lord." Aunt Lottie asked. "Were they as enamored with pigs as you?"

"No, Miss Maplehurst. No one else had the least interest in my pigs."

My pigs. He wasn't ashamed. Odessa found she liked that about him.

Stop liking him.

The carriage rolled to a stop, and she looked up, surprised to find they were in front of her father's house once more. She'd been so engrossed in Lord Emerson and his stupid pigs she hadn't paid the least attention to where they were.

Drat.

Two footmen rushed to the carriage to help her out. Thomas, the youngest, waved his hand in front of his nose when he caught wind of Odessa. His eyes widened at her thickened form, but wisely, after a stern look from Aunt Lottie, looked away.

"Thank you for the pleasure of your company." Emerson nodded to Aunt Lottie. "Miss Maplehurst." His gaze slid to Odessa. "Miss Whitehall."

"My lord." Odessa wobbled politely, not looking up until Emerson's carriage rolled away. The itch from the wool had her twitching and the taste in her mouth, interspersed with bits of tar, was atrocious. And still, Emerson was undeterred.

"He is more desperate than I thought," she said to her aunt.

"As I mentioned on his previous visit, Emerson may not be in any position to beg off. You should cease this foolishness. He is attractive. Intelligent. Not the least bit afraid of hard work if his pig farming is any indication."

"And he is my father's choice."

"Stubborn." Aunt Lottie took Odessa's arm, rushing her up the steps. "Hurry to your room before Burns catches sight of you. Or worse, smells you. He'll report back to your father. Thomas is already eyeing you with horror." Her aunt gave Odessa a tiny shove between the shoulder blades. "And Emerson *is* suspicious," she said in a low voice. "I wouldn't be surprised if he guessed at your game. He is clever, far more than the others."

Odessa hurried past her aunt and up the steps, shooing Thomas away with a stern look. As they entered the foyer, the sound of footsteps, Burns most likely, came from the direction of her father's study. Could today become any worse? "Papa is home."

"Go. I'll delay Burns." Aunt Lottie waved her hands. "Hurry."

"I'll need a strawberry," Odessa said over her shoulder as she quickened her steps. "For the next time Emerson calls."

CHAPTER ELEVEN

ROTTED TEETH. AN unfortunate skin condition, which only abated if she ate onions. A trunk like form full of fleshy hips and buttocks. He'd even caught a whiff of garlic on her breath today.

Incredibly unappealing.

Jordan drummed his fingers along the leather seats of his carriage and considered the almost *too* repulsive picture Miss Whitehall presented.

His future bride had taken the opportunity to smile broadly at Jordan a total of three times today, gleefully displaying the decay that waited if he dared kiss her. The sight, shocking at first, and combined with her breath, left no doubt that a bottle of whiskey would be required if he ever changed his mind about bedding her.

But the more he studied Miss Whitehall today, the more *curious* Jordan became.

He'd made the decision, that in order to continue to deal with his future wife without showing overt disgust at her appearance and smell, Jordan should try to focus on what he *did* find appealing about her physically. Despite deciding to discard her after the wedding, Jordan had no desire to be *cruel* to Miss Whitehall, even though his pigs smelled better than she did.

Miss Whitehall had lovely eyes. A mix of gray and blue. Unusual, to say the least. *That* was something. He found her fascination with the macabre, wax figures, and gruesome scenery to be strangely interesting. At least it was *different*.

And her skin was creamy. Smooth. Like fresh milk.

Jordan's brows drew together. There wasn't any sign of the skin affliction she spoke of kept at bay by onions. Surely, there would be…scars or marks of some sort. Discoloration, perhaps.

These observations led him to stroll with her along the pond. When he started to speak of the traveling troupe of performers who came to River Crest every year, that's when Jordan realized how *thoroughly* he was being duped.

The onions and garlic were merely diversion, meant to keep him from noticing Miss Whitehall's graceful neck, unblemished cheeks, and the fact that she possessed only *one* chin.

One chin.

Slender arms and shoulders. Nothing beefy at all about Miss Whitehall. The large mound of flesh on her hips bouncing about as they strolled, now appeared to be situated in a different position. And her enormous buttocks were…slipping.

Mother adored dressing up. Costumes. The uses of makeup to alter one's appearance.

A honeyed brown curl had escaped from beneath the hideous bonnet atop her head while she wobbled around the pond. No woman so repulsive should have a curl so lovely, Jordan decided. Nor be the owner of a sleek, pink tongue, which flashed when she pushed the tip against her rotted teeth.

A tiny black fleck was left behind on Miss Whitehall's *surprisingly* delectable bottom lip after she did so.

There were plenty of rotted mouths and stumps of teeth in Spittal, something Miss Whitehall couldn't possibly have guessed at. Some of the sailors who favored The Hen were missing so many teeth they were reduced to eating nothing that wasn't boiled to a mushy softness. The smell of such decay was noticeable when they spoke. *Nothing* covered it up.

Not a sprig of mint. Or ale. Or an *onion*.

Tar to make teeth appear rotted. That was what Miss Whitehall kept choking on. Padding to make herself rounded, wool he guessed, if her excessive itching in the heat was any indication. An onion to keep him at a distance. A bit of garlic in case the onion failed.

Miss Whitehall was *actively* avoiding marriage.

The irony.

A bark of laughter left him as the carriage turned a corner.

There were several reasons why a young lady might not wish to wed. Defiance, for one, at having her life dictated. Jordan understood that reason completely. Perhaps chart her own course. Pursue a talent. Maybe Miss Whitehall wished to sculpt in wax as Madame Tussaud did. Or a young lady might not care for men in general, though the way Miss Whitehall continuously studied Jordan's hands, cheeks blushing, led him to discard that possibility. Which left the obvious.

Her affections lay elsewhere with a man Whitehall didn't approve of.

What a pity. Miss Whitehall, much like Jordan, must accept the inevitable. There was no escape for either of them, not until they were wed. After restoring the family coffers with her dowry and the debt to her father erased, Miss Whitehall would be free to live her life as she wished.

The ruse *was* clever. As was Miss Whitehall. It was a daring thing to do, defying a man like Angus Whitehall. But she likely didn't *really* know her father. Jordan appreciated bold women. Determination. Intelligence. He even liked her strange hobby.

He'd deliberately challenged her with not consuming an onion, wondering what would happen if she didn't. There was no mysterious affliction, Jordan was quite sure about that. What sight would greet him when he next called upon Miss Whitehall? He'd give her the better part of the week to decide her next move.

There was a slim chance Jordan was incorrect and Miss Whitehall really was a smelly troll, but if that turned out to be the case, he'd drink whiskey and focus on her dowry.

River Crest needed a great deal of repair.

And Jordan meant to buy some pigs.

Chapter Twelve

"Y OU DIDN'T NEED to escort me, Jordy."

The stoic, adoring, and slightly terrifying Holly would have only been too happy to follow Tamsin about, but Jordan hadn't been inside a book shop in years. There were no book sellers in Spittal, only a peddler who came through every so often with a small box of used, tattered tomes. The books the peddler sold were half-falling apart and moth-eaten, but they had been a welcome addition to the small library at Dunnings all the same. Especially for Aurora, who adored books. Some would have questioned the wisdom of spending *any* coin on a battered copy of *Guy Mannering* given the circumstances of the Sinclairs, but the joy on Aurora's delicate features whenever Jordan handed her a book had been worth it.

"Aurora needs something new to read. Bentley's library is woefully lacking in anything remotely entertaining. Now that we've sold that horrid statue, we've more than enough for some luxuries."

The sum given for the hideous horse sculpture had been far more than Jordan expected, but he didn't possess an eye for valuing expensive items, having had so few in the last decade. "And Holly is guarding our door like some large mastiff. She's safe enough with him, even with Drew gone."

Drew had wrangled an invitation to yet another house party, this one in Surrey.

"I told you Holly is a marvel." Tamsin gave him a playful swat.

"We simply could not have gotten on so well without him."

"You were correct." The butler, with his enormous, menacing physical presence stared down every unwelcome guest the Sinclairs received, which included a recent visit by Lady Longwood. Bentley's aunt arrived unannounced again yesterday and forced her way past the new housemaid, who'd answered the door while Holly was down the hall instructing two of the recently acquired footmen. Lady Longwood barged into Jordan's home, with one of her own footmen, pointing out everything she claimed was promised to her by Bentley, which the footman trailing her was instructed to gather up and take directly to her waiting carriage.

Holly, hearing the ruckus, interrupted the pillage of Emerson House.

Lady Longwood didn't notice him immediately looming over her, too busy laying claim to two chairs covered in pale blue damask, a Grecian vase in the foyer, and a small figurine with wings gifted to Jordan's mother after the birth of Aurora. Father had always insisted it was a fairy, since Mother had once played Titania in *A Midsummer Night's Dream*.

Lady Longwood startled the entire household, and most of Bruton Street, when she shrieked out in horror at seeing that Bentley's portrait no longer resided over the fireplace. She screamed again at the sight of Holly.

Holly calmly instructed her ladyship's footman that if the lad touched one more item belonging to Lord Emerson, bodily harm would be imminent. A constable would be called at the attempted thievery of a lord's home.

"I can't believe that witch had the nerve to enter our home and attempt to intimidate our staff. By the time I arrived, she was puffing away like an outraged hen, daring Holly to put his hands on her person. So, I escorted her out myself." Tamsin grinned. "She *hissed* at me, Jordan. Like a coiled viper."

Lady Longwood's loathing of the Sinclairs, referring to them continuously as the *Five Deadly Sins,* was bearing fruit. The gossip columns had taken note and repeated the ridiculous moniker. The decades old scandal of his parents once more made the rounds.

London would continue to be an unwelcoming place for some time.

"We Sinclairs don't scare easily, Tamsin. Not after Dunnings. Lady Longwood will figure that out soon enough."

A bell tinkled above his head as he and Tamsin entered the book seller's. Nodding to the clerk at the front, Tamsin took a sharp left, heading for a tall stack of tomes at the back. "Aurora adores romantic novels. Princes. Pirates. Dashing gentlemen. I know just what will appeal to her."

As Tamsin perused the books looking for something wholly inappropriate to gift their youngest sister, Jordan wandered down another aisle, breathing in the smell of leather and old paper. Most of the books to be found in this direction were dustier than their brethren's. Animal husbandry, farming techniques and the like weren't popular among those perusing the shops along Bond Street, but Jordan wanted to expand his knowledge beyond raising pigs. River Crest needed him, as well as Miss Whitehall's enormous dowry, if the estate would be restored to its former glory. He planned on being involved, much more than many of his peers. After Dunnings, Jordan was intimately aware of what it took to create a working estate. The upkeep on a house the size of River Crest. The cost of repairs, animals, tenants. Jordan didn't plan on spending all his time in London, caught up in the goings-on of Parliament or a continuous stream of balls and parties.

He would cede London to Miss Whitehall.

Jordan had spent some time considering what his future wife looked like beneath all the onion and tar, but decided it didn't matter. She might become more tolerable to him, but she was still unwanted.

Picking up a book, Jordan moved to the large window along one wall where the light was better. The book had to do with sheep, a dull subject for anyone save Jordan. He leafed through it absently while watching the ebb and flow of the crowded streets outside. Pale blue skirts teased at the edge of his vision.

The book slipped from his hands, falling on his foot with a thud.

Well, I suppose that answers my questions on her disguise. Clever indeed.

Miss Odessa Whitehall looked spectacular in blue, a color more suited to her than the dull hues she'd worn on the last two occasions he'd seen her. She strode confidently about, just down the street, looking nothing like a well-rounded smelly troll.

Because she wasn't one.

He might have convinced himself it wasn't her, if not for the sight of Miss Maplehurst at her side. Without her aunt, Jordan might not have believed the willowy young lady speaking with such animation was his future bride. A bonnet shadowed her face, but Jordan caught sight of her unmistakable delicate features, impossible to miss now that he wasn't distracted by a bulbous padded body. A parasol was wielded adeptly in one hand, concealment nearby should she require it. She smiled up at her aunt, showing a row of pearly teeth.

Not a rotted tooth in sight. No surprise there.

Satisfaction filled him at knowing he'd been correct. The vision of Miss Whitehall, barren of subterfuge, dispelled any remaining doubts. Her dress nipped in at tiny waist, the modest neckline displaying a nicely rounded bosom. Her hips didn't flap about as she moved. The padding must have been extensive.

Clever Miss Whitehall.

Beautiful wasn't the first word Jordan would use to describe her. Pretty, perhaps. But when the light hit her face, the gleam of intelligence shone in her eyes. Joy, at being in the sunshine with her aunt. Miss Whitehall was striking, glittering like a diamond on Bond Street.

Arousal swiftly curled around the front of his thighs at the sight of his future bride, and he briefly reconsidered his decision not to bed her. Even if she hadn't been Whitehall's daughter, Jordan still would have been drawn to her. There was an innate vivaciousness to her as she strolled about. One that spoke of a passionate nature.

The plump curve of her mouth pursed at a comment from Miss Maplehurst.

A low growl left Jordan. Not annoyance. Well, at least, not *solely* that emotion.

After another moment, Miss Maplehurst took her niece's arm, hurrying her past a bakery to the end of the street, not once looking in the direction of the bookseller. Which was just as well, because the pair would certainly have seen him staring from the window. And Jordan had no intention of informing Miss Whitehall the ruse was up. At least not yet.

The twitching blue of her skirts garnered the attention of two passing gentlemen. Both paused to dip their hats.

Miss Whitehall ignored them.

Another sound came from Jordan's throat. One more possessive in nature. Odessa belonged to him, unwanted or not. He forced the resentment of her to bleed back into his veins. The absolute bitterness towards her father. Miss Whitehall would be relinquished by Jordan after they were duly wed and he had her dowry. Then her mysterious lover, the gentleman who she'd gone to such trouble for, could have her. Or any gentleman in London.

But not until then.

CHAPTER THIRTEEN

"ODESSA, DEAR. I don't think this wise." Aunt Lottie held up the bowl containing the lone strawberry. "It is only pure luck your father hasn't discovered your deception thus far. Burns was sniffing about." The silver curls at her temple quivered as she shook her head. "The rash will be noticeable for *days*."

"Maybe not. It is only *one* strawberry." She held up a finger. "If you'll recall, when I last utilized such a strategy to rid myself of unwelcome company, I ingested an entire handful. The rash at that time lasted an entire week. I imagine this will be much milder."

She stared with no small amount of trepidation at the strawberry. One would never consider that such an innocent bit of fruit would cause an eruption of itching and pustules. A reaction first made known to Odessa when she was eight. Strawberries had decorated an elaborate sponge cake to be served for an infrequent and unwelcome visit from Mama's relations. Wanting to avoid the entire afternoon since it would be spent with Odessa being looked down upon, and after being sternly instructed not to touch the sponge cake, Odessa plucked three strawberries off the top in defiance.

She was often defiant.

The itching, at first tolerable, became intense after a quarter hour. Small, pus-filled bumps spread rapidly over her skin. Mama gasped. Grandmother Maplehurst's unkind wrinkled face frowned in distaste. Odessa was rushed to her room and a physician summoned. Only her cousin, Hayden, didn't appear horrified. Instead, he started taking notes in a small book he always carried about. Later, he questioned her on the exact number of strawberries she'd eaten, the onset of the rash, and any other pertinent details.

Honestly, Hayden had been far more interested in Odessa's condition than Dr. Crandall.

"That was years ago," Aunt Lottie insisted. "You've no idea what could happen now."

"I have some idea. And that wasn't the last time I had to stoop to such tactics. Besides, Hayden assures me that one or two strawberries will cause a limited rash. He's taken careful note over the years."

"Hayden is not a physician. Or a scientist, though he claims to be one. A poor calling for a duke."

"I agree. But he hasn't always been a duke, has he?" Nor was he really Odessa's cousin, though the two of them had formed a close bond as children. Easy to do when you were both considered far too odd to be of any importance. Upon hearing of Odessa's obsession with murderous deeds and gruesome stories, something she wasn't supposed to talk about, Hayden had been delighted and offered up several tales of his own.

"No. I suppose not."

"He carefully transcribed what occurred when I ate exactly ten strawberries to frighten off Miss Flout." Miss Flout had been the ill-tempered governess who Papa had taken on after the death of Odessa's mother. She'd taken one look at Odessa's sores and packed her things while Papa was on one of his business trips. The next time had been during Grandmother Maplehurst's last visit. She'd ingested only six or seven at the time, careful to recount the entire episode to Hayden.

"I'm assured one strawberry will cause a rash, but it will persist only long enough to frighten away Lord Emerson."

Strawberries were a weapon for Odessa. One of last resort.

"Foolish," Aunt Lottie muttered.

"I have little choice. This might well be my last chance to avoid wedding Emerson. Phillips is sure to be at Lady Curchon's party in a few weeks."

"Yes, one of two invitations she issues to us each year. I can hardly wait."

"Sarcasm doesn't suit you, aunt."

After their carriage ride and walk in the park, Lord Emerson, thankfully, disappeared for a time, declining to call on Odessa for over a week. She waited patiently, hovering outside Papa's study door, for word that Emerson had visited and declined to pursue her further.

But then an enormous bouquet of flowers had arrived accompanied by a small box of sweets. A note, tied with red ribbon, was attached.

What harm could one more sweet cause? The flowers will brighten your drawing room.

"I've added an extra blanket today around my stomach, so Emerson can see the results of his gift. I may even blacken another tooth." Odessa stalked across the room, pleased that the extra padding made it seem as if her buttocks were flapping when she walked. "The gall, to send a woman with rotten teeth a box of marzipan and chocolate drops."

"Completely horrid of him," Aunt Lottie agreed. "I'll go down first and make sure Burns isn't hovering about. He's caught a whiff or two of your onion smell, but I convinced him Cook was experimenting with a new recipe. I'll make up an errand for him. Something your father wishes him to do so he won't refuse." Her aunt paused. "I do not believe you are fooling him."

"Burns? He pays me as little attention as possible. I'm sure he's already informed Cook not to use so many onions."

"Emerson. There was something in the way he looked at you during the carriage ride. He deliberately asked you not to eat an onion. He sent you sweets, Odessa."

"Perhaps he's as cruel as his brother. I'm certain he'll take one look at me today and flee, as Miss Flout did. Pustules or onions, neither is a decent choice. The balls of London are littered with wealthy girls, Aunt Lottie. Beautiful ones. He'll find another."

Odessa made a puffing sound, eyeing the strawberry. The rash would need to be sufficient to keep Emerson away, as she would not be able to depend on the smell of onion. She had rubbed some garlic on her skin. It might help.

"I've told you of Emerson's family. The scandal attached to his parents. He's made enemies in the *ton*. I don't think there *are* any other heiresses for him."

"You've given me even more reason to not wish this marriage. One would think Papa would see the futility of this endeavor. It will not give him what he wants if Emerson's poor reputation exceeds his own."

"I wouldn't go that far," Aunt Lottie mumbled under her breath.

Odessa gave her aunt a sharp glance. "What do you mean?" It was not the first time Aunt Lottie had made reference to Papa's standing. Yes, it was poor, but that was because the snobs of society refused to look past his birth. Mama's family had been well-respected, but even that hadn't raised her father up.

"Nothing, dearest." Aunt Lottie turned away.

Uneasiness, oily and slick, twisted in Odessa's stomach. Her father was a businessman, one who was determined in his dealings. Once, she'd overheard someone say Angus Whitehall belonged in the rookery, not a ball. She'd ignored the comment, but mayhap she should have paid more attention. Odessa made a note to question Aunt Lottie, *really* question her about Papa, and not be put off.

Once she got rid of Emerson.

"I can't possibly encourage Captain Phillips's suit with Emerson's betrothal hanging over my head. I plan to approach him at Lady Curchon's and make my affection for him clear."

Aunt Lottie turned back to her with a raised brow. "We saw him only the other day outside of the apothecary shop. While his greeting was warm, Odessa, it was not overly effusive. You've no idea if the good captain is committed elsewhere, yet you pin all your hopes on him."

Odessa bit her lip, staring at the strawberry once more. Captain Phillips might not be perfect, but at the very least, he was her choice, and not her father's. If Papa saw she was happy with Phillips, he would stop this nonsense of trying to wed her to a title.

"Phillips comes from a well-respected family. He's connected to a marquess." Her aunt waved her hand at Odessa. "Or someone equally impressive. Because of his connections, Phillips may be pickier than you imagine. And he did not ask permission to call on you when we spoke outside the apothecary, even though I certainly could have given it."

A bothersome fact Odessa tried not to think too much on. "Perhaps he's heard the whispers about Emerson calling on me. Our neighbors do like to gossip. In any case, I would rather focus on the problem at hand." Standing before the mirror, Odessa drew out the small container holding the tar for her teeth. Carefully, she blackened two on the top and three on the bottom.

"I prepared the ointment," Aunt Lottie said in resignation. "I've an entire jar in my room. It should help the worst of the itching. You may have to plead a stomach ailment if the rash isn't gone by the time your father returns. Though, if Hayden is correct, one strawberry shouldn't cause you great discomfort." She held out the bowl. "Go on then."

"Emerson gave me no other option. I said I wanted to please him. I hope he is wracked with guilt over my suffering."

"That is only somewhat dramatic."

A soft knock interrupted them. Her aunt crept to the door, opening it a crack, speaking to someone on the other side before turning to Odessa.

"Lord Emerson has arrived." Aunt Lottie paused before the mirror and patted a hair back into place. "I'll inform Burns of your father's errand before joining the earl in the drawing room. Listen at the door to make sure he's gone before you appear." Her aunt smoothed her skirts.

"You realize Emerson is here to see me, don't you? You are enamored with him."

"There is much to be enamored *of*, Odessa. I nearly fainted at the mere glimpse of his backside."

"Aunt Lottie." Odessa was aghast. Her aunt had always been...*vocal* in her appreciation of the male form. Admitted to having lovers, *discreetly*, in her youth. Sometimes when she had more than a nip of brandy, Aunt Lottie became rather talkative. Descriptive.

Odessa thought of Emerson's hands once more. Touching her. A prickling sensation slid over her skin.

Her fingers picked up the strawberry with determination.

"Your rash was caused by eating a pastry we purchased during our walk through the park. The woman who sold the pastry to us swore there were no strawberries in any of her goods, but she obviously lied. An unfortunate accident for which you must now pay the price." Aunt Lottie placed a palm over her chest. "I'll never forgive myself. My poor Odessa." She pretended to dab at her eyes before raising a brow. "Will that do should your father question me?"

Odessa gave a soft laugh. "You're quite good, aunt. Nearly as good as me."

"Practice." She sailed out of the room, shutting the door behind her.

Staring at herself in the mirror, Odessa checked her blackened teeth once more before plopping the strawberry into her mouth.

CHAPTER FOURTEEN

T HE TINGLING SENSATION along her skin heralded the beginning of the rash. Surprising, since it had only been one strawberry. But the berry had been overly large. Odessa scratched away before her slippered feet reached the door of the drawing room. As she entered, the sensation of pustules breaking across her cheeks greeted her, along with Aunt Lottie's muted gasp. The rash did make Odessa resemble a victim of some dreaded disease. Leprosy or the pox, perhaps.

She paused at the doorway, staring straight at Lord Emerson, and smiled politely. The wool tied to her backside flopped with every step, intensifying the burn of the rash against her skin. She wanted to roll about the floor like a dog trying to scratch itself.

"Miss Whitehall." Lord Emerson greeted her politely, those blazing hazel eyes with their sprinkle of green darted over the skin of her cheeks and neck before the left side of his mouth lifted in a half-smile.

No flicker of distaste.

Drat.

With no onion clogging her nostrils, Odessa finally caught Emerson's scent. Clean linen and leather with a touch of lime. He smelled wonderful. Masculine. Not like pomade or an equally revolting scent.

How annoying.

His coat, obviously new and tailored to his broad form, still pulled at the seams just a bit, enough to showcase the line of muscle covering his shoulders and arms. Dark hair lay in a thick tangle across his forehead and cheeks.

Emerson *was* breathtaking.

Odessa gave him a wide, welcoming smile full of tar-stained teeth. "Lord Emerson."

His gaze dropped to her mouth, but not on her supposedly rotted teeth. He appeared to be studying the curve of her lips.

She swallowed, telling her pulse to return to its usual rhythm.

Emerson took her fingers in his much larger, *naked* hand, and squeezed gently.

Where are his gloves?

Every gentleman wore gloves, especially when calling on a young lady, except it seemed, Emerson. He'd taken them off during their carriage ride and now, once more, had forgone gloves for some *inexplicable*, tortuous reason and—

Odessa shivered at the roughened skin brushing seductively along hers. A delicious, lazy sensation streamed across her well-padded stomach to shoot between her thighs. Belatedly, Odessa realized she hadn't put on her own gloves. Once the itching started, well, she couldn't scratch with her fingers covered. And that had been her only thought. The gloves were laying on her bed.

A hum, pulsing along her skin, vibrated into Odessa's core and along her limbs. From *only* Emerson's touch. Imagine if those callused hands trailed elsewhere over her body. What if—

Dear lord.

Odessa snatched back her hand.

"You are quite…flushed, Miss Whitehall."

"The rash reddens my skin." Panic laced her words as Emerson regarded her with a twitch of his lips. "I realize how awful it is. Repulsive. You see why I must eat a daily onion to avoid such a state." Absently, she scratched at her cheek.

"How terrible for you."

Odessa gritted her teeth. Soon she'd be twitching, scratching at herself like a madman if he didn't decide to leave. Hayden was incorrect. The smallest amount of strawberry caused a horrific reaction.

"There is no need for you to witness such an unpleasant display, my lord. I thought to please you, but I find—" Her lashes fluttered down.

"Please me?" The low timbre of his voice buffeted along her heated skin. "Hmm."

Dear God. Did he mistake her words as flirtation? She shot a look at Aunt Lottie, who was sitting perfectly still, her eyes on Emerson's backside. Odessa really needed to speak to her aunt about her incorrigible behavior. It was unseemly for a chaperone—

"No apologies are necessary, Miss Whitehall." He extended his arm. "Come, let us take a turn about the garden. There is a breeze. It will cool your skin." Emerson eyed an eruption at the end of her nose.

"But—"

"Should there be a part of your person which requires a scratch…" He lowered his voice until the rich sound singed her ears. "You've only to ask, Miss Whitehall, and I will comply."

Odessa stumbled as he pulled her in the direction of the doors leading outside. Large, warm fingers curled around her elbow, holding her firmly. The heat of his hand along her itching skin—

A searing tingle ran up her arm and down her neck, causing Odessa to suck in her breath. None of it related to her rash.

Drat.

"With your permission, of course, Miss Maplehurst." A lazy grin spread across Emerson's wide mouth with its full, sensual lips as he turned the full force of his charm, and it was significant, on her aunt.

As if Aunt Lottie, a woman in her sixth decade who looked as if she might swoon, would deny Emerson anything. "Of course, my lord."

"Are you sure that's wise?" Odessa gave Aunt Lottie a pointed look, more plea for help. She didn't want to be alone with Emerson in the garden. Or anywhere at all. Her reaction to him during this visit was already bordering on dangerous territory.

"The fresh air will help, my dear," her traitorous aunt replied. "I'm sure of it."

Odessa held back the scream of frustration threatening to escape her. Her appearance was horrid. Utterly disgusting. She did smell of garlic, if not onion. Her teeth were properly blackened. Small pus-filled pockets decorated her skin.

Why wasn't he making his excuses to leave?

She itched, rather impolitely, at the bump of wool over one hip.

Emerson didn't seem to notice, or if he did, paid her no mind. Leading Odessa into the Whitehall gardens, which weren't the least extravagant, he took a path curling about a willow tree. The bump at the end of her nose grew larger, begging for the tip of her nail. The wool tied over her backside slid around, tickling one leg.

Odessa glanced down, horrified to see one "lump" of flesh tilting down beneath her skirts as if one knee had suddenly grown in size.

Worst of all, *everything* itched. Terribly. Like having hundreds of ants dancing over your skin.

"I don't find your affliction that terrible." Emerson patted her hand. "You merely look as if you've been in the sun for too long without a parasol."

Odessa bit her tongue to keep from railing at him. Was he blind? She scratched at the end of her nose where the large bump at the end begged for her attention. "You don't find my appearance to be unattractive, my lord? Forgive me, but I find that difficult to believe."

"I admire your courage, Miss Whitehall."

She resisted the urge to stomp on his foot. "You do?"

"Most young ladies would hide themselves away in shame, yet you have gamely decided to show me a part of yourself. If I must grow accustomed to the scent of onions, so be it, for I do not wish you to be in pain." He patted her hand. "I think we should get on rather well."

Damn him.

Impulsively, she itched at her ear before inserting a finger into her nose, digging away as if she'd discovered gold. *Certainly*, that would disgust him.

"I took your advice, Miss Whitehall." He leaned closer and lime caught in her nostrils. "In taking my sisters to some unusual sights in London. Old Palace Yard. The Execution Dock."

"They allowed the accused a pint of ale at Turk's Head Inn before they were executed at the dock. And used a short rope to prolong the hanging," Odessa informed him, unable to help herself.

"How grim."

"You find me grotesque for my interests." Maybe Odessa should have discarded the tar and instead focused on treating Emerson to the execution of traitors. Or torture, perhaps. Though he didn't seem repulsed.

"Unusual. But it is refreshing to find a young lady with interests that are different from the usual reading, walking in the park, embroidery, and such."

Of course he did.

"How did you come to be fascinated by such things, if I may ask?"

Odessa scratched again with enthusiasm. "I'm not entirely sure, my lord. My cousin is also interested in such oddities, though his tastes lean more towards dissection."

Emerson's eyes widened. She'd finally managed to shock him. Over Hayden's habits, of all things. "I see."

She didn't bother to reassure him that Hayden's dissections were performed exclusively on insects, not people. "I'm hardly suitable, my lord, to be a countess. My affliction," she took the opportunity to flash a tiny smile at him, enough to show her blackened teeth, "and the steps I must take to avoid it make me a loner, of sorts. I would not want to add to the challenges your family already faces. You have two sisters who must come out."

Surely *that* would give him pause. Odessa didn't know much about

Lord Emerson, but he'd spoken of his sisters with great affection and would surely not wish them to be hurt.

"Only the younger. I fear Tamsin is well past such an entrance. But do not fear, Miss Whitehall. I expect both my sisters will welcome you with open arms. I've already mentioned the wax exhibit to them both. Aurora is especially excited."

Odessa nearly threw herself on the ground to roll about like a child in the throes of a tantrum. Nothing she did seemed to deter him.

"Won't you wish to entertain, my lord? I can hardly welcome guests in such a condition." Odessa jerked at the crawling sensation stretching across her stomach and thighs. The discomfort was growing by the moment.

"We'll manage. I've never cared much for dinner parties."

She struggled to keep from stomping her foot in frustration. "I fear," Odessa failed to keep the hostility out of her voice, "I will be the most disappointing of wives, my lord."

"I find you a most amusing companion."

Odessa coughed as bit of the tar on her teeth stuck to her throat. That was the problem with the tar. It kept slipping off, and the taste was nearly worse than that of onions. "Is that why you sent me sweets?"

"I assumed you liked them." A devastating grin crossed his lips. Unfortunately, Odessa was itching so much she couldn't appreciate it. Emerson stopped, pulling her beneath the willow tree, the one spot in the entire garden that wasn't completely in view of the drawing room.

If her appearance, smell, and morbid curiosity about the world didn't put him off, Odessa was doomed. The strawberry had been her last hope. Looking up at Emerson, their eyes caught. A soft exhale left her. What an arresting combination, all that brown and green mixing together. She'd always thought hazel eyes to be somewhat dull. Not worth mooning over. But—

Odessa's heart thumped inside her chest. He was staring at her with a great deal of intensity.

"I came to inform you today, Miss Whitehall, that I must depart London for a time. I didn't wish to convey my leaving in a note, but thought the news would be better received in person."

"You are *leaving*?" Odessa blinked at him and stopped scratching at her arm, stunned by finally hearing the words she'd longed for.

"Don't look so distressed, Miss Whitehall," Emerson said in a solemn tone. "I realize now may not be the best time to depart, when we are finally becoming accustomed to each other, but there are matters at my country estate which require my attention. Matters which cannot be ignored. Not even for you."

"Of…course not, my lord." The rash *had* worked after all. He was merely being polite. She allowed him another glimpse of her blackened teeth before he could change his mind. "I do hope it isn't anything serious, my lord."

"Nothing that cannot be fixed in a fortnight or so."

"A fortnight?" She tried to temper the excitement in her voice.

"Possibly longer. Depending." Emerson made a vague gesture with his free hand. "Estate matters can be complicated at times."

Oh, this was wonderful news. He *was* going to beg off. But not until he could depart London and the orbit of Angus Whitehall. The fortnight would stretch into another week, possibly more. From a safe distance, Emerson would inform Papa of Odessa's unsuitability. Cowardly, to be sure. She'd thought better of Emerson. But Odessa didn't care *how* she rid herself of the overly spectacular Emerson, only that she did.

He leaned over, nose mere inches from her face.

She had to keep from crossing her eyes at the enormous bump forming at the end of her own nose. Emerson's clean lime scent wafted over her in a warm rush, flooding her senses. She could do nothing but breathe in Emerson and his big, solid form.

He's too close. He's—

Going to kiss me.

Shockingly. *Impossibly.* Emerson's mouth lowered and brushed lazily over hers, his lips barely moving.

Odessa gasped, nearly sucking a piece of tar into her throat, stunned to the marrow of her bones. His lips trailed over her mouth with practiced decadence. Emerson, Odessa's dazed mind whispered, knew how to kiss a woman properly. The barest graze of his lips conveyed more promise than any kiss Odessa had ever experienced. Her hands floated upward, palms flattening over his chest, feeling the press of muscles beneath her fingertips. Odessa arched into Emerson, willing those roughened hands to take hold. Tug at her hair. Pull her beneath the willow tree and—

Emerson took a step back, taking his mouth from hers. The green of his eyes had deepened, mixing further with the brown. A ragged sound escaped him, but no regret for taking such a liberty. Emerson wasn't the sort of man who kissed a woman and then apologized.

A ripple caressed Odessa's skin, followed by a quaking sensation along the lower half of her body. She lowered her eyes to the path beneath her slippered feet, having no idea what to say, or even if she could speak.

"I'll show myself out, Miss Whitehall," Emerson said, saving her the trouble of deciding. "Until we meet again. Good day."

WHAT A RELIEF not to smell onions today. She must have rushed the application of tar because she'd blackened the wrong teeth. Jordan had toyed with taking hold of one fleshy lump, the one moving beneath her skirts in the direction of her ankle, but thought he'd be unable to stop laughing. Only the rash had been real. There was no faking the tiny bumps decorating her cheek, neck, and the end of her nose. She must have applied stinging nettles to her skin to cause such irritation, or something equally abrasive.

Had he not seen Odessa on Bond Street, one look at her skin would have sent Jordan back to his carriage. It wouldn't have stopped him from marrying her. Nothing would. But he would have been disgusted.

He'd only meant to tease her a bit with his false departure from London. Odessa had been so bloody hopeful. Plump lips parted, with no scent of onion on her breath to deter him.

Jordan smoothed down his coat as he jumped into his carriage. Tugging at the cravat circling his neck, he instructed his cock to stand down.

I shouldn't have kissed her.

That hadn't been his intent. Nor had Jordan thought one kiss would—arouse him to such an extent. Not even the taste of tar mixing with a bit of lemon and mint had put him off. But that plump bottom lip of Odessa's—he'd been consumed with dragging his teeth over the delicate bit of flesh since their initial meeting when Jordan had assumed her to be a troll.

He imagined Odessa in, perhaps, only her chemise. Honey brown hair spilling in a halo around her head as she lay beneath him. Legs and lips parted in welcome.

A small groan left him.

Part of the attraction for Odessa was that she didn't want *him*. A rare occurrence for Jordan where women were concerned. What manner of man *had* garnered her affections? One who didn't mind her gruesome observations. Or care that she was the daughter of Angus Whitehall.

Bedding Odessa, once improbable, was now a consideration, especially after that kiss. He reasoned the marriage had to be consummated to make it legally binding. It didn't mean anything. They would still live apart and lead separate lives. He would still abandon her.

Whitehall could not and *would not* win this game.

CHAPTER FIFTEEN

"**I** DON'T BELONG here."

"Nonsense, Tamsin," Jordan assured his sister. "We were invited by Lady Curchon."

His sister looked lovely tonight, in a gown of pale green, which brought out the emerald lights in her eyes. Although that could also have been scathing dislike glowing in their depths as well. With Tamsin, it was often difficult to discern the difference.

The invitation to Lady Curchon's gathering this evening had come as a bit of a surprise, considering Jordan had never been introduced to his hostess. It was Lord Curchon who had once been a close friend of Jordan's father and visited River Crest, but his wife never accompanied him, claiming she didn't care to be away from London.

Far more likely she didn't want to associate with the notorious Lady Emerson.

In either case, after Jordan found Lord Curchon, quite by accident, at the club Jordan's father had once frequented, the pair had become reacquainted over a glass of expensive brandy. Thus, the invitation to this evening's festivities. Freely given, no matter the opinion of Lady Curchon.

"I think I'll just join Drew at the card tables," Tamsin whispered from beside him. "I feel like a prize horse on display. Everyone's looking at me."

"Because you are stunning," he assured her. Truthfully, his sister *was* rather notorious. The story of her breaking the nose of the Marquess of Sokesby so many years ago was still making the rounds, as evidenced by the incident at Gunter's. And Richland's son, the boy she'd beaten in a horse race at Dunnings, took great delight in entertaining his cohorts with tales of Tamsin riding in breeches. "Joining our brother at the tables would only draw more attention. Besides, you're terrible at cards. You wear your thoughts on your sleeve."

Tamsin gave a puff of exasperation, but stayed by his side.

Lord Curchon was active in politics, and the guest list for tonight's event reflected his tastes more so than his socially ambitious wife. One or two of Her Majesty's ministers floated by, along with several members of Parliament. That wasn't to say that there weren't a handful of prominent titles sprinkled about the room, or that there weren't more than a few young ladies on the search for a suitable match. But Lady Longwood and her minions were unlikely to be in attendance.

"I almost prefer Dunnings to this," Tamsin murmured. "Or torture of some sort."

"Shh. Our hostess will overhear you."

Lady Curchon had welcomed the Sinclairs, if not with open arms, at the very least with excessive politeness. After a few moments of light, pleasant conversation, Lady Curchon announced she would introduce Tamsin to some of the other young ladies circling about, and Jordan was thankfully excused.

He'd have an earful from Tamsin on the carriage ride home.

Ignoring her angry glare, Jordan left Tamsin to the attentions of their hostess, thinking to join Drew at cards, but ultimately heading for the peace and quiet offered by Lord Curchon's terrace. He meant to enjoy a cheroot and contemplate where Miss Whitehall had been spending her evenings. Lord Curchon was far more open-minded than most, but he thought his father's old friend might draw the line at having Whitehall or his daughter here. Jordan toyed with the idea of informing Curchon of his situation with Whitehall, but decided to remain silent. All of London would know of his wedding Odessa Whitehall soon enough.

Since taking his leave of Miss Whitehall nearly a fortnight ago and allowing her to assume him gone from London, Jordan had visited Bond Street several more times, hoping to catch her unawares, but Odessa remained stubbornly absent. Assuming she must take leisurely walks with her aunt, Jordan made a habit of riding every day in the park. He'd also visited Madame Tussauds, thinking to catch Odessa and her mysterious lover gawking at the bloodstained wax figures, most of which were quite gruesome indeed, but there had been no sign of her.

Whitehall had sent Jordan a series of notes, demanding he call upon Odessa and the reason for his absence.

Jordan put him off with a deftly woven tale of estate matters.

Lamps had been lit along the terrace, attracting a great deal of flying insects, including a fluttering herd of moths. Small, papery wings flitted about, crowding around the torches. A young lady squawked, whispering in a terrified voice that she feared a moth would land upon her person or insert itself into her carefully styled coiffure. Or, she claimed in an innocent tone, one might land on her bodice.

Jordan snorted and lit his cheroot. The last declaration was merely an excuse for her companion to admire her bosom. She could use a lesson in deception from Miss Whitehall. But the gentleman finally took the hint and led her away from the light and deeper into the shadows.

Inhaling the cheroot, Jordan blew out a large, perfect 'O' and watched it float away into the night.

A large shadow suddenly loomed at his shoulder. "Do not move," a deep baritone instructed in a menacing tone.

"May I take my cheroot from between my lips?" Jordan asked,

peering over his shoulder.

The gentleman stood just to Jordan's left, but all that he could make out was a massive, lumpy shadow, the size of Holly. He doubted he was about to be accosted on Lord Curchon's terrace, though it wasn't completely out of the question.

"I beg you, do not move. You have an *opisthograptis luteolata* on your shoulder."

"A what?" Jordan's eyes turned.

"An *opisthograptis luteolata*," the condescending tone repeated. A small jar glinted in the muted light, followed by the light brush of fingers along Jordan's shoulder.

Good lord. He's bigger *than Holly.*

The rumpled giant standing in the shadows deposited something in the jar he held, which immediately disappeared into the folds of his coat. A massive pair of hands next took out a tiny notebook and pencil. He scribbled furiously, ignoring Jordan's presence completely.

"Was it a spider?" Jordan said in a hushed tone. He had an unnatural fear of spiders owing to an experience he'd had as a child. He'd been chasing Drew and Malcolm through the woods when the twins turned sharply, and Jordan ran into an enormous web. The creator of the web had been black with brilliant yellow streaks and didn't care for Jordan destroying her handiwork. She'd crawled up his forehead into his hair, but not before releasing a horde of baby spiders.

The feel of those tiny legs crawling over his body had never been forgotten. Malcolm and Drew found him screaming in the grass and tossed him in a nearby stream.

"A moth," said the bland tone. "I study *insecta* not *arachinda*."

Jordan had no bloody idea what his new friend was talking about. "You mean insects."

"Didn't I just say so?" the giant rasped.

"You study insects?" Jordan asked. What an odd sort of acquaintance to make on Lord Curchon's terrace, though there were quite a few eccentric characters inside sipping his host's punch and playing cards.

The massive head tilted to the side, looking very much like a shaggy dog Jordan once owned when he was a child. "I am an entomologist. And a duke. But that is less important. The ducal part."

"I see." Jordan bowed slightly. "Apologies, Your Grace."

A massive paw waved before Jordan. "I am Ware."

Ware? The name was familiar to Jordan, but he couldn't imagine they'd ever met. Dukes weren't exactly rushing to make the Earl of Emerson's acquaintance. Surely, he'd remember meeting this duke, given his size. Ware would be difficult to miss.

"Lord Emerson, Your Grace."

The duke leaned towards Jordan. His eyes gleamed like quicksilver in the torchlight. "Emerson? You're here for Miss Odessa Whitehall."

Jordan's teeth tightened on the cheroot. Was it Ware who had Odessa's affections? "You are acquainted with Miss Whitehall?"

"Oh, yes," the deep, raspy voice echoed in the night air. "We are quite close."

He frowned up at the duke. "Are you?"

Ware raised a brow at Jordan, lips curling in a moue of distaste, which was rather unsettling in such a large man. "Not like *that*, Emerson. What an utterly repulsive idea. Miss Whitehall is my cousin. Of sorts." The big shoulders lifted. "You've confused me with Captain Phillips." Ware started to move away.

How on earth was Miss Whitehall related to anyone of importance let alone a duke? Neither she nor her father were even received; that was the entire reason for Whitehall wanting a title for her. He should have paid closer attention to Patchahoo's recitation of the pedigree of Angus Whitehall's long dead wife; it was the only place from which the connection could come.

"Captain Phillips?" he asked the retreating Ware.

"Dashing cavalry officer." The duke paused and wiggled a pair of bushy brows at Jordan. "You should hurry before she does something stupid. Which I feel certain she is inclined to do. I don't like Phillips," he added. "Disingenuous. Not sure you'll be much better." He shrugged again. "You'd best hurry." Ware turned.

The entire conversation was confusing. *Ware*. Bloody hell. Tamsin. The duke's son. But surely *not*. His gaze took in Ware once more. Perhaps the duke had been smaller, years ago. He had to have been if Tamsin got in a punch. "Wait—"

The Duke of Ware never heard Jordan; he'd already started to make his way back inside, lumbering across the terrace with purpose, nearly toppling a whispering couple into the hedges.

CHAPTER SIXTEEN

ODESSA ENTERED LADY Curchon's extravagant residence, eyes immediately searching for Captain Phillips. He'd mentioned in passing he would be here this evening when she and Aunt Lottie had come upon him outside the apothecary the other day on Bond Street.

When he hadn't asked to call upon her.

Odessa pushed the thought aside. Merely an oversight on the part of Phillips. She was sure he *meant* to ask.

This event of Lady Curchon's, more of a gathering than a full-blown ball, was one of the few Odessa was invited to. No one of great importance was in attendance, unless you counted a few members of Parliament. The clustering of prominent titles and pedigrees was absent tonight. The presence of Angus Whitehall's daughter would largely go unnoticed.

She greeted her hostess, making sure to thank Lady Curchon profusely for the invitation. Complimenting Lady Curchon's gown, the floral arrangements, and the large table groaning under the load of refreshments, Odessa inquired after her health.

The last part may have been a bit much.

Lady Curchon, in turn, looked down her thin, aristocratic nose at the unwelcome product of her favorite cousin's marriage to Angus Whitehall. She sighed, half in resignation, half in disapproval as she took in Odessa, but nonetheless, pressed a brief kiss to her cheek.

"You look very much like Emily tonight." Sadness clouded Lady

Curchon's eyes for a moment. "Enjoy yourself, Odessa. Be discreet. Don't make me regret my invitation."

"Thank you, my lady."

"Whitehall isn't lingering about, is he?" A hard glint entered the eyes of her hostess. "You are welcome, but your father is not."

Odessa was *barely* welcome. Mama's family blamed Papa for many things, but mostly, for stealing Emily Maplehurst away from them.

"No, my lady." Odessa dipped obediently.

Cousin Alice, as Odessa was permitted to call Lady Curchon in private, didn't want anyone in London to know of the distant connection to Angus Whitehall and his daughter. She never acknowledged the relationship to Odessa publicly and barely did so even when the gossips weren't watching. Still, Cousin Alice did issue an invitation to Odessa several times a year to her smaller, less formal events.

She departed the presence of Lady Curchon, ignoring the sigh of relief from the older woman at her departure. Making her way around the perimeter of the ballroom, Odessa searched for anyone in uniform resembling Captain Phillips. Though there were several handsome officers in attendance, owing to Cousin Alice's diverse guest list for the evening and her youngest son's recently acquired commission, none were Captain Phillips.

And, more importantly, there was no sign of Emerson. Her unwelcome suitor had remained absent for the better part of two weeks.

Cerulean blue silk floated about Odessa's ankles as she passed through the crowd, few bothering to acknowledge her. A massive form in rumpled evening clothes was wedged in a small, darkened corner, one that couldn't possibly hide him from view. Unsociable to a fault, her cousin had picked a spot as far from everyone as possible while still being in the room. He must have promised Lady Curchon to make an appearance among her guests. A notebook was clasped in one hand, the other scribbling madly away with a tiny pencil.

"Your Grace," Odessa whispered, tapping one colossal shoulder.

He often reminded Odessa of an overly large, poorly-mannered bear, one you've unwittingly awakened from slumber, much to your detriment.

Nothing happened for several moments.

"Odessa." He continued to write, not bothering to look down at her. "Don't interrupt. A thought has just come to me, and I must commit it to paper."

She waited patiently, used to his little bouts of scientific focus. Hayden Redford, Duke of Ware, shouldn't have even been a duke. He was happiest tromping through the woods collecting insects, not fulfilling his ducal duties, which included, according to Lady Curchon, who was also his aunt, marriage. Thank goodness Papa hadn't even attempted to set his sights on Hayden. Angus Whitehall's fortune was a mere pittance to the Duke of Ware and his family. Odessa's dowry, no better than the amount the dowager duchess might spend on a month-long trip to the Continent. There was nothing Angus Whitehall could do to entice them.

"Cousin." She tapped her foot impatiently.

Hayden wasn't *truly* her cousin, of course. They weren't related by blood. But she and Hayden had found each other in childhood when both were declared too unsuitable by their families and a bond was formed. Odessa was unacceptable for the obvious reasons due to her birth, but Hayden, who had been the youngest of the Duke of Ware's sons, had earned his father's disappointment by being…different. Ironic that the eccentric, scholarly, third son had inherited the title after a tragic accident several years ago took the other males of his family. Poor Hayden was ill-prepared to be a duke. He wanted to study his beloved insects and not attend balls. At present, Hayden was compiling a book of his findings on the moths indigenous to England, an enormous undertaking which took up a great deal of his time.

After a few moments, Odessa tapped him on the arm once more. "Are you finished?"

"Odessa." Eyes like quicksilver turned on her. "Do *not* interrupt. I am documenting the *artica caja* I observed earlier in Lady Curchon's garden. Very unusual to have one flying about. Typically, they aren't found until much later in the summer."

"I see." Odessa rocked back on her heels, content to wait. "What is an *artica caja*?"

If Hayden had any other friends but Odessa, she had yet to meet them. He was a solitary creature. Neither duke nor a man of science, but a struggling blend of the two. Awkward in most social situations. He didn't have the easy charm of say…Lord Emerson.

Her eyes fluttered shut for a moment, remembering the press of his mouth on hers.

Drat.

"Tiger moth," Hayden informed her. "Did you know that no two are alike? The wings have a distinctive design." He opened the book to a sketch he'd done showing a pair of wings with a series of spots.

"I did not," Odessa admitted. She had absolutely no interest in the moth, or insects in general. When they'd been children, Hayden had often dragged her through the park to observe various insects in their natural habitat. Once, Odessa had brought Hayden a dead spider, hoping to please him. He'd informed her in a disappointed tone that the spider was *arachnida* and not *insecta*.

"Lady Curchon gave me leave to collect from her garden for an entire week if I agreed to attend tonight," Hayden said. "She even dismissed the gardener if I promised to be here."

Given that Hayden was an unmarried duke who was under the age of seventy, Odessa could see why her hostess might have resorted to such temptation. He wasn't unattractive, but his manner made him unapproachable.

A button was missing from Hayden's coat. Cravat hastily tied. He'd probably frightened off yet another valet and resorted to either dressing himself or enlisting his butler.

"I was surprised when Lady Curchon told me you were expected tonight. I assumed you would still be in disguise until you could get rid of the latest Lord Emerson." There was an amused glint in his silver eyes. "Aren't you worried he'll see you looking and smelling very unlike yourself?"

Odessa shot him a look. "You are the one who suggested onions."

Hayden shrugged.

"Keep your voice down." She nudged him with her elbow. Hayden was well aware of Odessa's efforts to dissuade her suitors. He understood, somewhat, since his mother and aunt were pressuring him to wed. "I managed to get him to depart London for his country estate, but had to take extreme measures."

"You used a strawberry. And that forced him to flee London?"

"The strawberry was quite large. The rash immediate."

Hayden brought out his little book once more. "How big exactly? What was the duration of the rash?"

Odessa dutifully made a circle with her fingers. "About so big. Very juicy. The rash lasted two days but stopped itching after one."

"Interesting." He wrote something down, shut the notebook, and tucked it back into his pocket.

"I believe he means to beg off, though he hasn't yet." She frowned. "But I expect a note from him any day explaining our unsuitability. Papa will be most distressed."

"Hmm."

"I've decided to encourage Captain Phillips tonight since I will soon be without a suitor. Do you think Lady Curchon would be horribly distressed if I am compromised tonight? I plan to convince Phillips of the benefits of doing so. I must see to my ruination before Papa brings me yet another lord with empty pockets."

"You're far too brazen, Odessa. And I don't care for Phillips."

"So you've said. I don't know why, Your Grace. He's perfectly acceptable. Dashing. Not titled. The sort of man I find appealing."

Hayden shrugged once more. "I've asked you not to call me that. Your Grace. Sounds ridiculous. I am the least graceful person I know."

"Apologies," Odessa murmured. Hayden had a point.

"Not all titled gentlemen are fops, Odessa. Look at me." Hayden turned slowly, showing off his massively disheveled form. "In fact, I plucked an *opisthograptis luteolata* from the shoulder of such a titled gentleman earlier, who did not strike me as limp-wristed in the least. He mistakenly assumed my specimen to be a spider. Which is ridiculous."

"How interesting." Odessa's eyes moved through the crowd. Hayden would drone on about moths forever if she allowed it. Where was Phillips? Now that she was sure she'd be rid of Emerson, time was of the essence.

CHAPTER SEVENTEEN

MISS WHITEHALL WAS at Lady Curchon's. Related to a duke who liked to pluck insects off of the shoulders of gentlemen on the terrace. And looking for a cavalry officer by the name of Captain Phillips.

He'd been correct.

Should he come upon Miss Whitehall in an indelicate situation with this Captain Phillips, the evening might well end in a brawl. Not out of any sense of possessiveness towards Odessa, of course, only her dowry. Besides, Jordan hadn't beaten anyone up since Spittal. A soldier might prove to be a challenge.

Jordan wandered back towards Tamsin who stood in a group of matrons at least three times her age, hands clasped, not bothering to hide her boredom.

"Why Lord Emerson, what a delight to see you this evening." Miss Maplehurst's sugary tone floated towards him. She was perched regally on the edge of a chair amid the small group clustered against the wall, silver curls bouncing at her temples. She shot Jordan a coquettish look. "It was my understanding you weren't in London at present."

"Miss Maplehurst." He took her fingers and bowed, declining to answer the question. "I see you've made the acquaintance of my sister, Lady Tamsin."

"Only moments ago." Miss Maplehurst raised a brow. "Lady

Tamsin quite reminds me of myself at that age, though I was more careful in showing my disinterest in those around me." She gave Tamsin a sideways glance. "We're going to be great friends, aren't we, my lady?"

"Assuredly." Tamsin's reply was stiff. "Lady Curchon introduced us with the admonition that Miss Maplehurst may be of some assistance to me, given our…circumstances, though I noticed our hostess didn't offer her own help."

"My dear." Miss Maplehurst patted Tamsin on the arm. "Lady Curchon has never cared for a challenge. Nor undue attention. She lacks courage. Not every lady is as bold as we are. I confess I am envious you possess such a scandalous moniker. *Embrace* it."

Tamsin made a disgruntled sound.

"You'll come around." Miss Maplehurst turned back to Jordan. "My lord, though it would please me—" Miss Maplehurst's eyes twinkled. "I doubt I am the quarry you seek. A wonderful ruse, pretending to leave town."

"Miss Whitehall is not the only one capable of deceit."

"True, my lord. You've proven yourself to be much more intelligent than your brother."

Another sniff from Tamsin. "My horse has more sense than Bentley."

"Don't speak ill of the dead, dear." Miss Maplehurst corrected her gently. "Though I believe your assumption is correct having been acquainted with the previous Lord Emerson. My lord, your search should continue on the other side of the room." The snowy white head inclined in that direction. "Do you see the splash of red?" Her grin broadened. "Dashing things, those cavalry officers."

"So, I've been told by the Duke of Ware."

"Oh." Miss Maplehurst clasped a hand to her throat. "His Grace has decided to attend this evening. How lovely for you to become acquainted given you have much in common. I thought Ware would be in the gardens plucking moths out of young lady's coiffures. The ladies in question usually pretend great offense until they find him to be a duke. And unwed."

"Ware?" Tamsin swallowed. "He's here?"

"Oh, not the one whose nose you broke, dear." Miss Maplehurst waved a hand. "Don't scowl, everyone in London knows the tale. The youngest brother inherited. You can't miss him. Oversized in the extreme. Broad. A little soft around the middle. His brothers are all...gone. Sadly."

Tamsin paled slightly. "Gone."

"A story for another time, perhaps." A sad smile crossed Miss Maplehurst's lips. "We must concentrate on you."

"If you'll excuse me, Miss Maplehurst, there is a matter of some urgency I must see to." Jordan bowed. "May I leave Lady Tamsin in your care?"

"Yes, be quick, my lord. And Lady Tamsin and I will do quite well." She patted Tamsin's arm once more. "I've so many interesting tidbits to relay to your sister. Useful things." Her kind eyes held a shard of something brittle. "I'll start with Lady Longwood, shall I?"

CHAPTER EIGHTEEN

O DESSA EDGED ALONG the wall of Lady Curchon's drawing room, popping up on her toes every so often to survey those around her. No sign of Captain Phillips. She wandered through each of the interconnecting rooms, some barren of furniture, the rugs rolled back for dancing, positive that Phillips had said he would be here tonight. The musicians were busy setting up behind a screen on the balcony, the sound of their instruments echoing above her. Turning back in the direction she'd come, Odessa caught sight of her aunt against the furthest wall, laughing uproariously.

A strikingly beautiful young woman stood at Aunt Lottie's shoulder, whispering in her ear.

Her aunt had to cover her mouth to stifle the sounds of amusement.

Odessa didn't recognize the girl, but that was no great surprise. She didn't have any friends in society.

Next, Odessa wandered about the refreshment table. The small group of gentlemen who'd been here earlier had since dispersed. She glanced out the terrace doors, half afraid she'd see Phillips with another young lady, but his tall, lean form was not there either. Making her way back down the hall, Odessa stopped in her tracks. She composed herself. Smoothed her skirts. Snuck a look in the mirror hanging next to her on the wall.

Finally. Captain Phillips.

Phillips looked exceptionally dashing this evening, the red of his uniform standing out among the more sedate formalwear of the other gentlemen in attendance. He was tall. Lithe. Danced gracefully. She assumed his hands to be properly callused.

Best of all, Phillips was not the choice of Angus Whitehall.

Odessa stopped short, taking a moment to admire the man she meant to coax into possibly compromising her. Ruination might be the only way to secure a future not of her father's making. She'd been so surprised to see him the other day outside the apothecary shop Odessa hadn't properly taken his measure. A frown tugged at her lips as she took in the handsome captain.

Hadn't Phillips been broader across the chest? She distinctly recalled his shoulders being...more muscular in nature. And his backside, as glanced from beneath Odessa's lashes, wasn't nearly as spectacular as she recalled.

Not at all as glorious as that of Emerson.

Odessa's lips pursed into a tight, irritated rosette. She pushed aside all thoughts of Emerson and his magnificence. It didn't signify. Tilting back her head, Odessa straightened her spine, so that her bosom jutted out in a fetching manner. Keeping her eyes focused as if intent on greeting someone on the other side of the room, she sauntered leisurely past Captain Phillips, making sure to show a bit of ankle.

"Miss Whitehall."

Turning, Odessa pressed a hand to her mouth as if unduly surprised. "Why, Captain Phillips." She tilted her chin, studying the close-cropped sandy hair, the too straight nose. He was in the military; surely, he'd brawled a time or two. Her glance fell to his hands. Gloved, of course.

Drat.

"Miss Whitehall, is aught amiss?" Captain Phillips bestowed a charming smile.

Flutter, she demanded of her heart which continued to beat at its normal pace, entirely unimpressed with Captain Phillips.

"Not at all. I was looking for my aunt." She held out her hand. "How lovely to see you."

His fingers curled around hers, squeezing gently.

Not so much as tingle. This was intolerable.

"You are a vision, Miss Whitehall. I confess, I didn't expect to see you this evening."

Odessa stared back at him. She'd seen him only recently. "But when we spoke outside the apothecary—didn't I mention I would be in attendance tonight?"

The expanse of his forehead rippled. "The apothecary?"

Captain Phillips didn't recall speaking to her on Bond Street. Nor remembered she'd be in attendance tonight. It was highly likely the dashing Captain Phillips hadn't given Odessa a second thought since stealing a kiss so long ago. While she—a burn of embarrassment filled her.

Odessa smiled back at him, waving a hand. "I must apologize, I was thinking of something else. Are you enjoying London?"

"Definitely." His gaze ran discreetly over her bosom. "I find I am enjoying myself immensely at the moment. Would you care to dance?" Phillips glanced up.

Odessa's lashes brushed her cheeks, hiding her annoyance at the good captain. The mild flirtation would have to do, she supposed. Phillips was busy. He had duties while in London. Their meeting on Bond Street had been brief and hurried. The interest in his eyes told Odessa that Phillips was happy to see her.

She opened her mouth to accept—

"There you are." A silky rumble, aristocratic accent slipping just slightly into that of a former pig farmer from Northumberland, came from behind her. "I don't mean to interrupt."

Odessa froze. In seconds, she was reduced to a young child caught stealing the last biscuit from the tea tray.

Oh. No. No. No.

Emerson had lied to her about departing for his country estate; instead, he'd laid a trap for her. He *was* smarter than the previous Lord Emerson.

Placing a hand on her chest, Odessa found she didn't have to fake the absolute shock of seeing him beside her, slightly wild and wind-blown in his dark-colored evening clothes. Emerson looked a bit more savage than usual.

The flutter from her traitorous heart was difficult to miss.

Emerson pierced Captain Phillips with an assessing look, as if sizing up the captain for a good brawl, which under the current circumstances, Odessa thought likely. Lime and clean linen caught in her nose, along with an undercurrent of cheroot. Emerson loomed inches away, big and warm, so terribly male. A delicious ache took up residence between her thighs.

"I don't believe we've been introduced." Emerson's smile was polite. Far too pleasant.

Captain Phillips straightened to his full height, which was significantly less than Emerson's. "Captain Phillips, 11th Hussars."

"Emerson. A pleasure to make your acquaintance, Captain. Did Miss Whitehall give you the good news? She's to be a countess. Mine, in fact."

Well, that was blatantly impolite. And rather possessive.

"My lord." Captain Phillips dropped Odessa's hand. "Congratulations to you both." The annoyance in his tone was difficult to miss and all of it directed at Odessa. "Miss Whitehall hadn't informed me."

"I—hadn't yet had the opportunity." Warmth seared her cheeks. She was mortified both at embarrassing Captain Phillips and that Emerson had caught her. There would be no going back to onions and tar. Her carefully laid plans, one in which she potentially compromised herself tonight with Phillips and traveled the world as an officer's wife, were rapidly crumbling.

"Captain Phillips has just asked for a dance." Possibly, if she could explain the situation to Phillips, he might understand. "Emerson isn't—

"Much of a dancer," Emerson interrupted. "And Miss Whitehall is often forced to find another gentleman to twirl her about." He allowed a chagrined smile to catch at his lips as if embarrassed by the admission. "But on rare occasions, like tonight, I am determined to make the effort. For Miss Whitehall." He gave her an adoring look. "My brother was in the 16th Lancers, Captain Phillips. Not the same as the Hussars. You might have encountered him, though. Major Sinclair."

Captain Phillips paled. The lines of his mouth hardened. "*Malcolm* Sinclair?"

Clearly, Phillips *had* heard of Emerson's brother and did not recall him with fondness. The affable smile disappeared.

"The very same." Emerson inclined his head.

"I made the acquaintance of Major Sinclair once. He is—quite proficient in his duties."

What a vague, slightly ominous comment to make about an earl's brother. Odessa's curiosity was immediately piqued about Malcolm, which wouldn't do at all because Emerson and his stupid family needed to become *less* interesting to her. She leaned away from her unwanted earl and Emerson firmly gripped her elbow.

"I envy my brother's finesse." Emerson's voice took on a slight edge. "I'm much better with my fists than a pistol. A pleasure, Captain Phillips. Enjoy your evening."

Captain Phillips bowed, barely casting another glance at Odessa. "Lord Emerson. Miss Whitehall."

Odessa was summarily dragged in the direction of the dance floor, the fingers around her elbow tightening, allowing her no opportunity for escape. She was surprised at his behavior towards Captain Phillips. If she hadn't known better, Odessa would have assumed Emerson to be jealous.

"Hoping to entice Phillips into a compromising situation on the terrace?"

Odessa tugged back on her arm, unsettled he'd guessed so precisely at her intentions.

"You insufferable…titled *dandy*. He is twice the man you are. At least Phillips is enticed by more than my dowry."

"Fair enough," Emerson snarled back at her as a wash of dark hair fell over his brow. The green lingering in the depths of his eyes gleamed like shards of emeralds. "Though I'm not sure that is the case."

Odessa tilted her chin up at him, refusing to be intimidated. "I need not explain myself to you, my lord."

Emerson, leaned in, sniffing deliberately along the exposed skin of her neck. He spun Odessa about as the musicians began to play. Clumsily, nearly tripping over his own feet. "I miss the stench of onion laced with garlic and tar. Your signature scent, though I doubt Phillips is familiar."

"You had no reason to—threaten Captain Phillips."

"I did no such thing, Miss Whitehall. I merely asked if he knew my brother."

"Clearly he had and did not recall him with fondness."

"No, only a great deal of fear. Malcolm is an expert marksman. I think his discharge was mostly honorable." Emerson spun her forcefully.

Odessa's skirts billowed out and she lost her balance. Fingers she knew to be wonderfully callused and scarred beneath their polite gloves pressed into her waist.

"Such a devious creature, aren't you?"

"You misled me." Odessa turned away. Her eyes kept landing on the scruff of hair along his jaw, a light dusting which would, should it come in contact with her skin, chafe in the most delicious manner.

"*I* mislead *you*?" A wicked sound came from him, one that raised the hair on her arms. "Oh, that's rich, Miss Whitehall."

"You claimed on your last visit, my lord, that you would be in the country," she said, though it wasn't much of a defense given her own actions.

"And you've been burping onion on me, swathed in a great deal of padding." The glints of green in his eyes trailed down over her breasts with shocking assessment. Blatantly sexual in nature. No man had ever regarded her with such…heat.

Her breasts, hidden beneath layers of cotton and silk, balked at their restraint. The tips of her nipples grew taut, tightening beneath Emerson's frank appraisal.

Odessa missed a step.

This won't do at all.

"Return me to my aunt, if you please, my lord. My temples ache terribly both from your inept dancing and having been forced into conversation with you. If you are expecting an apology from me, my lord, you will wait a lifetime."

Emerson gave her a jerky spin, stepping on her toe.

Odessa winced. "You're *terrible* at this."

"I haven't had much practice; I'll be the first to admit to it. I wasn't invited to many dances at Dunnings." A tiny grimace crossed his mouth as he tried to turn her properly. "You wasted all that effort on Phillips. Going about padded in wool, wearing tar on your teeth, eating onions, and doing whatever it was you did to cause the rash, so I would beg off and you could wed *him?*"

Another clumsy spin.

"I find myself insulted." Emerson stumbled through another step, barely missing her left foot. "Arms like sticks. Probably struggles to wield his sword. I suppose he must sit a horse well. Surely, you could have chosen someone better to bestow your affections on."

Odessa fumed, unwilling to look at him. "What do you care, my lord? Your only interest in me is the money attached to my skirts. How long have you known?" she demanded.

"Long enough to be annoyed at your ridiculous subterfuge. Only the rash was authentic. All those tiny sores. You looked like a victim of the pox."

"I was hoping for leper."

"Splendid. I'm sure you've read up on all sorts of horrid, disfiguring diseases, leprosy included. Where did you come by such a strange hobby, Miss Whitehall?"

"I find such things noteworthy. I opened the newspaper one day to an account of a mysterious creature lurking about the woods in the Peak District. Some said it was a devil, some the malformed son of a farmer's wife who sought revenge on his oppressors."

Emerson rolled his eyes. "You've got to be joking."

"I—next read of the ghost of Anne Boleyn," she stuttered feeling more foolish by the second. "She carries her head. And from there, accounts of executions written of in criminal broadsides, which in turn led to strange murders and—" Odessa sounded ready to be taken to Bedlam. She didn't know why such things fascinated her. "It doesn't matter."

"And the rash? What causes it?" Emerson had pulled her closer to the warmth of his body, and Odessa's skin tingled whenever her breasts came in contact with his chest. "Is that what scared Bentley off?"

"A strawberry." Odessa thought they'd been dancing for an eternity. She kicked Emerson in the leg. "Bentley never saw the rash. Your brother's accident precluded me having to resort to such an extreme measure."

A low sound came from Emerson. A growl, possibly. His gaze dropped to her lower lip for a moment, his teeth dragging over his own.

Something coiled tightly within Odessa, decadent and threatening to spiral out of control.

"Is that how you rid yourself of Bentley? Possibly with the help of

Phillips? You certainly have done enough research. Well, you won't get lucky a second time, you bloodthirsty little creature."

"You can't be serious," Odessa said in shock. "I would never do such a thing."

"Wouldn't you?" His palm flattened against the small of her back, fingers stretching along her spine. Warmth spilled down her buttocks and the backs of her legs along with the unsettling urge to mold her body to his.

"Let me apprise you of the situation, Miss Whitehall. I want to be perfectly clear should there be any other gentlemen, like Captain Phillips, lurking about. You could be dipped in horse manure," he annunciated every syllable, "and I would still wed you."

"How flattering," she snapped. "I see we find each other equally appealing."

"Appeal has nothing to do with it." The edge of his nose trailed once more along the slope of her neck, uncaring for the scene he created for Lady Curchon's other guests.

"Though I do prefer the scent of honey and lavender to that of an onion." Emerson's knee pushed briefly between Odessa's thighs, sending another pulse of sensation through her.

The crowd around them blurred, though not enough for Odessa to miss the dozens of curious looks cast in their direction. Lady Curchon's face came into focus. She wasn't smiling.

Cousin Alice will be most distressed. I'll never receive another invitation.

"What do you hope to accomplish with such antics? Dragging me about the dance floor. Behaving inappropriately. Good lord, neither of our reputations can suffer much more."

"I merely remind you of our circumstances." Emerson's cheek brushed along hers, sending a flood of warmth along her shoulders and neck. The feeling was one of intoxication, which Emerson ruined by stepping on her toe again.

Odessa kicked his shin. "Is your intent to make me lame?"

"It will make it that much easier to catch you." Emerson's features, harsh and cut with sharp edges, were softened by the light of the chandeliers above them. The hand at her waist drifted between them, fingers trailing lightly over her abdomen.

A ping sounded through her body, like the vibration of a fork striking a glass goblet.

Odessa's breath halted in her lungs, willing it to stop, less she lose herself in it. "You aren't a gifted dancer. You've stomped on my foot *twice*. But as you say, it is to be expected."

"Is it?"

He could cut wood with the hard edge of his jaw if he chose. Small curls, the color of chocolate, formed around his ears.

His stupidly beautiful ears.

A bleat of frustration left her at the inescapable fact that no matter what Odessa did, she would not be free of Emerson. And was no longer sure she wanted to be.

"Given your father married his mistress," Odessa said in a cool tone. "*I* was probably raised with better manners."

"Doubtful." Emerson trod on her foot deliberately. His heel caught in the delicate fabric of her skirts, tearing at the silk. "Angus Whitehall doesn't strike me as a stickler for rules and decorum. And his origins are far worse than mine."

Odessa kicked him in the ankle, though he spoke the truth. "All the more reason for us to end this hostile courtship. We don't like each other or trust each other. Neither of us wants this marriage. Make this easy, my lord. Find another heiress, one not so far beneath you."

"We are both in the *muck*, Miss Whitehall. And I very much doubt that your Captain Phillips cares for mud on his boots."

"Stop." She twisted away, pained at the truth in Emerson's words. Earl or not, his family's reputation forced him to the fringes of society, while Odessa's very name kept her from even getting close. "Let me go."

Instead, Emerson took Odessa's hand and stumbled his way through the other dancers, dragging her to the other side of the room. She did not look up to see where he took her. Nor did she care.

Emerson pulled her down a partially deserted hall before he stopped abruptly in front of a narrow space. A darkened alcove where no one would ever look.

Odessa caught sight of a small painting before he pulled her inside. A dog. The artist had done a poor job. "My lord," she started, gasping as Emerson pressed her back against the wall.

He pulled off one glove, using his teeth, and tossed it to the floor.

Oh, dear. Her entire form throbbed gently in response.

The tip of one roughened *naked* finger trailed along Odessa's cheek and traced the outline of her chin.

"What are you doing?" she gasped, unable to do anything other than inhale his warm scent. Odessa stretched along the wall, her breasts touching the edges of his coat. This was entirely wicked.

"Touching you," he ground out. "I've wanted to for some time, but you're always so distasteful. Covered in tiny bumps and smelling like a root cellar whenever I call." The finger rubbed along the edge of her cheek, and she turned into his hand. "I thought it strange, at first. The way your skin glows, like a freshwater pearl. It never fit with the rest of you," he whispered.

A wave of attraction for him washed over Odessa. Fierce. Sharp. And she was unable to push it away. She wanted so badly to be repulsed by Emerson. *Hate* him. Not be aroused by the lightest touch of his fingers. "I meant why did you take off your glove?"

"Because you like my hands. I'm not sure why. They aren't the hands of a gentleman." The finger fell to the edge of her bodice, dipping briefly beneath the silk at her neckline before his entire hand moved further, cupping the underside of her breast. Emerson squeezed gently, as if inspecting a plump peach. His thumb flicked over the satin covering her nipple, teasing at the spot.

Tiny halting breaths left her at the sight of those large fingers closing over the plump globe of her breast. The sensation of his thumb
brushing purposefully back and forth drove a lightning bolt down
between her thighs. "No, they are not the hands of a gentleman," she
agreed. Odessa should tell him to stop, but the words refused to form
on her tongue.

"I'm going to prove a point." Emerson didn't sound happy, as if he
caressed Odessa against his better judgment. But he never paused in
the careful, sensual perusal of her breast. "Has Phillips ever touched
you?" His voice was rough. "Anyone else?"

Odessa thought of Jacob, her father's groom. The collection of
stolen kisses over the years, all of which had failed to move her. "No."

A sliver of light fell over his mouth as he leaned forward, gilding
the sensual lines of his chin and lips. "We do not have to be at odds,
Odessa," he murmured. "I would prefer we were not."

Odessa jumped at the flick of his tongue along the curve of her ear.
The warmth of his breath falling over her neck. His thumb pressed
firmly, stroking over the silk where her nipple peaked and begged for
his attention.

"I—my affections lie elsewhere." She'd been so sure that was true,
but Captain Phillips left her unimpressed tonight. Nor did he bear her
any great interest. Another ruse of Odessa's, believing she could entice
Captain Phillips into compromising her.

"I don't believe you." He pinched at the silk, grazing, and circling
the taut peak of her nipple. "You wish to avoid marriage. I assume the
reason to be defiance. Disobedience." He drew his teeth over the skin
of her earlobe. "You don't want to wed a man of Angus Whitehall's
choosing. As it happens, I don't care for your father's manipulations
either."

Odessa sucked in a breath, her lips parting as Emerson's head tilted, his mouth mere inches from hers.

"No tar. No onion. Not an oozing pustule to be found. Much more to my liking." Soft heat descended on her mouth, moving with wicked deliberation across her lips. He took his time, savoring Odessa, drinking her in like a glass of fine brandy.

She sagged against the wall, hands clutching at the edges of Emerson's coat as her knees buckled at the onslaught of his mouth. His teeth grazed along her bottom lip, sucking the plump bit of flesh into his mouth.

Odessa whimpered, grabbing at him with desperation. She wanted more of him. All of Emerson.

"You are delicious," he rasped at the corner of her mouth. "So much better than that little peck in the garden allowed me to believe." His tongue dragged along the seam of her lips, coaxing her to open. "I want to taste every inch of you, Odessa."

Yes. Please.

Odessa had never given much thought to the sensual, sexual part of her nature despite having a chaperone like Aunt Lottie and Odessa's obsession with a gentleman's hands. Emerson awakened every depraved thought Odessa ever had. She moaned, trying to press herself as close to him as possible. Rubbing shamelessly against his chest, no longer plain Miss Whitehall, but some sensual creature Odessa hadn't known existed. The ache she'd felt earlier resurfaced with pulsing intensity. She kissed him back, moving sinuously as their tongues tangled together, moaning softly when he rocked their hips together.

Emerson broke away, the harsh sound of his breathing echoing in the small space.

A whimper left her. "Emerson."

"Damn," he swore softly, once more slanting his mouth over hers. His hand curled around her throat, the rough pads of his fingers pressing into the skin of her neck.

Yes. Please.

A sound came from Emerson. Primal. Raw. It conjured sinful thoughts of her and Emerson, his glorious hands trailing over Odessa's naked skin, their bodies sliding over each other as he pleasured her. When his free hand moved along the curve of her abdomen, she twisted in the direction of his touch. He cupped her sex through the silk of her skirts before pressing the heel of his palm firmly into the ache between her thighs.

Odessa's head fell back, meeting the pressure of his hand.

Emerson's mouth left hers, but nothing else. His grip on her neck didn't lessen, the pressure on her sex never stopped. The intensity between them, like rushing flood waters, threatened to drown Odessa.

His large body trembled beneath her fingers. Emerson was not unaffected.

"Unexpected, isn't it?" he rasped. "I never thought—" One hand fell away from her throat, but the other stayed fixed between her thighs, effectively pinning Odessa to the wall. His fingers stretching possessively over her sex through the silk.

Odessa took a long, shaky breath. How quickly she had forgotten herself, and with Emerson. A betrayal of herself, one she blamed Emerson for. Ashamed, she looked away from him. "Release me."

One finger pressed deeper into the folds of her skirts, finding the exact spot through all the layers of fabric with little effort. Emerson knew well how to pleasure a woman, that much was clear. That he could pleasure Odessa was not in doubt.

"Seduction does not change—" She cleared her throat. "The reality of the situation or make it more palatable to me. I am being wed against my will. My opinion not considered. You've no idea what it is like to have no say in your future." Odessa slapped at the hand groping her skirts. "We don't even care for each other, my lord. Fondling me will not change that fact."

"You liked me just fine a moment ago," Emerson drawled. "I could have had your skirts up over your head in a thrice, Odessa. I could fuck you in this alcove and you wouldn't say no."

She took a quick breath, shocked at the crudeness of his words.

"How eloquent you are."

"We should try to find pleasure in each other, if we can." There was a harsh note to his words, a grim resignation that he didn't want her but would bed her anyway.

A tiny pain pierced Odessa.

"As appealing as it is to be wed for my dowry, my lord" she said tartly, "and as appealing as your skills appear to be, you will never be a man I would choose as a husband. You've no idea what it is like—"

"The feeling is completely mutual," he interrupted in a clipped, furious tone. "You think you are the only one of us caught in a snare?"

"That isn't—" Emerson's sudden anger suffused the tiny space. The desire between them was viciously doused in an instant. "What I mean to say, my lord, is that *you* have no reason to be angry. *You* are not the injured party. *You* didn't have to suffer the calls paid upon you by a parade of fortune hunting fops. Men whose only interest in the odd, plain, and *low-born* daughter of Angus Whitehall was a dowry."

"You spoiled brat," he snarled. "Do you think I wanted to inherit an impoverished title? I've had an entire host of things forced upon me. Unpleasant duties. Unwelcome responsibilities. *You* being one of them."

"My lord—"

"Can you imagine," Emerson's voice slashed the air, "having the *entire* welfare of your family placed on you when you are barely seventeen? Sent off to Dunnings by your elder half-brother because *you* committed the unforgiveable sin of being born? Raising pigs to support your family because the Earl of Emerson fritters away all the wealth your family has accumulated in the last century on whores while you are scraping the ground for enough wood to keep your little sister warm? And he is revered for doing so. *You* are considered to be the ill-bred one."

"I think I should return to the party," she said quietly. "You are upset, my lord, and—"

"There's no time for anything else but worry over whether you can feed your siblings. Or if you've the money for a physician to tend your dying mother. But, of course, you've never experienced the least hardship, you who are the daughter of Angus Whitehall. A man who feeds off the misery of others. Instead, you spent your days sprouting nonsense about dead pirates. Who cares what they drank before they were hung? Reciting nonsense about ghosts and nefarious murderers, all while living your cosseted existence." He eyed her with disdain. "You would have done well with Bentley. He also did nothing the least useful."

Odessa fell back as if he slapped her. "I didn't know what your brother had done." But she had some sense of it. Aunt Lottie had alluded to Emerson and his siblings being banished from London. Told Odessa that Emerson might not be able to beg off, no matter whether he wanted to or not.

"Not only did I have my life *decided* for me, but I was told I must wed a spoiled, pampered little princess. Threatened with worse if I didn't comply. If you think this is a situation I *desire*, Miss Whitehall, you are sadly mistaken. Even with the largest dowry in London, I would never have *willingly* chosen *you*."

Odessa pushed at him, desperate to get away from Emerson, his anger, and especially the truth she heard in every word he uttered. What had her father done to secure this match?

Something awful. Terrible. Odessa felt it to the depths of her soul.

"Truthfully, I prefer my pigs to you." Emerson stepped aside and made a shooing motion with his hand. "Run back to your aunt, little heiress. If you think to compromise yourself with Phillips or anyone else to avoid marrying me, think again."

Odessa stumbled out of the alcove, shaken to the depths of her being. The ugliness of their argument after such a promise of pleasure left her mind reeling. She stumbled away from him and back down the hall, following the sounds of music and dancing. Her entire chest ached as if she'd been stabbed and wishing she had never come tonight.

CHAPTER NINETEEN

"**M**R. PATCHAHOO AWAITS you in the drawing room, my lord." Jordan looked up from his desk, exhausted with the ledger he'd been poring over. River Crest had a list of requests from his tenants, the few that were left. Bentley had managed to scare off nearly all except those who had nowhere else to go. There were requests for tools. Animals. Modern machinery.

"Was Patchahoo expected?" The solicitor had become something of a fixture at the Emerson home, though he had never appeared without first sending a note. He often dined with the Sinclairs, claiming Mrs. Cherry's cooking drew him to the earl's door. Jordan didn't mind. Patchahoo was invaluable. Brilliant and fiercely loyal to the Sinclairs.

"I don't believe so, my lord. Shall I tell him you are indisposed?"

"No. I need a moment away from these rows of numbers. I'll join him presently. Thank you, Holly."

Holly bowed and exited. Tamsin's choice of butler ran the Emerson household with military precision and little drama. He was fierce in his protection of the family, seeing it as his sworn duty to ensure the safety of Tamsin and Aurora. Important since Jordan was often caught up in the duties long neglected by Bentley. Lady Longwood had not been able to place her slippered foot inside Jordan's front door again thanks to Holly.

Drew was not often in residence. This week, it was to a house party hosted by Lady Robley. Jordan didn't want to know how his brother had received an invitation; he assumed it was while rolling about the sheets with the countess. His younger brother was going to get shot by a jealous husband one day if he wasn't more careful.

"Mr. Patchahoo," Jordan said in greeting as he entered the drawing room. "To what do I owe the pleasure of your visit? Mrs. Cherry is making a roast tonight. You're free to join us if you like."

"I couldn't, my lord." A small blush crawled up the solicitor's cheeks.

"Liar." Jordan strolled towards the sidebar, giving a fleeting glance to the portrait of his parents in a field of daisies, once more in its proper place above the fireplace. Holly found it beneath a sheet in the attic. Thank goodness Bentley hadn't sold it or destroyed it out of spite. "Brandy?"

Patchahoo nodded, studying the portrait of Lord and Lady Emerson before turning back to Jordan. "My lord, there is a matter of some urgency on which I must speak."

"Not the contract with Whitehall, is it? Did he try to add something else to it? That I must bed his daughter at least twice monthly or some nonsense? Consummation of the marriage wasn't included in the original agreement, as I recall. An oversight on his part."

Guilt he shouldn't feel gnawed at Jordan. Not for nearly lifting Odessa's skirts in that tiny alcove at Lady Curchon's; that particular desire hadn't abated. But his loss of temper after. Jordan had lashed out at her, the resentment towards Whitehall, Dunnings, and even Bentley erupting out of him in a great wave.

The solicitor's color deepened. "No, my lord. The contract, as I said before, only dictates your treatment of Miss Whitehall before and up to the wedding. Making her Lady Emerson seems to have been Whitehall's main concern. There is the provision that he will," Patchahoo cleared his throat, "reward you for every child. Handsomely. But that is more—"

"Inducement," Jordan interjected. "A reward for bedding his daughter and getting her with child. He mentioned it to me. I find it rather disgusting."

"As do I, my lord. But rest assured, the marriage contract is solid. Duly witnessed. Not a farthing can be added to the debt owed to Whitehall. The amount has been agreed upon. Miss Whitehall's dowry will transfer to you on the day of your marriage."

Every single pound, every marker of Bentley's, no matter how obscure, been accounted for and double checked by Patchahoo. No mysterious sums could suddenly make an appearance. No loans were to be made by Whitehall to any member of the Sinclair family. No business dealings of any kind. Whitehall assumed, wrongly of course, that paying Jordan for every child Odessa delivered would guarantee his influence for years to come.

Only a few days ago, Whitehall claimed to find yet another marker of Bentley's. A sleight of hand Patchahoo had firmly refused, referring to the already signed contract. Whitehall fumed. Threatened. But Jordan's solicitor held firm. The terms had been set.

"I cannot wait to be rid of Angus Whitehall and his daughter." The thought gave Jordan a slightly hollow feeling in the pit of his stomach. Things would have been much easier if Odessa had stayed a smelly, undesirable troll possessed of macabre tendencies. The desire for each other at Lady Curchon's, the *fierceness* of it, shocked Jordan. He had only touched Odessa to prove a point. That he could *have* Odessa but didn't choose to. Things may have gotten out of hand. Words were spoken that should not have been. Dunnings had been revisited.

Odessa's face, her shock at his tirade, had been genuine. She didn't know what Angus Whitehall had done to bring Jordan to her door. He accused her of causing Bentley's accident *and* threatened Captain Phillips. No good ever came of Jordan losing his temper.

"You plan to reside at River Crest, my lord? Not in London after the wedding? I will assume that Miss Whitehall will remain in town."

"Yes, but not here." Jordan circled his hand around the room. "Find her a house with a fashionable address. A small staff. A sum will need to be set aside for her every month. I want no further contact with Miss Whitehall or her father. Whitehall gets a title for his daughter and nothing else."

That was his revenge on Whitehall for beggaring Bentley and forcing Jordan to wed Odessa. He could not be allowed to win, under any circumstances. Thumbing his nose at Whitehall, assured that his adversary was not only powerless but beaten, was the only outcome satisfactory to Jordan.

The sound of Odessa in that small alcove, her muted cries of arousal and the press of her body against his, flitted through his mind. The unexpected desire for her twisted mercilessly around his cock. He should never have touched her.

"Find her a house," Jordan bit out, trying to staunch his arousal at the mere thought of Odessa. "I can't have her in this house if I'm in London." The knowledge that she would be under the same roof would be too tempting.

"I understand, my lord." Patchahoo turned once more to the portrait of Jordan's parents. "As I said, there is a matter of some urgency I need to discuss." He held up a hand. "Urgency may be incorrect, my lord. More curious, I think, in nature, but the matter requires your attention."

"I am most intrigued." Jordan handed Patchahoo a brandy before settling himself in a chair.

"Lord Emerson, your father, was a client of my firm for many years before his death. Bentley inherited us, so to speak, with the title. I was only a clerk when I met your father and the first time I learned of Dunnings. A useless, forgotten estate in Northumberland of little note, according to my superiors."

"I lived at Dunnings for over a decade, Patchahoo. I'm aware of the estate's limitations."

"But did you know." Patchahoo gestured to the portrait of Jordan's smiling father in a field of daisies. "That Lord Emerson refused to sell Dunnings?"

"Fortunate, else I'm not sure what other region of Hell Bentley might have sent us all to."

"There were at least two offers prior to your father's death, both for ridiculous amounts. Worth far more than Dunnings merited. I suppose that is what made him curious." Patchahoo regarded Jordan with an odd look. "And me, suspicious. I was put in charge of your brother's affairs roughly a year or so before his death. Bentley instructed me to sell Dunnings." The solicitor cleared his throat. He twitched, clearly uncomfortable.

Jordan shrugged. "As I expected Bentley would have. He cared nothing for us, Patchahoo, and would have been more than happy to see us tossed into the streets. You shouldn't feel bad about following his orders. He was your employer."

"Yes, but Bentley *did* receive a handful of offers for Dunnings, or rather, I did on his behalf. I declined them all without his knowledge."

Jordan's glass paused at his lips, surprised at Patchahoo's confession. The solicitor was one of the few honest gentlemen left in England. "How out of character for you."

Patchahoo glanced once more at the portrait of Jordan's smiling parents before pulling out a packet from his coat pocket. "When I was put in charge of Bentley's affairs, I did an extensive review of all the files pertaining to him and the previous Lord Emerson, your father, to familiarize myself. I don't know how this was missed by my predecessor, but—after reading the contents, I thought it best not to sell Dunnings. I did not inform your brother because—"

"You knew about me and my siblings by then, didn't you? Saw Bentley bleeding the estate. Knew he'd gotten himself involved with Whitehall. And you didn't like Bentley."

Patchahoo looked down into his glass of brandy. "I took liberties, my lord. Wrongfully. I am prepared to accept the blame and resign my position."

"Don't be an idiot, Patchahoo," Jordan said. "The client was Bentley. Selling Dunnings would have made me homeless." Jordan went to the sideboard and poured out another glassful of brandy, unsurprised to see his hand tremble slightly at what the mere thought of having Dunnings sold out from beneath Jordan and his family would have meant. "I'm sure you had good reason."

"Your father had the land Dunnings sits on surveyed," Patchahoo stated without preamble. "As I said, he was offered an outrageous sum for the estate by a fellow from Scotland. So, Lord Emerson decided to do his own research. He hired a survey company, one who dealt in finding mineral deposits. Your father was meant to review the results of that survey when he, unfortunately, died." He nodded to the packet. "I'm afraid, my lord, that I may have made additional decisions without your express approval."

"I'm not firing you as my solicitor, Patchahoo. I've no doubt that whatever you've done has been in the best interests of my family."

"I believe so, my lord. I met at length with the gentleman who conducted the initial survey of the land around and beneath Dunnings over ten years ago. Mr. Epps is his name. Studied geology at Cambridge. Highly respected. At the time, he was in the employ of a mining company but now provides independent appraisals, unbiased, so to speak. I asked him to once more survey and test the land at Dunnings. Epps recalled the previous survey and stood by the results, though he has agreed to perform another."

"What exactly did Epps find the first time and what is he looking for at present?" A strange sort of excitement filled Jordan. His father hadn't said a word to him, but at the time, Jordan was busy brawling and being thrown out of Harrow for insubordination. He would have been too young to have understood. And Father didn't trust Bentley.

"Coal, my lord. A great deal of it. At least, that is what Epps believes."

"And you agree." Jordan regarded Patchahoo. "Don't you?"

"I am not a miner, nor a geologist, my lord. But yes, I think Epps to be correct. Your father visited Dunnings in secret with Epps. He wanted to be sure, I suppose, before making any sort of announcement. At any rate, Epps found it strange, given Lord Emerson's interest, that your father didn't arrive for their meeting."

"Because my father died," Jordan replied.

"When Epps read in the papers that Lord Emerson had unexpectedly passed away, he came here, only to be turned away by Lady Longwood. Epps could do nothing further, so he handed off his findings to your father's previous solicitor, Hooks, who promptly filed it away. Everyone's assumption was that Dunnings wasn't good for anything. The land poor and worthless for farming. The estate falling apart. The day Bentley walked into our offices and demanded to know from Hooks which was the furthest, least profitable, most forgotten estate of the Earl of Emerson, he was told Dunnings. No one tried to dissuade him when he dictated that the belongings of his siblings and Lady Emerson were to be packed up from River Crest and sent to Dunnings. Certainly, Hooks didn't try to persuade Bentley to do otherwise." Patchahoo's mouth tightened. "Reprehensible."

"Lucky," Jordan murmured. "Because Bentley sold every other piece of property not entailed over the next ten years, but not Dunnings. He thought it worthless, which is why we were banished there. Until he became desperate. Epps will do another survey?"

"I convinced him to do so." Patchahoo looked relieved, as if the burden of carrying around the secret of Dunnings had weighed on him. "If the findings are positive, it will take time to excavate fully. I've taken the liberty of arranging funding to put a mining operation in place."

"Thank you." Jordan could only stare at Patchahoo, his mind already working around what coal at Dunnings would mean for the

Sinclairs.

"If this survey is in agreement with the first commissioned by your father…" Patchahoo hesitated. "Your worth will exceed the original value of the estate Bentley ruined. And the fortune your father held. *Combined.* You would have more than enough to restore River Crest, maintain this household lavishly, *and* repay the debt to Whitehall. Three times over, my lord. Possibly more."

Jordan sat back in his chair. "Patchahoo, if you don't mind, there's a bottle of whiskey beside the brandy. Would you bring it here and join me? I think whiskey much more appropriate for this conversation." He was going to be wealthy. Ridiculously wealthy. "If it weren't inappropriate, I believe I'd kiss you, Patchahoo."

"I would settle for being one of your investors." The solicitor gave Jordan a rare smile and obediently brought over the whiskey. "And there is one other matter."

"I don't think my heart can take much more, Patchahoo."

"Whitehall should fire his solicitor." Patchahoo cleared his throat. "The wording of the marriage contract states that the debt to Whitehall is to be erased upon marriage to Miss Whitehall or *other means if available.* Whitehall's man glanced over that part, or possibly, didn't think it important given you have 'no other means' at present with which to repay the debt. Whitehall foolishly tied your agreement to marry Odessa to the debt to ensure your compliance. It was simply a matter of rephrasing a few sentences."

Jordan would need to give Patchahoo a raise. "You added it because you knew about Dunnings."

"My lord, you asked me to find you a loophole, which I did. I cannot take responsibility for the fault of Whitehall's solicitor to review the contract as thoroughly as I."

"Devious, Patchahoo. I like you all the more for it." Jordan poured whiskey out for him and Patchahoo. Coal at Dunnings. He was nearly giddy with the knowledge.

"If Epps and his survey prove correct, my lord, the debt to White-hall can be repaid without wedding his daughter."

"Whitehall never assumes that anyone can outsmart him. A great weakness, I think." Jordan's thoughts went to Odessa and her own cleverness. She had outmaneuvered her father on several fronts. He had a great deal of admiration for her efforts, but as it turned out, they may well have been wasted. At least on him.

Such an odd, curiously desirable creature.

Jordan wasn't at all sure what he meant to do about her now.

Chapter Twenty

ODESSA DIDN'T BOTHER to look in the mirror before making her way to the drawing room to greet Lord Emerson. There was no onion to eat. Or wool to be wrapped in. No tar.

Her unwanted earl had been avoiding her since that night at Lady Curchon's a week ago. She didn't blame him. The storm of bitterness, lust, and resentment trapping them in the alcove didn't give Odessa much hope for their future union. Emerson's distaste for her and her father had been made abundantly clear. His rejection of Odessa required no disguise on her part.

She accepted her fate, though Odessa wasn't quite as distressed about Emerson as before. The anger hurled at her at Lady Curchon's had been distressing, but once taken away, something else remained.

Odessa had spent the days since being nearly ruined by Emerson pretending to read while sitting in the garden. A page or two into her book, Odessa would imagine the warmth of the sun was actually Emerson's broad form pressed to hers. The supple muscles of his chest moving beneath her palms. She would tilt her chin up, remembering in detail every moment of that kiss. Odessa's fancies became more erotic every day, with images of her naked and Emerson pressing her down into the grass. Yesterday, a whimper left her, frightening off a bird in a nearby tree.

Flushed and aroused, Odessa would limp back inside, embarrassed at her own behavior. Aunt Lottie cautioned her against reading so many romantic novels and told her to stay out of the sun for her cheeks were red.

I would never have willingly chosen you.

Such loathing filled those words. She had been arrogant in assuming herself a great prize not even considering the situation from Emerson's perspective. Had he any other option, Emerson would *never* choose her. Not even after sharing the most passionate, thrilling kiss of Odessa's life. Not to mention the fondling of her person.

Warmth curled inside her midsection at the thought, causing her to halt and catch her breath. It would do no good to be red-faced and mildly aroused when she faced the object of her improper thoughts.

If she must wed Emerson, and it appeared that was the case, then Odessa wanted more of what she experienced in that tiny alcove. And if Emerson gave her the opportunity, she meant to convince him that they should reach some sort of understanding.

Odessa had done a great deal of thinking since Lady Curchon's. She would never be completely comfortable with Papa dictating her future, but in all fairness to Emerson, he seemed to not have any choice either.

If I could beg off, I would.

Those words rang in her mind with greater frequency when she wasn't considering how splendid Emerson probably looked out of his clothing. Papa had done something Odessa wasn't ready to contemplate. Her entire life, she assumed that society's disregard for Papa was because he was a self-made man of business. One who had made himself wealthy by sheer will and intelligence. Yes, he'd been ruthless, but only because he'd had to be.

Threatened with worse if I don't comply.

But perhaps that wasn't the case. Odessa loved her father, but— her perceptions of him were clouded by that love. It was a difficult, painful truth. Looking back at the handful of events she'd been fortunate to attend, the forced greetings Papa received, even from Lord Norris, a clearer picture of Angus Whitehall was forming in

Odessa's mind. It was not favorable.

So it was with great trepidation that she made her way to the drawing room to greet Lord Emerson, a man who she hadn't wanted but was now sympathetic to. A titled lord who was anything but the foppish dandy Odessa once thought him to be. A man, who by all accounts, had faced a great deal of challenge in his life, raised pigs, worked with his hands, and survived by his wits.

In short, the very sort of man Odessa found incredibly appealing.

Had Emerson lifted her skirts at Lady Curchon's and decided to take her virtue, Odessa would not have protested. That was *her* truth, one she'd ignored from the first time Emerson sat across from her and tried not to cringe at the smell of onion. The worst part was knowing there *could* have been something between them.

Throwing herself at Captain Phillips. Honestly, his arms *were* too thin to hold a sword.

We must come to an understanding, Emerson and I.

Odessa was resolved to do so, no matter what it cost her. Continuing to be at odds with Emerson wouldn't serve her. She'd unwittingly touched a nerve at Lady Curchon's at the mention of his mother. The previous Lady Emerson had been *reviled*. The Sinclair children taunted endlessly over their mother's origins, according to Aunt Lottie. Emerson himself was considered no better than a savage. *The Deadly Sins.* That was how society referred to the Sinclairs.

She hadn't known. A poor excuse, but the only one Odessa possessed.

Pausing for a moment, Odessa clasped her hands before walking sedately into the drawing room to stand before the blindingly handsome man who came to his feet as she entered.

Emerson *couldn't* beg off. Papa had secured him. *Somehow.* The best course of action was to reach an understanding of sorts with Emerson. Because once wed, he would have control over her very existence. He could have her thrown into an asylum if he wished, particularly if she kept going on about ghosts, dead pirates, and the assortment of oddities she found so fascinating. Emerson *didn't* like her. He resented her. Found her strange. But there had been passion between them, a spark, that if nurtured might be enough so that Odessa had some hope of affection. Friendship, possibly. Children. A family.

Odessa briefly considered just running away. But then what? Her pin money would only last so long, and there was Aunt Lottie to consider. If Papa would stoop so low as to coerce an earl, what might he do to her elderly aunt?

She bobbed politely. "Lord Emerson." The flutter over her heart made itself known, gently pressing against the confines of her chest. Odessa decided to no longer beg it to ease.

"Miss Whitehall." Emerson greeted her as he normally did. Politely. Respectfully.

Odessa searched the depths of those hazel eyes, looking for any sign of emotion, but if Emerson felt anything towards her, disgust or desire, there was no sign.

CHAPTER TWENTY-ONE

JORDAN DIDN'T WANT to reply to Miss Maplehurst's request to call upon her and Miss Whitehall. He'd been toying with the idea for days of visiting Odessa, but kept putting it off. Part of him wanted to simply wait until Epps returned with his report and avoid seeing her again. But the need to apologize to Odessa for his loss of temper gnawed away at the joy in knowing he was about to become richer than Croesus.

And he *wanted* to see Odessa.

The unexpected longing for her came as a surprise. Last night, he'd dreamt of his limbs entangled with hers. The slate blue of her eyes gazing up at him as he fucked her senseless. Awaking with a jolt, he was unsurprised to find his cock tenting the sheets. Over a splendid breakfast from Mrs. Cherry, Jordan decided it was only that he hadn't had a woman in some time. His obvious arousal over Odessa wasn't really for *her*.

Now, standing before her in Whitehall's drawing room, Jordan realized how incredibly stupid that assumption had been. It was Odessa he craved for some inexplicable reason. Leaning forward, Jordan purposefully made a show of sniffing the air just to annoy her.

Odessa's willowy form arched towards him; a deep breath exhaled through her plump lips and pushed her delicate breasts up along the modest neckline of her dress.

Had Miss Maplehurst not been a few feet away, Jordan might have well buried his head between the valley so temptingly thrust out at him.

Odd, strange, lovely creature.

The air in the room snapped between them, drawing them closer until he and Odessa were mere inches apart. Why had he waited so long to come to her? He wanted to hear those soft noises of arousal she'd made in the alcove once more. Suck and nibble at her mouth. Most of all, Jordan wanted Odessa naked and laid out before him like a feast.

Desire was a tricky thing. It could be caused by nothing more than the shape of a woman's ear. Or the sight of her ankle. He could not have said exactly *why* Odessa Whitehall aroused him, only that she did. There had been that tiny shock at their first meeting when she appeared to be nothing more than a smelly troll. And when Jordan had seen her on Bond Street—

Miss Maplehurst cleared her throat.

Or possibly it was because now, Jordan knew he wouldn't have to wed Odessa if there was coal at Dunnings. There would be no debating whether he should bed her to consummate their marriage. He didn't have to bed her at all. Which made Odessa that much more enticing.

Jordan's fingers twitched against his thighs.

"How lovely of you to call, my lord." Odessa possessed a lovely voice; the sound of it flowed softly over his skin.

"I thought I'd escort you to Gunter's for an ice." It was the only excuse Jordan could think of to be alone with Odessa, something he greatly desired. Gunter's was one of the few places a gentleman might escort a young lady without causing undue talk, though the news of his betrothal to Odessa Whitehall had escaped at Lady Curchon's.

Captain Phillips, in addition to having arms no bigger than a pin, was a gossip.

Jordan neither confirmed nor denied the rumors making the

rounds. No official announcement of a betrothal had been made. He had spent several nights considering the look on Whitehall's face when the debt was paid in full. Possibly Jordan should take Odessa's virtue before jilting her.

Now *that* would really show the dirty sharker.

"Gunter's," Odessa said blithely. Her delicious bottom lip jutted out just a bit. She hadn't expected to be escorted for an ice.

"The carriage top will be down." He looked to Odessa's aunt. "You are welcome to join us, Miss Maplehurst. I will defer to your wishes."

The older woman waved him off with a smile. "I think you entirely trustworthy, my lord. And you are to be wed. I see no harm." Her gaze lingered far too long at the hem of Jordan's coat, obviously studying his thighs.

Jordan had come to like Miss Maplehurst, though he often feared for his own virtue in her presence. She had been terribly kind to Tamsin at Lady Curchon's, and the two had struck up a friendship.

Leading Odessa out to the waiting carriage, Jordan felt her hesitation as she reached the bottom step. "I thought you said your carriage would have the top down for propriety's sake."

Jordan helped her inside. "Did I? I may have misspoken."

Odessa allowed herself to be helped inside, a look of trepidation on her features as she turned to face the window. Her fingers clasped and unclasped themselves in her lap, tugging at the folds of her skirts. A tendril of honey blonde hair fell along one cheek, the curl spiraling to dangle near her chin.

Jordan wanted to sink his fingers into that heavy mass. Pull the curls free of pins. Spread them over his chest and lap—

Desire. Such an untamed emotion. He shouldn't want her so badly, yet he did. Taking revenge on Whitehall had nothing to do with it.

"We aren't going to Gunter's, are we?" The stormy eyes rose to his.

"No."

"What would you have done if my aunt decided to come along?"

"Then we *would* have gone to Gunter's. You would have availed yourself of an unappetizing ice, as would I. Miss Maplehurst might possibly have made an impolite comment about the cut of my trousers."

"Entirely true," she said without embarrassment. "My aunt is blunt about a great many things. Admiration of your person, for instance."

One of the things Jordan liked about Odessa, and he reluctantly admitted, now that the yoke Whitehall put around his neck didn't choke nearly so much, was he *did* like her. Odessa was clever in a way many women were not. Witty. She fairly sparkled with intelligence.

"You wish privacy to castigate me," Odessa informed him. "Or possibly you'll drive by the Thames and merely toss me into the waters. I wouldn't survive the shock of the cold. And I don't swim, but even if I did, my skirts would drag me down. I'd choke on all that filth. But the Thames often has a body or two floating about. No one would notice one more."

Jordan tapped his fingers along one thigh. "Did you read that in one of those dreadful pamphlets I've seen sold on the streets? Tamsin has a collection now. She shares your appreciation for oddities and strange crimes, though not the truly gruesome ones. I've no intention of tossing you into the Thames."

"But you do intend to inform me what I can expect as your wife, do you not? I suppose an asylum makes the most sense. The sort where they put the criminally insane. I'll be keeping rats as pets. Loraine Dunkirk did when her husband locked her away. Trained the rats in her cell to perform tricks. She eventually stabbed two of the orderlies with a fork."

"Can you not pick up a book of poetry? Possibly a romance of some sort?"

"Boring. I blame my cousin. He took me to see a two-headed

snake when I was a child."

"The Duke of Ware." Jordan tried to imagine that bear of a man as a child with Odessa trotting behind him, plucking insects out of the bushes and showing her a snake. "I made his acquaintance at Lady Curchon's."

Her brows lifted, surprised Jordan had met the duke. "His Grace isn't really my cousin; we aren't blood relations. But he is as odd as I am, something we both realized when we were children. He dislikes being a duke."

"He mentioned as much to me."

"At any rate, I developed a taste for oddities after that snake. We also visited a farmer who owned a goat with only one eye a few years later. My fascination for the grotesque was firmly formed. I've no actual talents, so I collect the strange here." She tapped on her temple and shrugged, turning once more to the view outside. "Separate lives, I think. Justified, my lord. I deceived you. I'm what politely is referred to as eccentric. And I did consider compromising myself with Captain Phillips to avoid marriage to you."

"You reconsidered after I pointed out his thin arms, didn't you?"

Her lips pursed. "I never told him about the German baker, or the two-headed snake. Or any of those other terrible stories I adore so much. It's possible he wouldn't have wanted to wed me either." A resigned puff of air left her.

"I did not call upon you today to—chastise you. I wanted to—offer an apology for my behavior."

"Apologize." She stared at him, incredulous.

"I lost my temper, something I rarely do. The headmaster at Harrow, if he is still there, would tell you differently."

"I provoked you."

"But others have said far worse." Jordan thought her beautiful, sitting across from him, with that curl of honey trailing along her skin. Arousal trailed over his thighs, making his cock lengthen and twitch. "I am sorry for spewing out such bitterness on to you. You didn't deserve it. I promise not to do so again."

She nodded, the curl bouncing gently against her cheek. "Your apology is accepted, my lord."

"I thought you might like to guide me through Madame Tussauds' bloodthirsty exhibit. Regale me with stories of gruesome death. Relate to me what the poor victims of the guillotine ate before having their heads leave their bodies. I'll consider it penance." He didn't bother to tell her he'd gone there once solely to catch her, undisguised.

"I see." A tiny smile lifted her mouth, causing Jordan's pulse to beat wildly. "You don't have a weak stomach, do you, my lord?"

"I endured onions, garlic, and tar. A trunk-like figure that reminded me of a forest troll. Raised pigs and butchered them myself. I believe I can tolerate an afternoon of wax with you." Another wave of longing for this strange creature struck him, curling along his waist and making him grateful his coat covered the worst of it.

"I am sorry, my lord." There was a sheen of moisture in her eyes. "Truly. I—didn't know."

Not for their argument at Lady Curchon's, he realized, but for Dunnings. For Jordan having to raise pigs. Bentley. The death of Jordan's mother. All of it. He wondered if Odessa knew that Angus Whitehall had beggared the previous Earl of Emerson and blackmailed the current. Something told Jordan she didn't.

"For your poor disguise?" He didn't want to discuss the past. Nor did he want her sympathy. "You *should* be ashamed Odessa. Anyone with sense could see right through your scheme."

"Jordan," she murmured, his name on her lips rippling down between his thighs. Her hand shot out and touched his knee.

Dear God.

He was going to *pounce* on her. Maybe Miss Maplehurst should have come.

"When I was a lad," he stopped her, hearing the patrician accent he tried so hard to maintain, slip to the rolling of near Scots. "We performed plays for my mother. I may have mentioned it before, but you were consumed with burping onion at me and might not have listened."

Another smile flitted along her delicious mouth.

"Aurora was little more than a baby, so she didn't get to play many parts. Mostly she laid on a blanket and cried. And the twins, Malcolm and Drew, weren't much better. Which left me and Tamsin to take over most of the roles. I was a witch in the Scottish play—" At her look of confusion he clarified. *"MacBeth."* Jordan lowered his voice to a whisper. "No actor worth his salt ever mentions the play by name. Bad luck and all that. Mother refused to name it, though she adored Shakespeare's words. That's where I learned about the various uses of tar and padding. I had a wart." He tapped his upper lip. "Affixed right here."

"I never fooled you." A wistful, soft smile broke across her lips, striking Jordan firmly in the chest.

"At first. My—dislike of the situation—"

"And your dislike of me," she added, biting once more on her delectable bottom lip. "Kept you from observing me too closely."

"The onion would keep anyone at bay. And those lumps of padding. I thought at first you were malformed. A troll of sorts with your oddly fleshy form. I expected hooves beneath your skirts or an overabundance of hair."

Laughter burst from her lips, a mirthful sound that jumped about Jordan's insides. Her eyes softened, the winter storm turning to a summer sky in an instant. "I wish I had thought to compare myself to a troll. Trolls as well as witches have warts. I should have adorned myself with a half-dozen, though given your experience, you would have known them to be false."

"You would have burped them off in any case." Jordan's mouth twitched.

"Onions really do cause me distress." She patted her stomach. "It is what made them so perfect. All the gases kept Malfrey from my side. When he arrived for tea, he sat as far from me as possible."

"Malfrey?"

"A horrid suitor. Very self-important. Before Bentley." Odessa gave a small roll of her shoulders. "There were several who suffered before you, my lord."

"Because you wanted Captain Phillips." Jordan watched her carefully. "Are you really so enamored of him that you would go to such great lengths?"

"What does it matter, my lord?"

"I want to know, Odessa, if your affections lie with Captain Phillips." Once Jordan wed her, *if* he wed her, fulfilling his bloody debt to Whitehall and had Odessa's dowry, and she wanted Phillips—

Jordan's fingers curled into fists where they rested on his thighs. The thought of the cavalry officer touching Odessa, eliciting those soft sounds of arousal from her, had a growl forming in his throat. What on earth was wrong with him? Yes, he wanted to tup Odessa. Badly given the way his cock pulsed between his thighs, but that was *all*. Phillips could have her.

Liar.

Odessa's brow furrowed. "They do not. But I *wanted* to be enamored of him. If given the chance, I might have been." She plucked at her skirts.

"Because of me."

She jerked her chin up, a startled look in her eyes. "Somewhat."

"Phillips would never have compromised you at Lady Curchon's. Too much of a gentleman," Jordan ground out, wishing he'd never brought up the cavalry officer.

"I believe I might have convinced him," she replied tartly.

That thread between them, the one formed without Jordan's express permission or knowledge, tightened sharply once more, pinging along the lower half of his body. "A kiss, possibly. But I doubt he would have lifted your skirts in that bloody alcove."

"Neither did you." There was a challenge as she glared back at him. "You merely kissed me."

Damn you, Odessa. Oddly magnificent, tempting little troll.

Jordan reached up and thumped on the roof. "Take us through the park. Slowly." He pulled off his gloves, tossing them to the floor. Then he slid off the seat to his knees before her.

"What if I raise your skirts now?"

CHAPTER TWENTY-TWO

T HIS WAS AN entirely unforeseen circumstance.

Odessa was unprepared for—she stared down into his eyes, the depths full of unrestrained heat. She'd pushed him again, pressed against Jordan's temper that always simmered beneath the surface, without knowing she'd done so.

His hands curled around her ankles, broad fingers teasing at the delicate bones. "Lift them."

"What?" she finally stuttered. "I'll do no such thing." A soft hum slowly made its way from her clasped ankles, across her calves to a point between her thighs. The hum stayed there, drawing out a delicious ache.

"Your damned skirts, Odessa. Lift them." His eyes blazed at her. "Now."

There was a coarseness to his tone, one that sent another fluttering pulse through Odessa. She tentatively lifted her skirts up to the middle of her calves.

Contrary to what Jordan assumed, Odessa did not spend all her time reading lurid tales of ghosts, murders, and the like. There were other books of a more sensitive nature that interested her as well. And Aunt Lottie was entirely too forthcoming for an elderly chaperone. A few nips of brandy and Odessa was nearly as well-educated as a courtesan.

All of which meant that she had a general idea of what Jordan meant to do to her. Not specifics, exactly. Another soft ache spilled moisture between her thighs. She couldn't stop it.

"I wish to reach an understanding, my lord." She sounded breathless and he'd barely touched her.

"An understanding?"

Jordan's hands curled around her ankles, his thumbs chafing pleasantly against her stockings. His fingers found the hollow of her knee before pushing her legs apart. "Higher," he ordered.

She tugged until the ruffle of her petticoats puffed up around her waist, exposing the lower half of her body clad only in her underthings. Not much protection. The cotton was very thin and there was a slit—

Heat stole up her chest to her cheeks.

His thumbs pulled and tugged at the cotton, tracing the stitching. "Lovely." He leaned in, his breath ruffling the hair of her mound. "I've found a part of you that isn't entirely odd." One callused finger trailed over her sex, teasing around the edges. "Now, about this understanding you wish to have." Jordan looked up at her, the bits of green in his eyes twinkling softly in the light of the carriage.

"I think—" The words choked out of Odessa as his tongue trailed along her wet flesh, flicking against a sensitive spot, already swollen. Another wick of moisture flooded between her thighs. This hadn't been what she'd imagined; it was better.

"I hadn't expected—" Her knees jerked at the soft press of his lips. "What I mean is—"

"Stay still, Odessa" His hands dug into her thighs. "We're having an important conversation, aren't we? Not the sort you'd have with Phillips else I might have to beat him with my fists. Or anyone else, for that matter."

Another wave of arousal struck her at the possessive nature of his words. Odessa belonged to no one but herself but—a small whimper sounded, *hers*—perhaps she could cede him ownership if the occasion merited.

Another slow draw of his tongue and Odessa's breathing faltered and the air escaping her lips came out in tiny gasps. The light, teasing pressure of his mouth elicited small waves of wondrous sensation across the lower half of her body, twisting about her legs to take up residence once more at the apex of her thighs.

"Put your hands on my shoulders."

Odessa's fingers curled in the fabric of his coat. Laughter sounded outside the carriage as it rolled past two gentlemen on horseback. They were in the park.

"You, Odessa." Another long draw of his tongue. "Are one of those rare women for whom arousal is quick. Dry kindling, which when struck with flint, immediately catches flame." He sucked her slowly into his mouth, tongue moving about in the most delicious manner, pulling Odessa towards an unbelievable peak of pleasure.

"Is that—" The words ended on a soft moan.

"Good?" His breath teased at her folds. "You cannot begin to imagine the things I will do to you, Odessa."

She bit her lip to keep from crying out; the pleasure, that hum between her thighs, had become almost painful as it thundered to a conclusion. Aunt Lottie, after three glasses of brandy, had tried to describe when Odessa asked what—a woman's release consisted of—but there weren't words to describe—"I feel as if I will come apart," she whispered.

"You will." He paused, his fingers and thumb replacing his mouth. "You'll climax with my mouth on you, Odessa. I believe this is the understanding you wished to reach, is it not?"

Another pleasurable ripple slid over her skin. "Yes. I think this could prove to be a benefit to our unwanted union."

"Agreed." His tongue once more eased over her, teasing and coaxing until Odessa shamefully writhed against his mouth. One hand stayed on his shoulder while the other cupped the back of his head.

Everything sharpened, became honed like the blade of a knife, curling inside her so tightly Odessa worried she would shatter into pieces.

And then she did.

Waves of the most indescribable sensation broke across her skin. One of his hands slid beneath her, pulling Odessa more fully into his mouth. As her eyes fluttered closed, two of his fingers pushed slowly inside her. "Jordan," she cried brokenly.

Odessa's legs trembled as her hips moved in tandem with his mouth as Jordan pulled wave after wave of sensation to crest over her body. When at last the pleasure slowly ebbed away, her head fell back against the leather seat, neck no longer able to hold her upright. A lazy, sated feeling stole over her. Opening her eyes, Odessa peered down at Jordan. There was something entirely erotic in watching him move those big, masculine fingers, which were still inside her. Another scar shown stark across the top of his hand near his wrist. One Odessa hadn't noticed before.

She traced her finger over the curved white line, gasping at the press of his forefinger. "What's this?"

"Tavern fight," he murmured, curling both digits inside her until her breath hitched and low, tingling sensation once more vibrated inside her. "Bottle." He gave her a half-smile before reluctantly easing his hand away and started to straighten her skirts.

"Don't," she said. Regret for this rash decision could come later. Tonight, alone in her bed, she could berate herself for giving Jordan her virtue in a slow rolling carriage. "I am not yet finished with our discussion."

A predatory look passed across his chiseled features. "What more do you wish to discuss?"

"I think you know, my lord." She gave him a defiant look. "You are not unintelligent."

Jordan slid onto the leather seat beside her. The fabric of his trousers stretched taut over what could only be a fairly large...*male appendage.* Of course, Odessa could only surmise. She'd never actually seen—her eyes met his. "And I am certain that I wish to continue." She nodded to the length clearly outlined beneath the fabric. "I believe you are in agreement."

Jordan's eyes grew shadowed, and he leaned forward, brushing his mouth over hers. She could sense his indecision at her offer. Would he reject her?

"Consider it a complete acceptance of your apology, if you must, my lord," she whispered against his lips.

He straightened, lifting an arm to rap at the roof once more. "Around the park again," he said loudly. Cupping her face between his big hands, Jordan slanted his mouth fiercely over hers. There was no other word for the near angry claiming of her lips, demanding she give herself over to him. The only regret, and it was minor, was that Jordan wasn't naked. She longed to see all the carved muscle hinted at beneath his clothes.

Jordan, unclothed, would be spectacular.

"This is insanity, Odessa." His lips left hers, trailing along the side of her jaw to nuzzle at the length of her neck. Teeth grazed and nipped at her skin. One of his hands jerked at the buttons of his trousers. Pulling her roughly into his lap, he pushed aside her skirts once more.

A blissful sigh followed the dip of his fingers inside her. "You weren't ready for Madame Tussauds." Her heart beat wildly in her chest, moaning softly as he positioned their bodies. His fingers fell away as he lifted her up. Heat pressed against her entrance before he carefully inched inside her.

Odessa's head fell to his shoulder as her body struggled to accommodate his. Her fingers tangled in his hair, tugging at the ends.

Jordan rotated his hips while one hand moved along her slit, forcing her pleasure to build once more. He pinched that small, sensitive bit of flesh between his thumb and forefinger, holding her in place, refusing to allow her to go further.

"Please, Jordan." Odessa's voice broke. "Please."

Aunt Lottie claimed there was plenty of enjoyment to be found when being bedded, if the gentleman knew what he was doing. Which Jordan most certainly *did*.

"Slowly, Odessa." He caressed the tiny nub before pinching gently once more. The painful stretch of her body mixed with the building pleasure he deliberately kept at bay. He stopped abruptly, pressing against the thin barrier inside her. His fingers rotated slowly over her as he finally allowed the first ripple of bliss to flow over her skin.

Grabbing her by the hips, Jordan pushed her down, thrusting upwards at the same time, tearing through Odessa's virginity to fully seat himself inside her. A startled whimper left her, though the pinch of pain was barely noticeable, hidden beneath the delicious pleasure erupting across her limbs. He stayed perfectly still, holding Odessa to his chest, as her release fell away until only the sensation of stretching, of fullness, remained.

Odessa opened her eyes; concern for her showed in every line of his face.

"Are you well, Odessa?" His palm flattened against her back, making a soothing motion along her spine. "I'm sorry. I tried to make it less painful."

"That is—so much larger than your fingers." She could make out the chafe of dark hair along his chin, saw the emerald lurking in the depths of his eyes. There was a tiny scar just above his lip.

A smile lifted the corner of his mouth. "So I've been told."

"No worse than pricking my finger on a needle," she assured him. The loss of her maidenhead seemed minor in comparison to having Jordan inside her. Odessa's muscles fluttered, clamping down on his body.

Jordan groaned. Cursed. Kissed her hard. "Now you've done it, Odessa." He rocked his hips, thrusting inside her again. "Now we are both lost," he whispered before his mouth caught hers.

"Jordan." Odessa bit into the side of his neck, just above the line of his collar. "Harder," she whispered into the curve of his ear. "I won't break. I promise."

Jordan's movements became rougher. One hand grabbed her thigh. His breathing strained. A rumble came from his chest as he took her in hard, furious strokes.

Odessa wrapped her arms around his neck to steady herself as the carriage rocked. The heat of his mouth, the intimate press of their bodies, sealed them together in this small space. Her release rolled softly about her midsection with Jordan buried inside her. She kept their mouths fused together, swallowing his cry of pleasure as a rush of warmth spilled between them.

Afterwards, with Odessa's body still throbbing from the ministrations of his, Jordan ordered the driver in a hoarse tone to make yet another circle of the park. He stayed buried, nose in the nape of her neck, making outrageous comments that she smelled of turnips and cabbage, while the carriage swayed along the path. But he did not let her go.

When at last he released her, reluctantly, Odessa thought, Jordan did so with great care. He asked her once more if she was hurt.

"No," she answered truthfully. "I feel wonderful." Better than she ever had her entire life. Whole. Complete. Odessa's heart thumped loudly, her fingers still curled in his coat.

Brandishing a handkerchief, Jordan cleaned them both. After straightening her clothing and his own, he pulled Odessa against his side, brushing his lips over her temple. He seemed pensive. Thoughtful.

"I suppose you think I'm overly bold, demanding you take my virtue in a carriage," she whispered.

"An odd request from a young lady to be sure." He pulled her against the warmth of his body. "But one I was happy to fulfill. Tell me your horrid fairytale. The one of the baker who put his wife in a pie."

Odessa breathed in his clean, warm scent, pressing her nose to his chest. She recited the tale, making it much less gruesome than usual. She didn't want to scare Jordan away.

Not anymore.

THE STORY ODESSA related was shocking to be sure, but Jordan sensed she'd tempered the most horrible details for his sensibilities. He'd learned quite a lot about Odessa Whitehall during this carriage ride, not the least of which was she possessed an uninhibited, passionate nature. Very few virgins requested their maidenhead be taken in a moving carriage.

Odessa wasn't avoiding marriage, exactly. She had been willing to compromise herself with Phillips, after all. But marriage to a man Angus Whitehall chose, all of whom were exclusively titled, snobbish and entitled, *that* was what Odessa didn't want. A gentleman from the echelons of the very society who had demeaned Odessa's origins her entire life. Why on earth would she want to embrace a lifetime of mockery, disdain and being looked down upon? Wed to a gentleman who would always think her beneath him?

Not to mention this titled lord's family who would *never* accept her.

Yet Whitehall hadn't shown an ounce of concern for what such a marriage would do to her. All he wanted was a title.

A wave of protectiveness for Odessa overtook him and Jordan pulled her more securely to his side.

She paused in her story and smiled up at him.

Odessa probably didn't see her motivations clearly, but he did. Jordan brawled. Fought with his fists. Whenever he was decried for being uncivilized, Jordan became that much more savage, flouting convention with a flip of his wrist. Brawling was a disguise of sorts, like Odessa's onions and padding. A way of rejecting those who were unkind first by becoming what they claimed you to be.

As a defense against the world, it was a good one.

He'd used it for years.

Jordan pressed a kiss to the top of Odessa's head while she gleefully detailed how the baker arranged the limbs of his wife into a pie. Incredibly distasteful. But he didn't mind her eccentricity. Or her.

Which made everything that much more complicated.

CHAPTER TWENTY-THREE

"I KNEW YOU would enjoy Gunter's with me." Jordan watched the movement of Odessa's mouth as she licked the spoon clean. She'd eaten her ice *and* his. Also, a tart filled with cream, which Jordan had sternly questioned the poor waiter to death over the possibility of strawberries.

The lad assured him the tart contained only cream and cinnamon.

"The loss of virtue stimulates the appetite." Odessa's expectations of marital duties and a wedding night hadn't been lofty, not when glimpsed through say...Malfrey. Captain Phillips had given her some hope, but after her recent experience with Jordan, Odessa thought she might have been disappointed. Losing her virginity in a moving carriage had been nothing short of magnificent. Odessa hadn't a hint of embarrassment over doing so. If she could, she would relive the entire event again.

Jordan gave her a half-smile. "Imagine how much you'd eat after an entire day at my mercy." His gaze dropped to the tops of her breasts, lingering long enough for her cheeks to bloom with warmth. "I must put my foot down, though, and not allow onions of any sort."

Odessa drew in a shaky breath. Marriage to Emerson wouldn't be terrible.

"I'll put the ice in my mouth and then kiss you." Pointedly, he looked at her lap. "Where I kissed you today."

Her heart, which had recently restarted its normal rhythm, took to beating like a drum. "That sounds…intriguing, my lord. I'll allow it."

Dark curls spilled over Emerson's forehead as he laughed, showing off the line of his throat and the tiny red spot beneath his ear where Odessa had bit him in the throes of passion. So beautiful, it hurt to look at him. If it hadn't been for a dismal reputation and whatever Papa had done—

Odessa firmly pushed that thought aside. *Not today.*

Emerson would have had his pick of any number of lovely, wealthy young ladies, none of whom would have given a fig for his reduced circumstances. He certainly wouldn't have looked in Odessa's direction.

The thought pressed against her chest.

"I would venture that you will allow a great deal, Odessa." Heat flared in his eyes as he looked at her. "If I insist upon it. Which I will. I promise you will enjoy every moment."

Purposefully, she ran her tongue over the edge of her spoon. Jordan's obvious desire for her gave Odessa a heady sensation. Only her cousin, Hayden, had ever found her acceptable.

"I've no doubt, my lord." She hesitated before placing her spoon down, wondering how much she should say. She wanted him to understand, a little.

"My mother was the daughter of a viscount. She was shunned by her family after wedding my father, even though I'm told her family insisted on the match. As a result," she said carefully, "I am considered beneath them all. The only reason I was at Lady Curchon's is because she was my mother's cousin and the event was one that no one of great importance had been invited to. She doesn't speak of our relationship. Lady Curchon is the Duke of Ware's aunt through marriage, in case you were wondering.

"I was curious as to how you were related to a duke."

"Distantly, my lord. And not by blood. I am tolerated, nothing more. My father not at all. Hayden is my dearest friend, the only one I possess. He has more eccentric tastes than I with his love of *insecta*. I tell you all of this because I have little desire to be part of a world that treated my mother so terribly. My grandmother was particularly horrible to her."

"And you. Your treatment at their hands has not been kind." Jordan nodded. "Did you deliberately relate the tale of the baker to your grandmother?"

"Unfortunately, I didn't know it when it was a child, or I would have. I settled on the hanging of several pirates. I was always treated as some exotic unwelcome animal come to burrow among them." She set down her spoon and looked up at him. "So you see why I have been averse to the courtship of a titled gentleman."

"I do. I've no great love for society given my own origins. I often wonder what I'm doing being an earl when I would be far happier in the country with my pigs. Less impoverished, of course, than I've been in recent years."

Odessa had the strangest urge to pull Jordan into her arms and press a kiss to his cheek. He'd been incredibly gentle in taking her virtue. Careful in a way she hadn't expected. "Thank you."

"I've no desire to curry the favor of those that find me less, nor should you," Jordan's hand, with those marvelous, powerful fingers, tugged gently on her skirts. "We have reached an understanding, Odessa. And our general dislike of our *betters*," there was a sarcastic edge to the word, "is part of it."

CHAPTER TWENTY-FOUR

JORDAN LOOKED DOWN at the woman beside him, admiring the graceful curve of Odessa's neck and the gentle rise of her small, perfect bosom. His desire for her had become near constant since that memorable ride in the carriage several weeks ago. Passion often proved fleeting between new lovers once the worst of their lust had been satisfied, but Jordan's want of Odessa had only increased. The longing for her had sunk deep in his bones and he doubted anything would dislodge it.

"She made death masks of those executed mere moments after the guillotine came down," Odessa whispered. "Blood still dripping from the cut." She drew her fingers along the line of her neck, the slate blue of her eyes filling with fascination. "Brave of Madame Tussaud, don't you think? Did you know she was imprisoned herself?"

Strange, unusual creature. Jordan had arisen this morning wishing Odessa was beside him, possibly recounting a ghost story to him before breakfast.

"You may have mentioned the fact to me," he replied. Odessa was enamored of Madame Tussaud. He'd heard the wax sculptor's history multiple times. "Her chosen occupation was not without risk."

He looked around at the vast collection of blood-soaked wax. The artistry *was* spectacular. Incredibly lifelike. None of it was real, of course. But still, incredibly gruesome. The Duke of Ware had his moths. Tamsin, her breeches and a wicked right hook. Jordan was afraid of spiders and liked to brawl. Odessa had…her morbid curiosity about the world.

He tried to picture Odessa as a child, with the enormous form of Ware next to her, deliberately tossing out grisly tidbits when her mother's family visited.

"Look. Robespierre."

Today's adventure was mild in comparison to some of Odessa's favorite spots in London. Tyburn and Newgate. The tombs beneath London Bridge. Highgate Cemetery where she pointed out grave-stones of unfortunate souls. Odessa had stacks of penny broadsides hidden in the drawing room at her home, all published in Seven Dials.

Jordan knew because he'd tupped Odessa on top of the pamphlets while Miss Maplehurst pretended to see to preparations for dinner.

Whitehall *still* rankled. The sharp bitter loathing for Bentley con-tinued to prick at his skin. The resentment would boil over and he then he would catch the scent of lavender on Odessa's warm skin. Or she would smile and trail her fingers along his arm. Angus Whitehall's unappealing daughter, the woman he'd been blackmailed to wed, was now the very thing that made Jordan happy.

"I wish I possessed an ounce of Madame Tussauds' talent." She held up two fingers pinched together. "A small amount. I would open my own exhibit, but focus more exclusively on murderous events." Her gaze flicked to him. "Like the scenes in a play."

Mother would have liked Odessa.

"You've many talents, Odessa." Jordan's lips dipped to the curve of her ear. "Though I am too much of a gentleman to say so in a public setting."

All true. Odessa had absolutely no reticence about anything of a sexual nature. He'd nearly fainted when she got down on her knees in the carriage and asked innocently if she could put her mouth on him.

A twist of arousal rushed down between his legs at the memory.

"Mmm." A slender hand trailed down the length of Jordan's coat, discreetly, as at least a dozen other patrons surrounded them. Her fingers wormed their way under his coat, tracing the outline of his cock.

Jordan's breath hitched, cock twitching and hardening at her touch. Odessa resembled a prim little flower but possessed a great deal of boldness. Vastly arousing.

"Naughty, Miss Whitehall." Madame Tussauds wasn't well-lit, but even so, her brazen behavior would be noticed if it continued. Especially if he threw caution to the wind and pulled her into a dark corner. "We should return."

"So soon?" She blinked up at him. "But we haven't seen—"

"You should have thought of that a moment ago, Odessa. I've little interest now in wax nor anything other than what lies under your skirts."

Jordan turned her abruptly and led her outside into the rapidly fading light, wondering if there was enough time to take her on the carriage seat before arriving at her home.

"Of course, my lord." Her fingers plucked at the edges of his coat but didn't attempt to touch him again. Just as well. The raging length of his cock already threatened to burst from his trousers.

"My aunt is out this afternoon," she breathed against his cheek before Jordan settled across from her in the carriage. "I think she is having tea with your sisters and gone for some time."

Miss Maplehurst was indeed at Emerson House, supposedly practicing decorum with Aurora and Tamsin, but according to Holly, all the three did was drink tea and gossip.

"Papa is in Manchester, once more. Burns is afraid of you."

"Good." Jordan didn't care for Whitehall's butler. The man was always snooping about. "Are you suggesting an assignation, Miss Whitehall? Do you mean to seduce me in the drawing room?"

"I was thinking I would sneak you into my bedroom, but if you prefer the settee in the drawing room, so be it."

Another wave of lust lashed Jordan.

In the end, Odessa had taken him to the drawing room, pretending, least Burns overhear, that she was going to read to him from one of her dreadful pamphlets. Once the butler departed, Odessa led him silently to her room. Jordan barely glanced at the four-poster bed with its counterpane of pale blue before Odessa was sliding off his coat.

"I'm going to seduce you, Jordan."

"If you must." His hands glided up her back to the buttons of her dress, trying not to pop them off in his haste. Their couplings in the drawing room and carriage had all been accomplished almost fully clothed due to the circumstances.

"I must." She fumbled with his trousers and boots. He had to help her with his shirt. But when Jordan finally stood naked before her, Odessa sighed deeply as if he were her heart's desire.

"I've never seen anything so beautiful." She lifted her lips to his.

"Now you," he whispered to her.

Jordan undressed her slowly, pressing his mouth to each spot of exposed skin. He caught her breasts in his hands, gliding his palms over the nipples. Bending, he sucked one taut peak between his teeth, rolling around the tiny bud until Odessa whimpered. His fingers grazed along her slit, unsurprised to find her wet and soft.

Laying her down on the bed, Jordan pressed his mouth to her stomach, enjoying the flush of her skin, the smell of her arousal. Her sex was a delicious shade of deep rose. He took his time, exploring every secret hollow of her body, hearing the small sounds she made. His tongue delicately traced her slit until Odessa begged and panted, pulling at his hair. Her ankles hooked over his shoulders as she strained against him, moaning out his name, climaxing with his mouth on her. She might have screamed.

As the last waves of her release ebbed away, Jordan thrust inside her, Odessa's small body surrendering to him in an instant. The feel of her naked skin gliding along his nearly undid Jordan. The press of her breasts catching against his chest so magical he nearly forgot to breathe. Jordan's heart, so long full of anger and the deep well of his own bitterness, filled with something else.

Odessa.

Kissing her tenderly, he sighed his release into her neck, hopelessly entwined with a woman he'd never wanted and had long meant to discard. One he'd been blackmailed into wedding. Now, he couldn't imagine a life without her.

Whitehall, though it pained Jordan greatly, would win. Odessa would be Lady Emerson. There would be children, a great many if their desire for each other was any indication. Jordan had no intention of leaving her. Or abandoning her.

Not for all the coal in Dunnings.

CHAPTER TWENTY-FIVE

ODESSA WHISTLED AS she made her way downstairs. She was joyful. *Blissfully* joyful. Much of it had to do with a certain, pig-raising earl. Titled, unfortunately, and her father's choice, but there wasn't anything she could do about that. Much could be overlooked when a man possessed such marvelous hands.

Two days ago, Odessa had snuck him into her rooms, nearly fainting at the sight of a naked Lord Emerson. The broad shoulders, the flat muscled stomach without an inch of spare flesh. His skin was lightly tanned from being in the sun, not the pasty white of so many gentlemen. A dusting of hair, a shade deeper than that on his head, covered his torso leading down between his thighs. She'd seen his cock before. Placed it in her mouth; her boldness in doing so still made her blush. But seeing him entirely unclothed—*breathtaking*.

Jordan had kissed the clothes from her body; there was no other way to describe the urgent press of his mouth as dress, petticoats, corset, and chemise all slipped away. He had insisted on leaving her stockings on. When Jordan thrust inside her, he'd raised her hands above her head, threading their fingers together, looking down at Odessa as if she were the rarest of jewels. Something fine and worth cherishing.

I'm in love with him.

The knowledge drew her up short. No use denying it. Odessa had suspected for some time, well before their infamous carriage ride. But now the knowledge filled her with a sense of peace. There would be affection in her marriage. A great deal of it.

"How dare you listen at the door while I'm conducting business." Her father's voice boomed down the hall.

"Angus. Dear God, what have you done?" Aunt Lottie's horrified words came to Odessa.

Odessa halted, her fingertips pressing into the wall. Aunt Lottie and Papa were arguing, something that rarely happened.

"What I had to do. What I will continue to do."

"Angus—"

"Odessa will be a countess. After which, the news will reach Emerson that he's sitting on a fortune in coal. But not before. Can't have him jilting her at the altar. They're to be wed at the end of the week."

"But you can't—"

"Now look, Lottie." Her father interrupted in a coaxing tone. "I want the best for Odessa, as do you. She deserves to be a lady, a real lady. I tried to find a titled gentleman willing to take her on, dangled the largest dowry in London, but no one came to the table. I had to resort to other methods. I thought I'd succeeded with that foppish brother of Emerson's, but he drove a barouche with the same skill he wagered on horses."

"Oh, my God. Tell me you didn't—*You* beggared him. *You* impoverished him. But I suppose it isn't the first time you've done so to get what you want, is it? Viscount Maplehurst, Emily's father—"

Odessa pressed a hand over her mouth lest the horror bubbling up her throat erupt from her lips. Shocked to the core of her being, her feet stayed firmly rooted in place.

The study remained silent as the question hung in the air.

"The other Emerson was a wastrel." Papa ignored her aunt's question. "He would have squandered away the family fortune on his own. I merely helped him along. Fool had no choice but to wed Odessa. He owed everyone in London, including me, and yet he dithered," Papa spit out. "But with his brother, *this* Emerson, I took the precaution of purchasing *all* the outstanding markers. The entire debt is owed to *me.*"

A small, wounded cry sounded. Aunt Lottie.

"I thought that would be the end of it. But his solicitor gave him a bloody loophole and I never expected the coal—I will not have my plans ruined again." The slap of her father's palm against his desk cracked through the air. "I. Will. Not."

Odessa forced herself to take deep breaths else she feared she might faint. And Burns would find her body in the hall. Papa would be summoned.

Blind. I have been blind to his ambitions all these years.

He *bankrupted* Jordan and his brother, all so that one of them would wed Odessa. Forced them as surely as he'd put a pistol to their backs.

Threatened if I don't comply.

Jordan's words to her that night at Lady Curchon's. A sob threatened to erupt, and Odessa swallowed it down. Her father's casual words had her lightheaded and her knees buckled.

Papa had done this before. Viscount Maplehurst. Odessa's grandfather.

No wonder Mama had hated him.

"Odessa wouldn't want this, Angus." Aunt Lottie's voice trembled. "Think of your daughter."

"I am thinking of her. Honestly, do you think a man like Emerson, despite his reputation, would look twice at Odessa if I didn't hold a pile of markers over his head? She's *odd*, Lottie. Only passably pretty. Certainly not intelligent, if her hobbies are any indication. But Odessa is the only child I have. My heir, whether I like it or not."

A flare of anger surged through the pain beating in Odessa's chest. "I was clever enough to have outsmarted you for several years," she whispered, fists clenched at her sides. How could she have been so blind?

Not blind. You *chose* not to see.

"When Odessa finds out, she'll hate you," Aunt Lottie, weeping now, hurled at him.

"Emerson won't tell her. I'll have his hide if he does. Put it in the contract that he had to treat her well. Respectfully. And he receives a lump sum for the birth of every child. Incentive, so to speak." An ugly chuckle lit the air. "I'm holding the man's markers as well as his bollocks."

Odessa clutched at her stomach, willing the contents roiling about inside to stay put. Jordan's treatment of her had been in a bloody contract. Every kindness and smile. Even the tolerance and amusement at her eccentric interests had been dictated by her father. And their physical relationship—

A wave of anguish struck her.

How could she ever believe any of it was real? Worse, how could Jordan not despise her? He had to dance attendance on her like a well-trained dog.

"Odessa—*cares* for Emerson," Aunt Lottie said in a low, pleading tone. "This will destroy her, Angus. You terrible, horrible—"

Her father pounded on the desk. "I'm her Papa. She loves me. When Odessa is surrounded by my grandchildren one day and addressed as Lady Emerson, she will be grateful I went to great lengths to secure her future."

"No, I won't," Odessa sobbed quietly to herself. "Not ever." She straightened, meaning to march into the study and confront her father. Every fiber of her being dictated that she tell Angus Whitehall what she thought of him. She would *never* call him Papa again. Never believe he loved her. She'd only been a tool to further himself. And Jordan—

"And you will refrain, Charlotte Maplehurst, from expressing your opinions to me further, and to Odessa, not at all."

The menacing tone stopped Odessa in her tracks.

"You're quite ancient. Elderly. A tumble down the stairs and those old bones will shatter into pieces." A growl came from the study. "I'd hate for you to take a tumble."

Odessa swallowed. She steadied herself. Tiptoed quietly back the way she'd come. She could not be discovered. If Odessa confronted the madman in the study, he would hurt Aunt Lottie. Lock Odessa in her room. Threaten Jordan's sisters. Angus Whitehall would do *anything* to get what he wanted. She felt foul. Ruined. *Utterly* horrified.

Jordan, I'm so sorry.

She had to make this right. Fix the mess her father's unbridled ambition had created. Make sure Jordan wasn't forced to wed her all so that he could erase a debt he had nothing to do with. But help would be required. She and Aunt Lottie must leave this house.

So instead of storming into the study and confronting the monster who had been her father, Odessa returned to her bedroom. Seated at her desk, she wrote a short but pointed note to her cousin, the odd, but very powerful Duke of Ware.

CHAPTER TWENTY-SIX

"EPPS HAS APOLOGIZED for the delay, my lord. The packet became misplaced on the way to the train station. Thankfully, precautions were taken to make multiple copies of the survey, as you suggested. All the copies have been certified. One has even been filed at the solicitor's office in Spittal, as you requested."

Jordan nodded. The entire affair of the misplaced survey, among other random problems which had arisen, smelled of Whitehall, who must have found out about the coal at Dunnings despite the precautions Jordan and Patchahoo had made.

"How fortuitous Epps made it to the train station at all given the wheel of his carriage broke on the way." There had been a fire at Dunnings, burning the ruin of a house to the ground. No great loss there. Two of the assistant surveyors requested by Epps had gotten lost on their way to Northumberland. The survey had been misplaced by the very man Patchahoo specifically hired to deliver it.

"Odd that that the Duke of Ware's man was out on the same road as Epps and intercepted him. The duke's estate is in the other direction," Patchahoo mused.

"Fortuitous." Epps and his survey had been delivered to Jordan this morning. The news was as expected. Coal, a great bloody mound of it, was hidden beneath the barren landscape of Dunnings. A team of men were already on their way, dispatched by Patchahoo.

"I wish to properly thank you," Jordan said. How far he and

Patchahoo had come from that first meeting at The Hen. "The Sinclairs are incredibly grateful."

A blush snuck up the edge of Patchahoo's collar. "I am your solicitor, my lord. I am merely doing my duty."

"You are more than that, you are my friend," Jordan said, meaning every word. "An honorary Sinclair, though I'm not sure you'll wish to spread that news about."

"Bent never knew." Drew, settled in an overstuffed chair, lifted his glass. He'd recently returned from a visit to the country and the arms of Lady Robley. "Thank God. Else we might have found ourselves on a boat destined for a distant shore. Lady Longwood will be beside herself when she realizes we aren't impoverished rats anymore. And best of all, you won't have to dance to Whitehall's tune and wed his unappealing daughter."

Slate blue eyes floated before Jordan, along with a swathe of skin like satin, her hair spread out over the coverlet of her bed. He'd been paying a great deal of attention to her left breast when Odessa told Jordan the story of a wife poisoning her husband by grinding up apple seeds into his biscuits, meticulously, over an entire year.

I miss her. Desperately.

It had been a mere two days since he'd seen her, but Jordan didn't want to endure a third. A note had been sent, asking if he could call, but his request remained unanswered. He'd been so mired in Dunnings, Epps and the survey…he hadn't given it much thought until now.

"You don't have to wed her and can now beg off, thanks to Patchahoo and his way with words," Drew said needlessly. "Remind me, Patchahoo, to never sign a contract without you reviewing it. Whitehall, as intelligent as he is, never considered you'd have the funds to repay him. Now you won't need to worry about sticking his daughter in some house in London that you'll never visit. Or bumping into her at a ball and making awkward conversation. Cheers." Drew drained his glass.

"She isn't invited to many balls as Whitehall's daughter." Lady Curchon's had been an exception. His original plans for Odessa had not been a secret to Drew and Tamsin. He doubted anyone, even Patchahoo, assumed Jordan's relationship with Odessa had become—

Real. Very real.

"Jordan isn't going to beg off. Or jilt Miss Whitehall." Tamsin regarded Jordan over her glass of ratafia, trying not to grimace with each sip. "Are you?"

A knock sounded on the door before Jordan could answer his sister.

"My lord." Holly's massive form filled the doorway, a silver tray in his hands on which sat a slim packet. "This was just delivered. The messenger was instructed not to wait."

Jordan stood and took the packet, not recognizing the seal.

"From the Duke of Ware, my lord," Holly informed him. "So claimed the messenger."

Tamsin stiffened and peered into her ratafia. "I haven't done anything, Jordan. I promise."

"I know, Tamsin. You've become a shadow of your former self. An insipid flower growing in London where you once boldly marched about."

His sister frowned at him. "I will not have Aurora's debut ruined."

Jordan waved a hand. "You're becoming quite proper." He looked at the packet. "I'm sure it is merely the duke ensuring that Epps arrived safely and wondering why I haven't thanked him profusely. I met Ware at Lady Curchon's, Tamsin, if you recall." Jordan didn't mention the duke's relationship to Odessa since she'd mentioned it wasn't common knowledge. "He's as big as Holly and obsessed with insects. You wouldn't attract Ware's notice, unless you were a moth."

Tamsin resolutely took a sip of her ratafia.

Jordan took the packet, cracking the seal as he opened it. Paper torn to bits fell to the floor, scattering across the rug and his feet. Another document was wedged inside the envelope. The paper slid out and landed near Patchahoo.

Jordan stared at the tiny squares of torn paper. A hole seemed to open beneath his feet. Odessa hadn't answered the note he'd sent her. Miss Maplehurst had been unavailable for her usual walk with Tamsin and Aurora.

Odessa.

Stooping, Patchahoo picked up the document near him, his shrewd gaze running over the cramped writing. "Your debt to Whitehall has been expunged." The solicitor looked at Jordan in surprise. "*Gone.* As if it never existed. Legally witnessed by the Duke of Ware no less. Your brief conversation with the duke must have made an impression. Congratulations, my lord."

Ware, who Jordan didn't know, had mysteriously found Epps. Made sure the survey arrived at Emerson House. Witnessed the cancellation of his debt to Whitehall.

"Expunged." Jordan fell to one knee, picking up the bits of torn paper strewn over the rug. Even without piecing it together, there wasn't any doubt it was the marriage contract binding him to Odessa Whitehall. Ripped apart. Destroyed.

"Jordan." Tamsin came forward and kneeled beside him.

He stared at the tiny squares, but all he saw was Odessa and the desperate need to comfort her. There wasn't any doubt she knew what her father had done to him. The proof lay scattered over the floor. One torn piece of the contract bore her name and Jordan picked it up, fingers running over the letters.

"Why aren't you happy?" Drew said. "If the debt is erased, you don't have to wed the troll."

"Shut up, Drew." Tamsin placed a hand on Jordan's shoulder. "You are forgiven your ignorance because you've been attending an endless stream of house parties. But I believe that despite our good fortune, and terrible Angus Whitehall, Jordan has decided he wants to wed Odessa after all. Haven't you, Jordy?"

A well of pain broke over his heart.

I should have told her. Whispered it to her when she was in my arms.

"Yes." Jordan rubbed his finger over Odessa's name once more. He had stupidly assumed Odessa *knew* what was between them. That the contract no longer mattered. Their reasons for marrying no longer mattered. But she *did*.

"Stop referring to Miss Whitehall as a troll, Drew. She's perfectly lovely," Tamsin admonished him. "And Jordan loves her."

He folded up the tiny piece of paper with her name and clutched it in one hand. He had to find Odessa. The Duke of Ware was an excellent place to start.

CHAPTER TWENTY-SEVEN

ODESSA WANDERED ABOUT the hall of Orchard Park, the Duke of Ware's estate, admiring the exorbitant amount of statuary that Hayden's mother, the dowager duchess, had managed to acquire in her lifetime. There was a great deal of winged goddesses, togas, and sandaled feet. Her Grace favored antiquities from Greece, but there were also a few Egyptian gods mixed in for good measure. Anubis was a favorite of Odessa's. Head of a jackal and all that. She'd amused herself all week by reading about mummification. Horribly gruesome.

She turned in the direction of the lawn, spying the head of Zeus as he stood guard at one end and Athena, clad in armor at the other. A massive black cat, tail twitching, sat atop the Greek god's head, watching Odessa as she roamed about.

In addition to statues, the dowager duchess also collected cats.

A window seat sat tucked in one corner of the gallery, near Odessa's favorite sculpture, Persephone and Hades captured in a tortured embrace.

Her fingers traced the folds of Persephone's gown, the stone cold beneath her fingertips.

"Murder of a peer. I'm a duke, Whitehall. No one will believe the word of a charlatan like you over me."

It was the first time Odessa had really seen Hayden for what he was. Not her beloved cousin or insect collector. But a duke. One whose influence stretched across England.

She had stood silently beside Hayden's massive form as the threat was issued, carefully watching her father's face for any sign that it could possibly be true. Only his left eye twitched. A tell of sorts. He may not have caused the death of Bentley Sinclair, but at the very least, he'd considered it.

"The marriage contract," Odessa had said calmly with her hand held out. "Is declared void."

He'd snarled at her. "No. Now get out of my study before I lose my temper, Odessa. And take him with you." A rude gesture was thrown at Hayden.

"Summon your solicitor, Whitehall," Hayden had drawled, looking far more menacing than Odessa had ever thought him capable. "Or I will. Along with the constable. You have no power. Not with me," Hayden's tone was so icy Odessa shivered. "You keep forgetting, I'm a bloody duke," he growled, taking a step forward.

Her father's eyes narrowed into slits.

Once Mr. Hall, the solicitor, arrived, Odessa took the marriage contract and tore the horrible document into tiny, impossible pieces. Putting the torn paper into a packet, she waited for Mr. Hall to produce another document, this one stating that all debts owed Angus Whitehall by Jordan Sinclair, Earl of Emerson, had been erased.

The document was witnessed by the Duke of Ware and a reluctant Burns.

All the while, her father glared at Odessa, but was wise enough not to issue a single demand in front of Hayden. She could see his mind working, trying to find a way to stop what was happening.

Odessa could barely look at the man who'd raised her.

"Least you think to undo this, Whitehall..." Hayden regarded her father with chilly indifference. "You should be aware that I have shared certain pertinent facts with Lord Curchon and, of course, my mother, the dowager duchess. Lord Curchon, in turn, has taken the precaution of informing his connections in the ministry of certain events. At my request. You haven't many friends in London, White-hall. Far fewer now. I will ensure that you make no others."

Her father's skin paled, the brackets at the corners of his mouth digging into his flesh, blue eyes full of impotent rage with just a flicker of something that looked like fear.

"How does it feel to be powerless?" Hayden had continued in that same icy tone.

"I am not powerless," her father had snarled.

"A matter of opinion. There are also the attempts at bribery, the theft of a packet containing a survey for a coal mine, and," Hayden tapped his lip, "Arson at Lord Emerson's estate, Dunnings. Emerson may wish to press charges. I'll support him if he does."

"Odessa—" Papa growled and reached for her, but Hayden pulled her away.

"You daughter and Miss Maplehurst are now under my protection and that of the Duchess of Ware. You are no match for a duke, Whitehall, and certainly not my mother."

"Goodbye." Odessa whispered. "I do not wish to see you again, Angus Whitehall. Feel free to disinherit me. I am sickened that I have lived so well on the misery of others. I will never forget what you did to Mama. *Ever.*"

A wild look had entered her father's eyes. "You'll regret this, daughter. When you are forced to live on charity. Unwed. A spinster like your worthless aunt. I did all of this for you. So you could be a lady, like your mother."

Odessa turned away. Hayden took her arm.

"Odessa," her father thundered. "You will not leave this house. Don't you dare—"

Hayden slammed the study door shut.

The entire ride to Orchard Park, Odessa wept on Hayden's shoulder, her cousin assuring her with a clumsy pat to her shoulder, that all would be well. Epps had been found. The survey was on its way to

Emerson. Associates of Lord Curchon would be descending upon her father. His affairs would be combed through. Examined. He might retain some of his wealth, but Angus Whitehall was now a bigger pariah than ever before. Hayden would see to it personally.

Odessa berated herself for hours, for her blindness at not seeing what was before her. How could she ever have assumed the animosity directed at her father was only because of his birth and the wealth he'd acquired? At least Jordan would now be free to marry as he wished. A girl of his choosing. One who didn't carry the taint of Angus White-hall. One he wasn't forced to wed.

Hayden had deposited her and Aunt Lottie at Orchard Park, a place where her father would never dare to venture, before returning to London.

"I'll see to everything, Odessa. I hope you like cats."

A tear rolled down Odessa's cheek and she wiped it away, wishing her cousin was here to comfort her now. She'd done the right thing. The *only* thing. Jordan couldn't possibly ever want to see her again.

"Odessa, there you are." Aunt Lottie came into view with one of the duchess's cats trailing behind her. "Moping about Hades and Persephone. Though I can honestly say, Hades is exceptionally well-formed. The sculptor did a marvelous job. Splendid backside."

"Aunt Lottie," Odessa admonished. Her aunt was incorrigible. "I am thankful Her Grace is not in residence at the moment else she might take offense to your ogling of her statuary." Hayden's mother was in London, which was just as well. She'd given her support to Odessa grudgingly.

"Pah. Might give the old dragon something to think about. I'm assuming those tears are not because you've stubbed a toe in this mausoleum." Aunt Lottie crossed her arms.

Odessa looked away, ignoring the ache in her chest. "The marble is tough on one's slippers."

"You should write to Emerson," Aunt Lottie sighed. "You jilted him, after all. The gossips have had great fun with the news. Lady Longwood was heard to exclaim that not even Angus Whitehall's daughter wanted one of the Deadly Sins."

"I didn't jilt him. Nor was my intent to hurt him further. I gave Emerson his freedom."

"Possibly he didn't require you to make such a sacrifice. In fact, I'm certain he didn't." The silver curls batted about her temples. "He did not call upon you nearly every day and listen to your horrible stories because he was forced to do so." She tilted her chin. "I believe there is affection between you, Odessa. Possibly a great deal more."

"How could there be? My father blackmailed him into wedding me, after bankrupting Bentley. Concocted a scheme to keep the information of Emerson's newfound wealth from him. Fraud, aunt. *Theft*. Although, I suppose that is the least of my father's sins." Odessa thought of Mama and Viscount Maplehurst.

"Angus did those things, not you, Odessa. Emerson knows that."

"How could he possibly look at me and not hate me, Aunt Lottie? Had the marriage happened under threat of my father, Emerson would have eventually grown to resent me, a wife foisted upon him. One he could never hope to care for. I overhead everything that was said in the study. A gentleman such as Emerson." Pain pinched her at the sound of his name. "Would *never* have chosen me. Not without proper inducement, which in this case, included threats. I'm only passably pretty. Mildly intelligent. My bosom isn't overly spectacular. I'm...odd. All I ever had to recommend me was my dowry."

Booted feet echoed on the marble of the gallery floor behind her. "I completely disagree." The words, uttered in that rolling, not quite patrician accent, made their way to Odessa.

Jordan stood a few feet away, big hands gloveless, stretching along his thighs as if he wished to strangle something. Probably her. He didn't look the least pleased to see Odessa. Had something gone wrong with the dissolution of the marriage contract?

Impossible. Hayden took care of everything. He's a duke.

Odessa straightened her shoulders, ready to bear whatever distaste Jordan hurled at her. She must. "My lord."

Jordan's eyes shifted to her aunt before nodding politely. "Miss Maplehurst, will you excuse Miss Whitehall and me for a moment?"

"Of course, Lord Emerson." Aunt Lottie, never one to refuse a handsome man, blushed delightfully and scurried off. A cat appeared, a tabby this time, and trailed behind, swatting at her skirts. "I'll be having tea in the drawing room."

"How unexpected to find you here, my lord." Odessa drank in the sight of him, dark hair curling about his temples, big and male, standing out dramatically against the stark white of the dowager's statues.

He looks very angry.

Yes, of course he was angry. Furious, she imagined. He'd come all this way to tell her so. Rail at her a bit. Make himself feel better. She could hardly blame him for seeking out the source of so much unhappiness. Perhaps he'd come to inform Odessa he meant to spread the news all over London that he'd taken her virtue in a carriage. It was an excellent way to jab at Angus Whitehall. Destroy any future ambitions her father might be considering for Odessa.

Hayden has assured me I can live here forever as his spinster cousin.

Jordan took a step forward, strong fingers curling at his sides. "You jilted me. Left me at the altar, as they say." The words rang against the marble. "Unacceptable, Odessa."

"Well—I didn't—"

Another step in her direction. Menacing. Jordan looked every inch an enraged pig farmer and not an earl at the moment. "You made me a *laughingstock* in London. I can barely show my face."

"Well, you weren't actually received before so—"

"You didn't even have the decency to warn me," he bit out. "Couldn't spare a moment to write a bloody note. Have you *nothing* to say for yourself?"

Why didn't she ever listen to Aunt Lottie? She had said the gossips were mocking Jordan.

"I—That was not my intent, my lord." She swallowed. "I only wanted to release you from Angus Whitehall." The name soured in her mouth. "You must hate me. *I* would hate me."

"I do not."

Odessa didn't believe him. "You should be relieved. Thrilled to be rid of me." She paced a few feet away, well out of reach. Jordan had a temper. "If your concern is that our physical relationship—"

"You mean the tupping? Coupling? Bedding? Bending you over the settee in the drawing room?"

"Yes, my lord." Heat seared her cheeks at the remembrance. "And there is no need to be crude. You may rest assured that any concerns you may have in that regard are without merit." Odessa had her courses two days after arriving at Orchard Park. A relief. Of sorts. Given circumstances.

"I don't know what is worse, Odessa." He strode towards her, stretching those marvelous hands in her direction, his jaw taut. "Having you assume that I am so dishonorable that I wouldn't wed a woman I've ruined or that you assume I did so only to get you with child and earn a bit of coin from your father. Do you think so little of me?"

"You were to receive an additional sum for each child I bore." She was nearly shouting at Jordan. "It was in the contract. What else should I believe?" She held up her hands. "I don't blame you, Jordan. Any man in your position would have done the same."

Jordan's nostrils flared, like a bull about to charge. "Don't say *another* word, Odessa."

She placed a statue between herself and Jordan. "I know you are angry, Jordan. But you are *free* of me."

"I don't want to be free of you." He tried to grab her. "I miss the smell of onions. I consider it an aphrodisiac. Tales of murdered husbands arouse me."

Odessa paused and took a deep breath. She pressed a palm to her heart, which was fluttering about. "But Jordan, there is coal at Dunnings. You don't need to wed me."

"Not just coal, Odessa. *Massive* amounts of coal. More than enough for two lifetimes. Makes your bloody dowry look like a pittance." He flicked his wrist. "Admittedly, my reputation is still tarnished, owing to the fact I've been left at the altar and Lady Longwood going about calling me a *Deadly Sin*. But I have a lovely home on Bruton Street. Needs updating. Nothing crimson, please. Tamsin and Aurora are firmly under the tutelage of Miss Maplehurst, which I haven't decided is wise. Drew hasn't been shot yet for fleecing anyone at cards yet—"

"Don't forget Malcolm," she said quietly, winding her way towards him.

"I was getting to him. He's alive and well in Paris. Or Venice. Shooting pistols and I've no idea what else. But you see the one thing I do not possess is a woman who breaks out in a rash if she eats a strawberry. A wife who will likely grind apple seeds into my biscuits one day if I annoy her. Or create beheaded wax figures in the kitchens and call doing so art."

"It *is* art." Odessa took his hand, feeling the warmth of his fingers close over hers. "I'll convince you one day."

"I've resigned myself to seeing every obscure landmark in London even if it is only a church where a half-dozen actors are buried."

"The resting place of Richard Burbage. He was the first actor to play MacBeth. I thought you would appreciate the sentiment."

"I can't wed some ordinary, wealthy girl. She must be unusual. Odd. *Rare*." He pulled her close. "One who has no qualms about being tupped in a slow-moving carriage."

"I prefer a bed on occasion." Odessa smiled up at him, trying to blink back the moisture gathering in her eyes.

"Duly noted." Jordan leaned in and pressed his forehead to hers. "Don't you love me, Odessa?" He sounded uncertain. "You are the only woman in all of England who would get on with my pigs."

A choked sob came from her. "I do love you, but—"

"But what?" Cupping the side of her face, Jordan's thumb gently caressed the length of her chin. "Think of the pigs. They'll be terribly disappointed if we don't wed." His lips brushed hers.

"So, you are going to wed me for the sake of your pigs?" Her heart swelled inside her chest. Jordan loved her. He'd come for her. "I'm not sure," she hiccupped, "how I feel about that."

"For *my* sake, Odessa. Strange, wondrous creature that you are." His mouth found hers, tongue licking at the tears covering her cheeks. "I am afraid your best efforts have failed, Miss Whitehall. You will have to tolerate the title of Countess of Emerson no matter how much you don't wish it."

"I do wish it."

"I stopped caring about the marriage contract well before I was even sure of Dunnings," he whispered. "After your seduction in the carriage, I had little room in my mind or heart for anything else." Jordan kissed a tear from her cheek.

They slid to the ground, his body curled around hers, holding her tight. Lips and tongues entwined about each other. The duchess's cats, thrilled to have company, purred around their ankles. One of the footmen found them sometime later. He cleared his throat. Several times.

"My lord. Miss Maplehurst requests you and Miss Whitehall join her for tea. I'm to escort you."

"Your aunt has decided it is time to admire me." Jordan stood slowly, unwinding his limbs from hers, and took Odessa's hand, pressing a kiss to the palm. "Just as well. The marble is a bit hard for tupping. Then there is the matter of all the cats."

"Orchard Park has beds, my lord." She pressed her forehead to his chest.

Jordan pressed a kiss to the top of her head. "I love you, Odessa Whitehall. You may doubt many things in your life going forward, but you may never question that. Are we agreed?"

She nodded, tugging at his coat. "Agreed."

Trailing behind the footman, Jordan murmured, "I don't think I can tolerate your father. Bad enough he's getting what he wants after all." His mouth drew firm. "But if you must see him—"

"I won't. I can't at present, at any rate. I reserve the right to change my mind one day, Jordan. But I will not ask you to welcome Angus Whitehall into our home. Agreed?"

"If he causes you a moment's grief—"

"He won't." At least, Odessa didn't think he would. "My father is rather caught up in the snare Hayden set for him. He'll be far too busy to concern himself with me."

Odessa threaded their fingers together, loving the sensation of his roughened skin against her own. Impossible to believe this splendid man loved her. Aunt Lottie was going to be incredibly pleased.

"Did you know, Orchard Park is haunted." Odessa shot him a grin. "There's a rather lurid tale of a maid, a footman, and a visit from Henry Tudor."

Jordan laughed and kissed the tip of her nose. "I see. Go on."

She told him the story, which wasn't very lurid at all, as they slowly made their way to Aunt Lottie. Cats dotted nearly every inch of the drawing room, sleeping on pillows and purring around the tea tray.

Jordan whispered in her ear he loved her. And he planned on sharing a bed with her that night, no matter the scandal it might cause.

"I'll assume everything has been worked out to your satisfaction, my lord." Aunt Lottie grabbed a cat stalking a mound of scones and placed the animal on the floor. Her eyes caught Odessa's.

"Indeed, aunt." Odessa squeezed Jordan's fingers. "Lord Emerson and I have reached an understanding."

About the Author

Kathleen Ayers is the bestselling author of steamy Regency and Victorian romance. She's been a hopeful romantic and romance reader since buying Sweet Savage Love at a garage sale when she was fourteen while her mother was busy looking at antique animal planters. She has a weakness for tortured, witty alpha males who can't help falling for intelligent, sassy heroines.

A Texas transplant (from Pennsylvania) Kathleen spends most of her summers attempting to grow tomatoes (a wasted effort) and floating in her backyard pool with her two dogs, husband and son. When not writing she likes to visit her "happy place" (Newport, RI.), wine bars, make homemade pizza on the grill, and perfect her charcuterie board skills. Visit her at www.kathleenayers.com.

Printed in Great Britain
by Amazon